Honeymoon

Books by James Patterson

THE ALEX CROSS NOVELS

London Bridges
The Big Bad Wolf
Four Blind Mice
Violets Are Blue
Roses Are Red

Pop Goes the Weasel
Cat & Mouse
Jack & Jill
Kiss the Girls
Along Came a Spider

THE WOMEN'S MURDER CLUB

3rd Degree (with Andrew Gross)
2nd Chance (with Andrew Gross)
1st to Die

OTHER BOOKS

santaKid
Sam's Letters to Jennifer
The Lake House
The Jester (with Andrew Gross)
The Beach House (with Peter de Jonge)
Suzanne's Diary for Nicholas
Cradle and All
Black Friday
When the Wind Blows
See How They Run
Miracle on the 17th Green (with Peter de Jonge)
Hide & Seek
The Midnight Club
Season of the Machete
The Thomas Berryman Number

For more information about James Patterson's books, visit www.jamespatterson.com

BOOKS BY HOWARD ROUGHAN

The Promise of a Lie
The Up and Comer

Honeymoon

A NOVEL BY

James Patterson

AND

Howard Roughan

Doubleday Large Print Home Library Edition

LITTLE, BROWN AND COMPANY

NEW YORK   BOSTON

For Suzie & Jack.
Love, Jim

For my beautiful bride, Christine.
Love, Howard

This Large Print Edition, prepared especially for Doubleday Large Print Home Library, contains the complete, unabridged text of the original Publisher's Edition.

Little, Brown and Company
Time Warner Book Group
1271 Avenue of the Americas, New York, NY 10020

ISBN 0-7394-4967-2

Printed in the United States of America

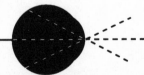

**This Large Print Book carries the
Seal of Approval of N.A.V.H.**

Prologue

WHODUNWHAT?

THINGS AREN'T ALWAYS *as they appear.*

One minute, I'm totally fine.

The next, I'm hunched over and clutching my stomach in sheer agony. *What the hell is happening to me?*

I have no idea. All I know is what I feel, and what I feel I can't believe. It's as if the lining of my stomach is suddenly peeling away with a corrosive burn. I'm screaming and I'm moaning, but most of all I'm praying—praying for this to stop.

It doesn't.

The burning continues, a blistering hole forms, and the bile trickles out of my stomach with a sizzling . . . drip . . . drip . . . drip . . . over my entrails. The smell of my own melting flesh fills the air.

I'm dying, I tell myself.

But no, it's worse than that. Much worse. I'm being skinned alive—from the inside out.

And it's only just beginning.

Like a firework, the pain shoots up and explodes into my throat. It cuts off all air and I struggle to breathe.

Then I collapse. My arms prove useless, unable to break the fall. Headfirst I hit the hardwood floor and bust open my skull. Blood, plum red and thick, oozes from above my right eyebrow. I blink a few times, but that's all. The gash doesn't even factor in. Needing a dozen stitches is the least of my current problems.

The pain gets worse, continues to spread.

Through my nose. Out to my ears. Right smack into my eyes, where I can feel the vessels popping like bubble wrap.

I try to stand. I can't. When I finally manage to, I try to run. All I can do is stumble forward. My legs are leaden. The bathroom is ten feet away. It might as well be ten miles.

Somehow I make it. I get there, lock the door behind me. My knees buckle and, again, I collapse to the floor. The cold tile greets my cheek with a horrific *crack!* as my back molar splits in two.

I can see the toilet but like everything else in the bathroom it's moving. Everything is spinning and I reach for the sink, arms flailing, to try and hold on. No chance. My body begins to thrash as if a thousand volts are coursing through my veins.

I try to crawl.

The pain is officially everywhere, including my fingernails, which dig into the tile grout and inch me forward. I desperately grab the base of the toilet and drag my head up over the lip.

For a second, my throat opens and I gasp for air. I begin to heave and the muscles in my chest stretch and twist. One by one, they tear as if razor blades are slashing through them.

There's a knocking on the door. Quickly, I turn my head. It's getting louder and louder. More a pounding now.

Were it only the grim reaper to put me out of this excruciating misery.

But it's not—not yet, at least—and that's the moment I realize that I may not know what killed me tonight, but I know for damn sure *who did it.*

Part One

PERFECT COUPLES

Chapter 1

NORA COULD FEEL Connor watching her.

He always did the same thing when she packed to leave on one of her trips. He'd lean his six foot three frame against the doorway to his bedroom, his hands buried in the pockets of his Dockers, a frown tugging on his face. He hated the thought of their being apart.

Usually he wouldn't say anything, though. He'd just stand there in silence as Nora filled her suitcase, occasionally taking a sip of Evian water, her favorite. But that afternoon he couldn't help himself.

"Don't go," he said in his deep voice.

Nora turned with a loving smile. "You know I have to. You know I hate this, too."

"But I already miss you. Just say no, Nora—don't go. To hell with them."

From day one, Nora was captivated by how vulnerable Connor allowed himself to be with her. It was in such sharp contrast to his public persona—a very rich and hard-driving hedge-fund manager with his own successful company in Greenwich, with another office in London. His puppy-dog eyes belied the fact that he was built like a lion. Powerful and proud.

Indeed, at the relatively young age of forty, Connor was pretty much king of all he surveyed. And in Nora, thirty-three, he'd found his queen, his perfect soul mate in life.

"You know I could tie you up and keep you from leaving," he said jokingly.

"That sounds like fun," said Nora, playing along. She lifted up the top of her suitcase, which was lying open on the bed. She was searching for something.

"First, though, could you maybe help me find my green cardigan?"

Connor finally chuckled. He got such a kick out of her. Good jokes, bad jokes—it didn't seem to matter. "Do you mean the one with the pearl buttons? It's in the master closet."

Nora laughed. "You were dressing up in my clothes again, weren't you?"

She headed for the cavernous walk-in closet. When she returned, green sweater in hand, Connor had moved to the foot of the bed. He stared at her with a grin and a twinkle in his eye.

"Uh-oh," she said. "I know that look."

"What look?" he asked.

"The one that says you want a going-away present."

Nora thought for a moment before flashing a grin of her own. She dropped the sweater on a chair and slowly walked up to Connor, purposefully stopping just inches from his body. She was wearing only her bra and panties.

"From me, to you," she whispered in his ear, leaning in.

There wasn't that much to unwrap, but Connor took his time anyway. He gently kissed Nora's neck, then her shoulders, his lips tracing an imaginary line downward to the jutting curves of her small, pert breasts. There he lingered. One hand stroking her arm, the other reaching around to remove her bra.

Nora shivered, her body tingling. *Cute,*

funny, and very good in bed. What more could a girl ask for?

Connor knelt and kissed Nora's stomach, his tongue lightly drawing circles around her little wink of a belly button. Then, with a thumb resting on either side of her hips, he began to roll down her panties. He charted the progress with kiss after kiss after kiss.

"That's . . . very . . . *nice*," whispered Nora.

Now it was her turn. As Connor's tall, muscular frame straightened out before her, she began to undress him. Quickly, deftly, but sensually.

For a few seconds they stood still. Perfectly naked. Gazing at each other, taking in each and every detail. *God, what could be better than this?*

Suddenly Nora laughed. She gave Connor a quick, playful shove, and he fell back onto the bed. He was fully aroused. A prodigious human sundial lying there on the duvet.

Nora reached into her open suitcase and removed a black Ferragamo belt, pulling it taut in her hands.

Snap!

"Now, what was that about tying somebody up?" she asked.

Chapter 2

THIRTY MINUTES LATER, donning a plush pink terry-cloth robe, Nora descended the sprawling staircase of Connor's 11,000-square-foot, three-story neoclassic Colonial. Even by the standards of Briarcliff Manor and the other surrounding towns of tony Westchester, his home was impressive.

It was also impeccably furnished—every room a superb blending of form and function, style and comfort. The very best New York City antiques shops meet the best of Connecticut—Eleish–Van Breems, New Canaan Antiques, the Silk Purse, the Cellar. Signature works by Monet, Hudson River

School star Thomas Cole, Magritte. A George III secretary in the library that had once been owned by J. P. Morgan. A humidor originally presented to Castro by Richard Nixon, with provenance documentation. A walk-in wine cellar that held four thousand bottles and was nearly full.

True, Connor had hired one of the very best decorators in New York. In fact, he was so impressed with her, he asked her out on a date. Six months later she was tying him up in bed.

And he'd never felt happier, more excited, more alive in his entire life.

Five years before, he'd found love, marveled at it, treasured it, but his fiancée, Moira, had died of cancer. He'd thought he could never find love again, but suddenly there she was, the amazing Nora Sinclair.

Nora walked through the marble foyer and past the dining room. Before she had to leave, there was just enough time to take pity on the appetite she'd worked up in Connor.

She entered the kitchen, her favorite room in the house. Prior to enrolling at the New York School of Interior Design, she'd thought about becoming a chef. Even gone as far as taking courses at Le Cordon Bleu in Paris.

Though she chose to decorate homes instead of plates, cooking remained one of Nora's passions. It relaxed her. Helped clear her mind. Even making something as basic as Connor's favorite: a big, juicy double cheeseburger with onions—and inside, caviar.

Fifteen minutes later, she called out to him, "Honey, it's almost ready. Are you?"

Back in cutoff Dockers and Polo shirt, he made his way downstairs and ambled up behind Nora at the stove. "No place else on earth . . ."

". . . I'd rather be," she said, taking her cue. It was one of their things. A shared mantra. Little testaments of making the most of their time together, which, given their bustling careers, was always at a premium.

He peered over her shoulder as she sliced into a large onion. "They never make you cry, huh?"

"No, I guess they don't."

Connor took a seat at the kitchen table. "When is the car service picking you up?"

"Less than an hour."

He nodded, fidgeted with a place mat. "So where is this client of yours who's making you work on a Sunday?"

"Boston," she answered. "Retired guy who just bought and renovated a huge brownstone in the Back Bay."

Nora cut a kaiser roll and loaded it up with the sizzling double cheeseburger and onions. She grabbed an Amstel Light for Connor and another Evian water for herself from the fridge.

"Better than Smith and Wollensky," he said after the first bite. "With a far more attractive chef, I might add."

Nora smiled. "I've got some Graeter's for you, too. Raspberry Chip." Graeter's was the best ice cream she'd ever tasted, good enough, great enough, to have it shipped all the way from Cincinnati.

Nora took a sip of water and watched him make quick work of her cooking. He always did. Such a healthy appetite! Good for him.

"God, I love you," he suddenly gushed.

"And I love you." Nora stopped and stared into his blue eyes. "I do. I adore you, actually."

He raised his palms in the air. "Then, really, what are we waiting for?"

"What do you mean?"

"I mean, you've already got more clothes here than I do."

Nora blinked a few times. "Is that your idea of a proposal?"

"No," he said. "*This* is my idea of one."

He reached into the pocket of his shorts and removed a small box, Tiffany blue. Dropping to one knee, Connor placed it in her hand. "Nora Sinclair, you make me incredibly happy. I can't believe that I found you. Will you marry me?"

With a completely stunned look on her face, Nora opened the box to see an enormous diamond. Tears welled in her green eyes.

"Yes, yes, yes! Yippee-yes!" she cried out. "I'll marry you, Connor Brown! I love you so much."

Pop! went the champagne. Dom Pérignon '85 that he'd chilled in anticipation. He'd also bought a bottle of Jack Daniel's for himself, just in case Nora said no.

With two glasses poured, Connor raised his high and made a toast. "To happily ever after," he said.

"To happily ever after," echoed Nora. "To yippee-yes!"

They clinked glasses, they sipped, they

held hands. Madly in love and giddy with excitement, they hugged and kissed.

Soon, though, the celebration was interrupted by a horn in the driveway. Nora's car service had arrived.

She quickly dressed, and moments later, as the limousine started to drive away, Nora called to Connor out the open back window. *"I'm the luckiest girl in the world!"*

Chapter 3

NORA COULDN'T STOP staring at the dazzling ring for most of the ride to the Westchester airport. Connor had done well. The diamond was at least four carats, a brilliant round stone, at least D or E color, and flanked by baguettes. All set beautifully in platinum. It looked amazing on her, she thought. *It looks like it belongs.*

"Will you be needing a pickup upon your return, Ms. Sinclair?" asked the driver, guiding her out of the Lincoln Town Car in front of the terminal.

"No, I'm all set," she said. "Thank you." She handed the man a handsome tip, popped up the handle on her suitcase, and rolled on inside—past the exceedingly long line for coach check-in and right up to the first-class counter. With each step she could practically hear Connor's voice and the start of one of their other shared mantras.

"Less hassle . . . ," he'd say.

"Is always worth more money," she'd respond.

After a smooth takeoff and a climb to cruising altitude, Nora finally took her eyes off her engagement ring. She opened up the latest issue of *House & Garden.* One of the feature pictorials was a home she'd decorated for a client out in Connecticut. DARING IN DARIEN, read the title. The shots were glorious, and the accompanying article glowing with praise. The only thing missing was any mention of her name.

Precisely how she wanted it.

An hour later, the plane touched down at Logan Airport. Nora picked up her rental car, a Chrysler Sebring convertible. With the top down and her sunglasses on, she started on her way toward the Back Bay section of Boston.

The presets on the radio led her to believe two things. First, Beantown had too many all-talk stations. Second, the previous driver had no business renting that car. A convertible requires music.

She hit the SEEK button and found a tune to her liking. With her hair blowing freely in the wind and her tan skin soaking up the mid-June sun, she sang along with a classic. "I Only Have Eyes for You" by the Flamingos.

Soon Nora pulled up to a magnificent old brownstone on Commonwealth Avenue just down from the Public Garden. The relative quiet of a summer Sunday afternoon had lent itself to a bit of luck: a visitor space in front. "Goodie," Nora said.

She shifted into park and spent a moment making a minor adjustment to her hair. Barrette? No barrette? *Barrette!* Before reaching for the door, she glanced at her watch. It was showtime.

Chapter 4

AS SHE WALKED up to the oversize double doors of the old brownstone, Nora reached inside her purse for the key she'd been given when Jeffrey Walker first hired her. With the place so big and the buzzer a little temperamental, he'd asked that she just let herself in. A little voice in her head whispered, *Sweet.*

"Hello? Is anyone here?" Nora called as she stepped inside. "Hello? Mr. Walker?"

She stood in the center of the foyer and listened. Then she heard the distant sound of Miles Davis and his magnificent trumpet trickling down from the second floor.

She called out again. This time she heard footsteps overhead.

"Nora, is that you?" came a voice from atop the stairs.

"Were you expecting someone else?" she answered. "You better not be."

Jeffrey Walker hurried down to the foyer. Then he swept Nora up in his arms. He twirled her around as they kissed for a full minute. Then they kissed again.

"God, you're so *beautiful!*" he said, finally lowering her back to the floor.

She gave him a playful punch to the stomach with her left hand. Connor's four-carat diamond had already been replaced by Jeffrey's six-carat sapphire set with diamonds in a three-stone arrangement.

"I bet you say that to all your wives," she said.

"No, just the gorgeous ones like you. God, I missed you, Nora. Who wouldn't?"

They laughed and kissed again, deeply and passionately.

"So, tell me, how was your flight?" he asked.

"Good. For commercial anyway. How's the new book coming?"

"It's no *War and Peace.* No *Da Vinci Code,* either."

"You always say that, Jeffrey."

"It's always true."

At age forty-two, Jeffrey Sage Walker was an international bestselling author of historical fiction. He had fans numbering in the millions, the majority of them women. They liked his writing and strong female characters, but his rough-hewn handsomeness on the dust jacket certainly didn't hurt. Never had tussled bleached-blond hair and razor stubble looked so good.

Suddenly he swooped Nora up and threw her over his shoulder. She howled as he climbed the stairs.

Jeffrey was headed for the bedroom, but Nora grabbed a doorjamb and made him turn into his library. She had her eye on his favorite chair—the one he did his writing in. "You always say you do your best work in it," she said. "Let's see about that."

He lowered her into the worn brown leather seat cushion and changed the music. Norah Jones, one of their favorites.

As the singer's strong smoky voice began to build slowly and engulf the room, Nora leaned back and lifted her legs. Jeffrey removed her sandals, her capri pants, her panties. He helped her off with her favorite green cardigan while she reached down into his jeans.

"My handsome, brilliant husband," she whispered as she pulled down his pants.

Chapter 5

THAT EVENING NORA COOKED, a penne with a vodka sauce she made from scratch. A tossed salad and a bottle of Brunello from Jeffrey's private cellar. Dinner was served. Everything just so. The way he liked it.

They ate and talked about his new novel, which was set during the French Revolution. Jeffrey had only just returned from Paris days earlier. He was a stickler for authenticity in his writing and insisted on traveling for research. With Nora having her own busy work schedule, they were apart more than they were together. In fact, they had been married on a Saturday, in Cuernavaca,

Mexico, and had flown home on Sunday. No mess, no fuss, no records in the States, either. It was a very modern marriage.

"You know, Nora, I was thinking," he said, digging his fork into the last of his penne. "We should really take a trip together."

"Maybe you can give me that honeymoon you've been promising."

He put a hand to his heart and smiled. "Darling, every day I spend with you is a honeymoon."

Nora smiled back. "Nice try, Mr. Famous Writer, but I'm not letting you off with a cute line."

"Okay. Where do you want to go?"

"How about the south of France?" she offered. "We could shack up at the Hôtel du Cap."

"Or Italy?" he said, holding up his glass of wine. "Tuscany?"

"Hey, I know—why don't we do both?"

Jeffrey threw his head back and roared laughter. "There you go again," he said, his index finger waving in the air. "Always wanting it all. And why not?"

They finished up dinner, talking more possible destinations for the honeymoon. Madrid, Bali, Vienna, Lanai. The only thing settled as they split a pint of Ben & Jerry's Cherry Garcia was to get a travel agent involved.

By eleven they were snuggling in bed. Husband and wife. So very much in love.

Chapter 6

THE NEXT DAY at a few minutes past noon, on the corner of Forty-second and Park in front of Grand Central Station, a woman screamed. A second woman turned her head to look and she screamed, too. The man beside her muttered, "Holy shit." Then they all ran for cover.

Something very bad was happening. A train wreck, so to speak, just outside one of the most famous train stations in the world.

The chain reaction of fear and confusion quickly cleared everyone from the sidewalk. Everyone, except for three people.

One was a fat man with dense sideburns,

thinning hair, and a dark mustache. He was dressed in an ill-fitting brown suit with wide lapels. Wider still was his shiny blue tie. On the ground by his feet was a medium-size suitcase.

Next to the fat man was a young woman, perhaps mid-twenties, attractive. She had red hair that hung straight down to her shoulders, lots of freckles on her face. She wore a short plaid skirt and a white tank top. A beat-up knapsack hung over one shoulder.

The fat man and the young woman couldn't have looked any more different. However, at that moment they were very much connected.

By a gun.

"If you come any closer, I'll kill her!" barked the fat man with a thick, Middle Eastern accent. He jammed the cold steel of the barrel hard against her temple. "I swear, I'll shoot her dead. I'll do it in a second. No problem for me."

The threat was directed at the third person remaining on the sidewalk—a guy standing maybe ten feet away, wearing baggy gray khakis and a black T-shirt. He looked like a typical enough tourist. From the Pacific Northwest, perhaps. Oregon? The state of

Washington? A runner maybe. Somebody in decent shape anyway.

And then *he* pulled a gun.

The Tourist took a step closer, his gun pointed at the forehead of the fat man with the mustache. Dead center, actually. The Tourist didn't seem to care that the young woman was in his line of fire.

"No problem for me, either," he said.

"I said stop!" said the fat man. "Don't come any closer. Stay where you are."

The Tourist ignored him. He took another step.

"I swear, I'll fucking kill her!"

"No, you won't," said the Tourist calmly. "Because if you shoot her, I'll shoot you." He took another step forward but then stopped. "Think it through, friend. I know you can't afford to lose what's in that suitcase. But is it worth your life?"

The fat man squinted and suddenly looked to be in great pain. He appeared to be thinking about what the Tourist had said. Or maybe not. Then a maniacal smile filled his face. He cocked his gun.

"Pleeeeease," begged the young woman, trembling. *"Pleeeeease."* Tears poured from her eyes. She could barely stand.

"Shut up!" the fat man yelled in her ear. *"Shut the hell up! I can't hear myself think!"*

The Tourist stood his ground, his flinty blue eyes locked on one thing: the man's trigger finger.

He didn't like what he saw.

Twitching!

The fat bastard was going to shoot the girl, wasn't he? And that just wasn't acceptable.

Chapter 7

"WHOA," the Tourist announced with a raised palm. "Take it easy, my man." He took a step backward, chuckled to himself. "Who am I kidding, right? I'm not that good of a shot. No way I could be sure to get you and not the girl."

"That's right," said the fat man, hugging the young woman even tighter with his puffy right arm. "So, you tell me now, *who's in charge?*"

"You are," said the Tourist with a deferential nod. "Just tell me what you want me to do, my friend. Hell, if you want, I'll lay my gun down on the sidewalk, okay?"

The man stared hard at the Tourist. His squint returned. "Okay, but slowly you do this," he said.

"Of course. Easy-peasy-Japaneasy. Wouldn't have it any other way."

The Tourist began to lower his gun, and a gasp could be heard from behind a nearby telephone kiosk. Another gasp followed from behind a parked delivery van on Forty-second Street. The looky loos who'd run for cover but still *had* to watch the unfolding events were all thinking the same thing: *Don't do it, buddy. Don't give up your gun. He's going to kill you! And her, too!*

The Tourist bent his knees and crouched down. He gingerly placed the gun on the sidewalk.

"See, nice and easy," he said. "Now what do you want me to do?"

The fat man began to laugh, his fluffy, unkempt mustache bunching up beneath his nose. "What do I want you to do?" he said. The laughing grew even louder. He could hardly contain himself.

Suddenly he stopped laughing. His face went rigid. The man removed the gun from the side of the young woman's head and aimed it straight in front of him. "What I want you to do is *die.*"

That's when he made his move.

The Tourist.

In the blink of an eye, in one fast, efficient move, he reached up his pant leg and pulled a Beretta 9 mm from his shin holster. He whipped his arm forward and fired, the *crack!* echoing before anyone knew what had happened. Including the fat man.

The hole in his forehead was about the size of a dime, and for a moment he froze like a statue, an oversize Buddha. The onlookers screamed, the young woman with the knapsack fell to her knees, and with a horrific thud, the fat man collapsed to the dirty, littered sidewalk. His blood spurted like a water fountain.

As for the Tourist, he returned the Beretta to his shin holster and the other gun to his fanny pack. He stood up and walked over to the suitcase. He picked it up and carried it to a blue Ford Mustang that was double-parked on the street. The engine had been running the entire time.

"Have a nice day, ladies and gentlemen," he said to the people who'd been watching

him in stunned silence. "You're a lucky girl."
He saluted the woman holding the knapsack
tightly in front of her chest.

The Tourist then climbed behind the wheel
of the Mustang and drove off.

With the suitcase.

Chapter 8

THE LIGHT TURNED GREEN and the New York City cabbie hit the gas pedal as if he were trying to squash a bug. What he really almost squashed was a bike messenger—that rare breed of daring and death wish for which red lights and stop signs are merely a crazy suggestion, an un-joke.

As the cabbie slammed on his brakes in the middle of the intersection, the messenger swerved and kept right on going, his speeding bike missing the bumper of the cab by no more than an inch.

"Asshole!" screamed the messenger over his shoulder.

"Up yours!" the cabbie yelled, flipping him the bird. He glanced at Nora in the backseat and shook his head in disgust. Then he floored it again as if nothing had happened.

Nora shook her head and smiled.

It was good to be home.

The cabbie continued his mad dash south on Second Avenue toward lower Manhattan. After a few blocks of relative silence, he switched on the radio. It was 1010 News.

A man with a deep, mellifluent voice was just finishing up a report on the latest city-budget crisis when he announced that there was breaking news in midtown. He turned it over to a female reporter who was at the scene.

"Just about a half hour ago, a tense, if not somewhat bizarre, situation unfolded here at the corner of Forty-second and Park Avenue outside Grand Central Station."

The reporter described how a man took a young woman hostage at gunpoint, only to be shot dead by *another* man whom onlookers believed to be an undercover police officer.

"Except when the police finally did arrive, it became clear that the man was not affiliated in any way with the NYPD. In fact, at this time, no one seems to know who he is. After

the shooting he fled from the scene—but not before first absconding with a large suitcase belonging to the dead man."

As the reporter promised more on the story as it developed, the cabbie let out a long sigh and glanced in his rearview mirror. "Just what this city needs, huh?" he said. "Another vigilante on the loose."

"I doubt that's what it is," Nora said.

"Why's that?"

"The suitcase. Whatever happened—and why—obviously has to do with what's inside it."

The cabbie shrugged his shoulders, then nodded. "Yeah, you're probably right. So what do you think it is?"

"I don't know," said Nora. "But you can bet it wasn't dirty clothes."

Chapter 9

THERE WAS A QUOTE from someone, somewhere, that Nora loved and also believed with all her heart: One's real life is almost always the life one doesn't lead.

Well, not this girl's life.

At the corner of Mercer and Spring in SoHo, she paid the cabbie and wheeled her suitcase into the two-story, all-marble lobby of her apartment building. It was a deluxe converted warehouse. An oxymoron everywhere but in New York City.

Hers was the penthouse loft, half of the entire floor. In a word, huge; in another, stylish. George Smith furniture, polished

Brazilian wood floors, a Poggenpohl-designed kitchen. Calm and quiet and elegant, this was her sanctuary. Her true "no place else on earth I'd rather be."

Actually, Nora loved to give tours of the place to those few people who interested her.

At the front door was Nora's sentry—a six-foot clay sculpture of a male nude by Javier Marin.

There were *two* intimate sitting areas—one in sumptuous white leather, its complement in black—all Nora's design.

She adored everything in her place and had scoured antiques shops, flea markets, and art galleries from SoHo to the Pacific Northwest to London and Paris, and tiny villages in Italy, Belgium, Switzerland.

Her collectibles were everywhere.

Silver: several Hermès treasures; a dozen or more silver bowls, which she loved.

Art glass: French Gallé picture frames; opaline boxes in white, green, turquoise.

Paintings by a select handful of up-and-coming artists from New York, London, Paris, Berlin.

And, of course, her bedroom: so vivid—very heavy on the beta waves—dark wine-colored walls, gilded sconces and mirrors, a chiseled block of antique scrolled wood over the bed.

Go ahead, figure me out if you can.

Nora grabbed a bottle of Evian from the fridge and then made a few calls, one of them to Connor, which she called her Man Maintenance. A bit later she made a similar call to Jeffrey.

At a little past eight that evening, Nora walked into Babbo in the heart of Greenwich Village. *Yes, it is definitely good to be home.*

Never mind that it was a Monday, Babbo was packed. The mingling sounds of silverware, glasses, plates, and hip city people filled the split-level restaurant with a pulsating hum.

Nora spotted her best friend, Elaine, already seated with Allison, another dear friend. They were at a table along the wall of the more casual first floor. She bypassed the hostess and headed over. Cheek kisses all around. God, she adored these girls.

"Allison's in love with our waiter," announced Elaine as Nora settled in.

Allison rolled her big brown eyes. "All I said was that he is cute. His name is Ryan. Ryan Pedi. He even has a cute name."

"Sounds like love to me," said Nora, playing along.

"There you have it, corroborating testimony!" said Elaine, who was a corporate lawyer with Eggers, Beck & Schmiedel, one of the city's preeminent firms. Above all else they specialized in billable hours.

Speak of the devil. The young waiter, tall and dark, appeared at the table to ask if Nora wanted anything to drink.

"Just water, please," she said. "With bubbles."

"No, tonight you're drinking with us, Nora. That's it. She'll have a cosmopolitan."

"Coming right up." With a quick nod, he turned and walked off.

Nora put a hand to the side of her mouth and whispered, "He *is* cute. . . ."

"I told you," said Allison. "Too bad he's barely old enough to drink."

"I was thinking more like *drive*," said Elaine. "Or is it we're getting so much older that they're looking younger?" She dropped her head. "Okay, now I'm depressed."

"Emergency change of subject!" declared Nora. She turned to Allison. "So what's the new black for this fall?"

"Believe it or not, it may actually be black."

Allison was a fashion editor at *W,* or as she liked to call it, the only magazine that could actually break your toe if you ever dropped it. Their business model was simple, she explained: big ads featuring skinny models wearing designer clothes never went out of style.

"So what's new with you, Nor?" asked Allison. "Seems like you're always out of town. You're a ghost, girl."

"I know, it's crazy. I just got back today. Second homes are all the rage."

Allison let out a sigh. "I've got enough problems paying for my first—oh, that reminds me, did I tell you about the guy who moved in on my floor?"

"The sculptor who played all that weird New Age music?" asked Elaine.

"No, not him. He moved out months ago," she said with a dismissive wave. "This new guy just bought the corner apartment."

"What's the verdict?" asked Elaine, ever the lawyer.

"Single, adorable, and an oncologist," said Allison. She shrugged. "I suppose there are worse things in life than marrying a rich doctor."

The words had barely left Allison's mouth

before she raised a desperate hand to cover it.

A quiet fell over the table.

"Guys, it's *okay*," said Nora.

"I'm so sorry, sweetie," said Allison, embarrassed. "I wasn't thinking."

"Really, you don't have to apologize."

"Emergency change of subject!" declared Elaine.

"Now you're both being silly. Listen, just because Tom was a doctor doesn't mean we can't ever talk about doctors." Nora put her hand on top of Allison's. "Tell us more about your oncologist."

Allison did and the three carried on, the idea being that they'd been friends long enough not to let a terribly awkward moment stand in their way.

The young waiter returned with Nora's cosmopolitan and went over the specials. The three friends drank, they ate, they laughed, they gossiped wickedly. Nora looked completely at ease. Comfortable and relaxed. So much so that neither Allison nor Elaine could tell where her thoughts really were for the rest of the evening: the death of her first husband, Dr. Tom Hollis.

Or rather, his murder.

Chapter 10

A TALL GLASS of water and some aspirin—a little preventive medicine in the wake of her after-dinner drinks with Elaine and Allison. Nora never got drunk, abhorring the idea of ever surrendering control. But thanks to the high spirits and good company of Elaine and Allison, she had gotten a nice buzz on.

Two glasses of water, *two* aspirin.

Then she changed into her favorite cotton pajamas and pulled out the bottom drawer of her oversize dresser. Buried beneath several cashmere sweaters from Polo was a photo album.

Nora closed the drawer and turned off all

the lights, save for the lamp on her night-stand. She climbed into bed and opened the album to the first page.

"Where it all began," she whispered to herself.

The pictures were arranged chronologi-cally, a photographic time line of her rela-tionship with the first love of her life, the man she called Dr. Tom. Their very first weekend away together in the Berkshires; a concert at Tanglewood; shots of them in their suite at the Gables Inn in Lenox.

On the next page was a medical confer-ence he took her to in Phoenix. They had stayed at the Biltmore, one of her favorites, but only if they put you in the main building.

After that were some candids from the wedding in the Conservatory Tent at the New York Botanical Garden.

Those pages were followed by their hon-eymoon down in Nevis. Glorious, one of the best weeks of her life.

In between were memories along the way—parties, dinners, funny faces mugging for the camera. Nora touching her tongue to her nose. Tom curling his upper lip like Elvis. Or was that supposed to be Bill Clinton?

Then the pictures stopped.

Instead, there were clippings.

The last pages of the album were filled with nothing but newspaper items. The various stories and the obituary—tinted yellow now from the passage of time. Nora had kept them all.

TOP MANHATTAN DOC DIES IN MEDICAL MIX-UP, wrote the *New York Post.* MD A VICTIM OF HIS OWN MEDICINE, declared the *Daily News.* As for the *New York Times* there was no hyperbole. Just a simple obituary with a matter-of-fact heading: DR. TOM HOLLIS, NOTED CARDIOLOGIST, DEAD AT 42.

Nora closed the album and lay in bed alone with her thoughts about Tom and what had happened. The beginning of everything, really: the start of her life. Nora's thoughts then turned naturally to Connor and Jeffrey. She glanced down at her left hand, which was sporting neither ring at the moment. She knew she had a decision to make.

Instinctively, Nora began compiling a mental list. Orderly and concise. All the things she loved about being with one versus the other.

Connor vs. Jeffrey.

They were both so much fun. They made her laugh, made her feel special. And there was certainly no denying that they were wonderful in bed—or wherever else they chose to have sex. They were tall, in wonderful shape, handsome as film stars. No, actually, they were more handsome than the film stars she knew.

The fact was, Nora loved being with Connor and Jeffrey equally. Which made her decision that much harder.

Which one was she going to kill?
First.

Chapter 11

OKAY, THIS IS WHERE it gets really tricky.
And also really hairy.

The Tourist sat at the corner table inside a Starbucks on West Twenty-third in Chelsea. Just about every table was in use by slackers and moochers, but the environment felt safe and secure. Probably because there *were* so many moochers and hangarounds; hell, for three dollars and change you ought to get something with your coffee, some added benefit.

The suitcase he had appropriated outside Grand Central was on the floor between his legs, and he already knew a couple of things about it.

One—it was open, not locked.

Two—there were men's clothes, mostly wrinkled, and a brown leather Dopp kit inside.

Three—the Dopp kit had the usual shaving crap, but also something interesting: a flash drive, a DiskOnKey—one of those USB external storage devices you can attach to any computer. Costs about $99 at CompUSA. The flash drive was what all the trouble was about, wasn't it? Ironic—it was smaller than his finger.

But the little sucker could hold a lot of information. Obviously, this one did.

The Tourist already had his Mac out. Now came the moment of truth. If he had the guts. Which, it so happened, he did.

Here we go!

He plugged the flash drive into the Mac.

Why did some miserable fat guy have to die for this on Forty-second Street?

The drive icon appeared—E.

The Tourist began a drag and drop of the files stored on the flash drive. *Here we go. Here we go, loop-de-loop; here we go, lu-de-lu.*

A couple of minutes later the Tourist was ready to look at the files.

Then he stopped himself.

A pretty girl—only with spiked black and crimson hair—was trying to sneak a peek from the next table.

The Tourist finally looked her way. "You know the old joke—I could show you what's in the file, but then I'd have to kill you."

The girl smiled. "What about the joke—you show me yours, I'll show you mine?"

The Tourist laughed back. "You don't have a laptop."

"Your loss." She shrugged, got up from her table, and started to leave. "You're cute, for such an asshole."

"Get a haircut," the Tourist said, and grinned.

Finally he looked back at the computer screen.

Here we go!

What he saw on the screen made sense—sort of. If anything made sense in this crazy world.

The file consisted of names, addresses, names of banks in Switzerland and the Caymans. Offshore accounts.

And amounts.

The Tourist did a quick tally in his head.
Ballpark figure, but close enough.
A little over one point four.
Billion.

Chapter 12

NEW YORK MAY BE the city that never sleeps, but at four in the morning there are definitely parts that are barely awake. One such was the dimly lit basement of a parking garage on the Lower East Side. Buried five stories beneath the street, it was a picture of stillness. A concrete cocoon. The only noise was the numbing buzz of the fluorescent lighting overhead.

That and an impatient middle finger tapping on the steering wheel in an idling blue Ford Mustang.

Inside the Mustang, the Tourist glanced at his watch and shook his head. His finger tapping continued, his *middle* finger. His contact was late.

Two days late, actually.

A missed appointment.

Trouble brewing? No doubt about it.

Ten minutes later a pair of headlights finally lit up the far wall by the ramp to the next level. A white Chevy van appeared. On the side was a sign for a florist. FLOWERS BY LUCILLE, it read.

Oh, c'mon, the Tourist thought to himself. *A flower delivery truck?*

The van slowly approached the Mustang, stopping twenty feet away. The engine was cut and a tall, rail-thin man stepped outside. He was wearing a gray suit, white shirt, and tie. He began walking toward the van. There was somebody else in the van, but he stayed inside.

The Tourist got out and met the Thin Man halfway. "You're late," he said.

"And you're lucky to be alive," said the contact.

"You know, there are some people who actually think of it as skill."

"I'll give you points for the shot. Dead-center forehead, I'm told."

"Well, the guy did have a receding hairline. Bigger target. Is the girl all right?"

"Shaken up. But she'll be fine. She's a professional. Just like you."

The Thin Man reached inside his jacket pocket. Not good! He pulled out a pack of Marlboros, offered one to the Tourist.

"No, thanks. Gave it up for Lent. 'Bout fifteen Lents ago."

The man lit up. He shook the flame from his match.

"What are the New York police saying?" asked the Tourist.

"Not a whole hell of a lot. Let's just say they're dealing with conflicting eyewitnesses."

"You sent someone over, didn't you?"

"*Two* eyewitnesses, actually. We had them both claim that you had a scar on your neck and a goatee."

The Tourist smiled, rubbed his bare chin. "That's pretty good. How about the working press?"

"They're all over it. The only bigger mystery than who you are is what's in the suitcase. Speaking of which . . ."

"It's in the trunk."

The two walked to the back of the Mustang. The Tourist popped the trunk. He lifted out the suitcase, placed it on the ground. The other man looked it over for a moment.

"You tempted to open it up?" he asked.

"How do you know I didn't?"

"You didn't."

"Yeah, but *how* do you know?"

The man blew a smoke ring. "Because we'd be having a much different conversation right now."

"Am I supposed to know what that means?"

"Of course not. You're not in the loop."

The Tourist let it go. "So, what now?"

"Now you get lost. You've got another gig, right?"

"A *gig?* Yeah, I'm already on something interesting. Who's in the car?"

"You did good on this one. He said to tell you that. Leave it at that."

"I *am* good. That's why they called me in on this."

They shook hands and the Tourist watched as the Thin Man carried the suitcase back to the van and drove off. The Tourist wondered if they would be able to figure out that he'd looked at the contents of the flash drive. Any which way, he was definitely in the loop now. Even if he wished to hell that he wasn't.

Chapter 13

IT WAS A BUSY morning for Nora. First, she shopped for a very delicious hour at Sentiments on East Sixty-first, and now she had work to do for a client at ABC Carpet & Home near Union Square. After that it was off to the D&D Building showroom and, finally, Devonshire, an English garden shop.

She was shopping for Constance McGrath, one of her first clients. Constance—who was definitely not a "Connie, for short"—had just moved from her posh East Side two-bedroom to an even more posh two-bedroom on Central Park West. The Dakota, to be exact, where they had filmed *Rosemary's Baby* and

John Lennon was murdered. A former stage actress back in her day, Constance still possessed a flair for the dramatic. She explained to Nora her move across Central Park as follows: "The sun sets in the west, and in this, my last apartment, so will I."

Nora liked Constance. The woman was feisty, forthright, and fond of invoking a decorator's favorite expression: *Money is no object.* She had also outlived two husbands.

"As I live and breathe!" came a man's voice.

Nora turned to see Evan Frazer with his arms outstretched wide in full-hug mode. Evan represented Ballister Grove Antiques, which occupied a large portion of the fifth floor.

"Evan!" said Nora. "It's so good to see you."

"Even better to see you," he replied. He kissed Nora on both cheeks. "So, what fabulously wealthy client are you shopping for today?"

Nora could almost see the dollar signs flashing in his eyes. "She'll go nameless, of course, but lucky for you she's ditching some of her ornate French for a more traditional English look."

"Then you've come to the right place," he

said with a toothy grin. "But then again, you always do."

For the next hour or so, Evan walked Nora through his entire inventory of English furniture. He knew the drill: what to say and what not to say. *Especially* what not to say to Nora Sinclair.

Nora hated to be told by a salesperson that something was beautiful. As if that would influence her opinion. She had her own aesthetic. Her own taste. Part innate, the rest developed and honed by experience. She trusted it implicitly.

"Does this come with one leaf or two?" she asked Evan while hovering over a mahogany dining-room table with satinwood banding.

"It comes with one," he said. "But it can accommodate two, and we can easily have the second one made."

"The one should be fine." She glanced at the price. Again, it was a perfunctory move when shopping for Constance McGrath. With a step back and a final peruse, Nora delivered her signature variation on "I'll take it." Why say three words when she could be far more emphatic with one?

"Done!" she declared.

Evan immediately pulled a sold card from his clipboard and slapped it on the table. It was the fourth and final slap of the morning. Combined with the breakfront, highboy, and settee that were also "done" deals, Nora was satisfied.

The two took a seat on a large sofa as Evan wrote up the invoice. Not a word was spoken regarding Nora's 10 percent kick-back. It was understood.

After saying good-bye to Evan, Nora stopped for a quick bite at one of the in-store restaurants, La Mercado. She realized she didn't need to visit D&D or Devonshire after all. She'd accomplished everything she had to at Sentiments and Ballister Grove. Over a Cobb salad and a dulce de leche crepe for dessert, she worked her cell phone.

She placed a call to Constance to rave about the morning's purchases. She also returned calls from both Jeffrey and Connor to fulfill her Man Maintenance for the day.

Chapter 14

NOW SHE HAD some important work to do at a lawyer's office on East Forty-ninth Street near the East River.

"So, Ms. Sinclair, what can I help you with?" asked Steven Keppler, Esq.

Nora smiled warmly. "Please, call me Olivia."

"Olivia it is, then." Keppler smiled back at Nora a little too broadly from behind his large desk. "You know, I have a boat named *Olivia*."

"No kidding!" said Nora, feigning amazement. "I'll take that as a good sign."

What she took as a better sign was the

way Steven Keppler—middle-aged, midtown tax attorney with a bad comb-over—was ogling her breasts and legs.

It all but guaranteed smooth sailing.

The other male attorneys on Nora's list were booked solid for two to three weeks. The same would've been true for Steven Keppler, were it not for a sudden opening in his schedule due to an ill client. Fortuitous timing for her. In less than twenty-four hours, Nora had her appointment. Or rather, "Olivia" had her appointment. For what Nora was attempting, she needed to borrow her mother's name.

She continued: "What you can help me with, Steven, is setting up a business for me." *And by the way, that business isn't located in my brassiere.*

"It so happens that's something I specialize in," said the lawyer.

Nora tried not to cringe when he actually ended the sentence by combining a wink with a loud, double-clicking noise from the side of his mouth.

"Where will this business be located?" he asked.

"The Cayman Islands."

"Oh," he said, pausing. A slight look of

concern came over his face. His very attractive new client in the silk blouse and short skirt was undoubtedly looking to sidestep the law and not pay her taxes.

"I hope that's not a problem," said Nora.

Keppler's disgusting ogling went into overdrive. "Ah, no, I don't see why it . . . uh . . . has to be," he stammered. "The thing is, establishing a business down there requires the cooperation of what's called a registered agent. In simple terms, it's a resident of the Cayman Islands who, in name only, acts as a representative of your company. Am I making myself clear?"

Nora knew all of this but didn't let on. She nodded her head like a rapt student.

"As luck would have it," Keppler added, "I have just such an agent under my employ."

"That *is* lucky," Nora said.

"Now, I assume you'll be needing a bank account opened for you down there as well, right?"

Bingo.

"Yes, I think that would be a good idea. You can do that for me?"

"Actually, you're supposed to do that in person," he said.

Again, Nora shifted in her seat. "Oh, what a horrible inconvenience," she said.

"I know, isn't it?" He leaned over his desk. "Maybe I could pull a few strings and save you the trip."

"That would be wonderful! You're a lifesaver."

He reached into a file drawer and took out some forms. "I'll just need to get a little information from you, Olivia."

Chapter 15

THE LINCOLN TOWN CAR turned off busy Route 9, then sped along picturesque Scarborough Road, eventually making it to equally pretty Central Drive, finally pulling into Connor's Belgium block driveway a little before dusk that Friday. The driver had barely stepped out to open the door for Nora when he was beaten to it by Connor, who was obviously beyond eager to see her.

"Come here, you!" he beckoned. "I've been just about crazy, thinking about you."

Nora swung her feet out of the car and immediately leaped into his arms. They kissed while the driver—a robust, older

Italian man—popped the trunk and lifted out Nora's suitcase. He tried not to stare but he couldn't help it. With the sun setting on a beautiful day, and in front of one of the most gorgeous homes he'd ever seen, here was this lovely couple clearly head over heels in love. He thought to himself, *If this ain't the top of the mountain, I don't know what is.*

"Here you go," said Connor. He reached into the pocket of his trousers and pulled out a wad of cash. He slid the driver a twenty-dollar tip.

"Thank you, sir," the man said through a thick accent. "You're too kind."

"And too cute!" chirped Nora as she hugged Connor around the waist.

He really is cute, isn't he? she couldn't help thinking.

The driver jiggled with a hearty chuckle and returned to his car. "Have a nice night, kids," he called over his shoulder.

Nora and Connor laughed, then watched for a moment as the Town Car turned out of the driveway and disappeared.

Nora peeled herself away from Connor. "So how was work?" she asked. "On second thought, I don't want to talk about work."

"Me, either," he said. "Besides, all work and no play . . ."

". . . makes us *very fucking boring!*"

That was one of their very first mantras—and still one of their favorites.

"We should do it right here," she said, and winked. "Right here on the front lawn! To hell with the neighbors. Let them watch if they want to. Maybe they'll be inspired."

Connor reached for her hand. "Actually, I've got a better idea."

"Oh? Better than sex with me? What would that be?"

"It's a surprise," he said. "Follow me."

Chapter 16

"YOU WANT TO do it in the *garage?*" Nora asked with a giggle.

Connor could barely contain his laughter. "No," he said. "That's not the surprise. It's not such a bad idea, though."

He'd led Nora around the side of the house, stopping about ten feet in front of his five-car garage. All the doors were closed. Nora stood there with him, not knowing what to expect.

"Are you ready?" he asked.

He reached into the other pocket of his trousers—the one without the wad of cash—and pulled out the garage door opener. It had five buttons. He pressed the middle one.

The door began to rise slowly.

"Omigod!" shrieked Nora.

Behind the door, facing out, was a brand-new bright red Mercedes SL 500 convertible with a huge white bow strapped across the hood.

"Well?" said Connor.

Nora was speechless.

"Thing is, if you're going to be my wife, you're going to need your own set of wheels, don't you think?"

Nora was still speechless.

He was getting a big kick out of this. "I take it you're surprised?"

Nora leaped into his arms. The words came, and very loudly. "You're absolutely amazing! Thank you, thank you, thank you!" She flashed her left hand. "First a beautiful ring and now—"

"A key ring," he said as if it were another one of their mantras. "Which, by the way, is waiting in the ignition."

Connor carried Nora into the garage and placed her gently in the driver's seat. Then he raced around to the other side, removing the bow along the way. "Shotgun!" he yelled like a schoolboy, hopping over the door into the passenger seat.

Nora sat admiring the car's interior, running her fingers along the stitched leather of the steering wheel. "What do you think? Should we break it in?" she asked.

"Absolutely. That's what it's for."

She looked at him, the corners of her mouth curling mischievously. Her hands were suddenly nowhere near the ignition. They were playing between Connor's legs.

"Oh," he said happily, his deep voice cracking.

Nora nimbly climbed out of her seat and over to Connor. On top of him, knees bent, she began to run her fingers through his thick black hair while gently kissing his forehead, both cheeks, and finally his mouth. She unbuttoned his sports shirt.

"How far back do you think these seats go?" she asked.

"I'll have to check that out."

He reached down along the side of his seat, and like that, it began to recline with a low-pitched hum. They began to undress each other, and it was as if their clothes were on fire. His shirt, Nora's blouse and bra. Trousers and skirt, briefs and panties.

"I love you," Connor said, staring up into her eyes. There was no way not to believe him and to feel something for him.

"I love you, too," she replied.

And right there in the garage, Nora went for a ride in her new car.

Chapter 17

"DO YOU REALIZE there's only one room left in this house we haven't made love in?" Connor asked. He looked as if he was doing the math in his head.

"Well, I suppose the night is still young," said Nora.

He pulled her tighter in his arms. "You're insatiable."

"And aren't you the lucky one."

They'd finally come in from the garage and were standing in the kitchen, holding their clothes as well as each other.

"Speaking of insatiable . . . ," he said.

She stifled a laugh. "How did I know that

was coming? All right, naked boy," she said. "How does an omelet sound?"

"It sounds fantastic. Or we could just go out? I could call the Inn at Pound Ridge? Or the Iron Horse?"

Nora shook her head.

"What do you want in your omelet? I want to cook for you."

"Surprise me," he said. "In fact, we'll make that the theme of the evening—surprises."

And for the first time, Nora felt a pain in her stomach. *This is it.*

He went off for a quick shower but not before bringing in her suitcase, which had been sitting out in the driveway. She opened it in the kitchen and removed a neatly folded pair of jeans and a white cotton T-shirt.

Then, like an old friend, a little voice inside her head showed up.

C'mon, Nora, keep it together now.

She got dressed and began preparing the omelet. With a look in the Sub-Zero she found half a Vidalia onion, a whole green pepper, and some Virginia ham, a quarter-inch thick. That was settled. She'd make a western omelet.

You've already made your decision. It's

*just nerves, that's all. You know you can get
past this—you've done it before.*

The kitchen had a magnetic strip along
the backsplash for holding large knives.
Nora stared at them. They all hung in a perfect row, razor-sharp. She reached for the
biggest one and gripped it in her hand, her
fingers adjusting to the slight curve of the
handle before squeezing tight.

*Forget about the car. And the ring. Es-
pecially the ring.*

The eggs were cracked open and
whipped, the green pepper diced. Nora was
making small cubes of the ham. She stood
at the cutting board by the sink, her back
turned to the entrance of the kitchen. She
could hear Connor.

"I'm so hungry, I could eat a restaurant,"
came his voice, getting louder by the word.

Do it, Nora!

He was walking right toward her.

Do it, now!

She cut off another piece of ham and
stared intently at the knife, her knuckles
going stark white as she gripped it tighter.
The lights from the ceiling shone down and
danced off the blade.

There was still time to change her mind.

Connor's footsteps were just behind her now, getting closer and closer. She felt his warm breath on the back of her neck. He was right there, within reach. She spun around quickly, her hand raised high.

Chapter 18

"DOES THIS TASTE okay to you?" she asked.

Connor opened his mouth for the piece of ham hanging from her fingertips. He chewed for a few seconds. "Delish."

"Good, because I didn't know how long you've had it," she said. "How was your shower?"

"Felt great. Not as good as you feel, though."

Nora finished cubing the ham and began slicing the onion. *Still time to change your mind.*

Connor, wearing only sweatpants, his wet

hair combed back, went to the fridge and grabbed an Amstel. "You want one?" he asked.

"No, thanks. I've got my water." She raised a bottle of Evian for him to see. "Watching my waist—for you."

He opened his beer and took a swig. He looked at Nora from the side. "Honey, are you all right?"

She turned to him, a lone tear streaking down her cheek.

"Oh," she said, realizing it was there. She wiped it away and forced a smile before averting her eyes. "I guess onions make me cry after all."

Nora cooked up the western omelet soft, no burn on the outside, the way he liked it. She placed it in front of Connor at the kitchen table. He doused it with salt and pepper and dug in his fork.

"Fantastic!" he declared. "This could be your best."

"I'm glad you like it." She sat down next to him. He took a few more bites and she watched.

"So, what do you want to do tomorrow?" he asked.

"I don't know. Maybe we can take my new car out for a spin."

"You mean actually leave the garage?"

He laughed and raised his fork for another bite. But with his hand halfway up to his mouth, Connor froze.

In a split second the color drained from his face. He was as white as milk. His head began to weave. The fork dropped to the plate with a noisy clang.

"Connor, what is it?"

"I don't . . ." He could barely talk. "I don't know," he said, his voice straining. "All of a sudden I feel really . . ."

He immediately grabbed his stomach as if he'd been viciously punched. Or stabbed. His eyes rolled back into his head. He lurched in his chair before falling off with a horrific thud.

"Connor!" Nora sprang from her seat and tried to help him off the floor. "C'mon," she said. "Try to get up."

He struggled to his feet, his legs like rubber. She guided him to the bathroom in the hall. Connor fell to the floor again, nearly passing out. Nora lifted the seat of the toilet, and he tried to crawl to it.

"I'm . . . I'm . . . going to be sick," he muttered between gasps of air. He was beginning to hyperventilate.

"Let me get you something to take," she said, her voice ripe with panic. "I'll be right back."

She ran into the kitchen while Connor labored to raise his head above the lip of the toilet. His body was an inferno, and not just his stomach anymore. Sweat gushed from every pore.

Nora returned with a glass in her hand. In it was a clear liquid, fizzing. Looked like Alka-Seltzer. "Here, drink this," she said.

Connor took the glass, his hands trembling. He could barely lift it to his mouth, so she helped him. He took one sip, then another.

"Take more," she said. "Finish."

He took another sip before clutching his stomach again. Connor clamped shut his eyes and clenched his teeth, the jaw muscles so taut that they looked ready to burst from his skin.

"Help me," he begged. "Nora!"

Seconds later, it was as if his prayers had been answered. The awful trembling began to subside. As quickly as it started, it was ending.

"I think the medicine is working, honey," said Nora.

Connor was back to breathing normally. Some of his color had returned. He opened his eyes, slowly at first, then wide. He breathed out a long sigh of relief. "What was *that?*" he asked.

That's when it all started again.

Only ten times worse. The trembling was now a series of brutal spasms that shook his body. The gasping became a quick and horrible suffocation. Connor's face turned blue, his eyes fully bloodshot.

The glass fell from his hands and shattered. His body violently convulsed, and he was writhing in pain. His hands reached for his neck, desperate for air.

He tried to scream. Couldn't. Nothing came out of his mouth.

He tried to reach for Nora. She took a step back.

She didn't want to watch and yet she couldn't turn away. All she could do was wait for the shaking and convulsing to stop again, which it finally did.

Permanently.

Connor was lying on the floor of one of the bathrooms in his 11,000-square-foot Colonial. Dead.

Chapter 19

THE FIRST THING Nora did was to clean up the broken glass off the bathroom floor.

The second thing was to scrape the remains of the omelet down the disposal, turn on the disposal, then thoroughly wash the plate, fork, and omelet pan.

The third was to fix herself a stiff drink.

Half a glass of Johnnie Walker Blue, straight up, and it was gone in about half a second. She poured herself a little more and sat down at the kitchen table. She gathered her thoughts. Went over her lines. Drew a deep breath and exhaled slowly.

It was showtime.

Nora calmly walked over to the phone and dialed. She reminded herself: *The cleverest liars don't give details.*

After two rings, a woman picked up and said, "Nine-one-one Emergency."

"Oh, God!" Nora screamed into the phone. "Please help me, he's not breathing!"

"Who's not breathing, ma'am?"

"I don't know what happened, he was eating when all of a—"

"Ma'am," the operator interrupted. "*Who's* not breathing?"

Nora sniffed, her lungs heaving. "My fiancé!" she wailed.

"Is he choking?"

"No!" she cried. "He just started to feel sick and . . . and . . . then he . . ." Nora stopped. She thought unfinished sentences might be more convincing on 911 tapes.

"Where are you, ma'am? What's your address?" asked the operator. "I need an address."

Nora alternated between sputtered words and more crying until she'd finally given Connor's address in Briarcliff Manor.

"Okay, ma'am, stay put. Try to be calm. An ambulance will be there right away."

"Oh, please hurry!"

Nora hung up the phone. She figured she had maybe six or seven more minutes to herself. Plenty of time for the last bit of cleanup.

The bottle of Johnnie Walker would stay out, she decided, as would the glass she poured it in. After all, who could blame her for having a drink at a time like this? The pill bottle, on the other hand, would definitely *not* stay out.

She placed it back in her suitcase, burying it deep in her medicine bag, which itself was buried deep beneath her clothes. Were anyone ever to find it and read the label, they'd see that she took 10 mg tabs of Zyrtec for her seasonal allergies. Asking to borrow one would be extremely ill advised, though.

Nora zipped the suitcase closed and carried it up to the master bedroom. There, she applied the finishing touches in front of a full-length mirror. She untucked her T-shirt from her jeans and yanked on the collar a few times. She followed that by vigorously rubbing her eyes to make them red. With a flurry of blinks she forced out a few more tears to further streak her makeup.

There, that ought to do it.

Nora was ready for the next act.

Chapter 20

KIND OF EXCITING, actually. A rush. The all-important third act of the drama.

Flashing lights and the ascending scream of a siren filled the driveway. Nora ran out the front door, hysterical, screaming, "Hurry! Please, hurry! Oh, please!"

The paramedics—two young men with short-cropped hair—quickly grabbed their bags and hustled into the big house.

Nora rushed them to the hallway bathroom, where Connor's large frame was sprawled out on the floor.

Suddenly she fell to her knees, weeping uncontrollably, her face flush against Connor's chest. One of the paramedics, the shorter of the two, had to drag her back out to the hallway to make room for himself and his partner. "Please, ma'am. Let us work in here. He might still be alive."

For the next five minutes, every effort was made to bring Connor Brown back to life, and every one of those efforts failed. Ultimately, the two paramedics exchanged that knowing glance, the silent recognition that there was nothing more they could do.

The older of the two turned and looked back over his shoulder at Nora, who stood by the doorway in a seemingly shock-induced haze. His face said it all, no words were required, but he uttered the redundant "I'm sorry."

She took her cue and burst into more tears. "No!" she yelled. "No, no, no! Oh, Connor, Connor!"

Minutes later the Briarcliff Manor police arrived. It was routine procedure, Nora knew. Connor being pronounced dead at the scene meant they got the call. Another screaming siren and more flashing lights in the driveway.

A few of the neighbors had gathered to look on. It seemed that Nora and Connor had just been joking about their watching them have sex only moments ago.

The police officer who did most of the talking was named Nate Pingry. He was older than his partner, Officer Joe Barreiro, and clearly the more experienced of the two. Their purpose was simple: prepare a report detailing the events leading up to, and the circumstances surrounding, the death of Connor Brown. In other words, the necessary paperwork.

"I know how hard this must be for you, Mrs. Brown, so we'll try to do this as quick as possible," said Pingry.

Nora had her head buried in her hands. She was sitting on the ottoman in the living room, where the paramedics had practically carried her. She looked up at the policemen, Pingry and Barreiro.

"We weren't married," she said through a sob. She saw both officers glance at her left hand and the four-carat diamond ring Connor had given her. "We were just . . ." She paused and dropped her head back into her hands. "We were just recently engaged."

Officer Pingry trod lightly. As much as he hated this part of his job, he knew it had to be done. Of all the skills it required, there was none more important than the right amount of patience.

Slowly, Nora took him and his partner through everything that happened. Her arrival at dusk, to the omelet she made for Connor, to the moment he said he was feeling sick. She described helping him to the bathroom, and the trauma his body seemed to suffer.

Nora rambled and, a few times, corrected herself. Other times she spoke with great clarity. As she'd read in books on forensic psychology, the major similarity among "grief-stricken" people was their ever-shifting cognitive and emotional states.

Nora even admitted to the officers that she and Connor had just made love. In fact, she was sure to mention it. The county medical examiner wouldn't have a report for a day or so, but she already knew what the autopsy would show. Connor died from cardiac arrest.

Maybe the sex, even at the age of forty, had triggered it. That would be one theory. Stress from his job would be another. Perhaps there was a family history of heart disease. The bottom line was that no one would ever know for sure.

Exactly how she wanted it.

After Officer Pingry asked the last of his questions, he read back the notes he'd taken. It was an outline of what Nora had told him—which was everything he needed to know. Except, of course, the little part about how she poisoned Connor, then watched him die on the bathroom floor.

"I think we have everything we need, Ms. Sinclair," said Officer Pingry. "If you don't mind, we'd like to take one last look around the house."

"Okay," she said softly. "Whatever you need to do."

The two policemen went down the hallway, and Nora remained on the ottoman, which she'd purchased for slightly over seven thousand at New Canaan Antiques. After a minute she got up. Pingry and his partner may have seemed nice and flashed what seemed to be genuine looks of concern, but the moment of truth had yet to come.

What do they really think?

With furtive steps, Nora fell in line behind the policemen as they went from room to room. Close enough to overhear them, far enough away not to be noticed.

Along the second-floor hallway, she got what she was looking for. The two had stopped to chat inside Connor's media room. The early reviews of her performance were in.

"Shit, will you look at this setup?" said Pingry. "I think the TV alone is worth more than my salary."

"That girl was about to marry very rich," said his partner, Barreiro.

"No kidding, Joe. Now she's shit out of luck."

"Tell me about it. She was this close to grabbing the brass ring."

"Yeah, and then the brass ring drops dead."

Nora turned in the hallway and quietly padded back down the stairs. Her eyes were bloodshot and she looked a mess. But on the inside the feeling was relief. *Brava, Nora! God, you're good.*

The police didn't suspect a thing.

She had committed the perfect murder.

Again.

Chapter 21

THE SHUFFLING OF mostly solemn strangers in and out of the house, the cacophony of noise and commotion created by it, lasted for nearly two hours. The irony was never lost on Nora: *Things really get lively when someone dies suddenly.*

Eventually it came to an end. The paramedics, the local police, the morgue wagon—they all left. Nora was finally alone in the house.

Now it was time to get down to business. This was what the police really needed to know but would never find out.

Connor's study was on the far end of the

house, practically a separate wing. As per his instructions when they'd first met, Nora had decorated it like a private men's club: tufted leather sofas, cherrywood shelving, oil paintings depicting hunting scenes, which were all the rage with the boys. In one corner was a full suit of medieval armor. In another, a display case housing an antique snuff bottle collection. *What a load of over-priced crap, and I should know.*

Nora had even joked upon the study's completion, "This room is so manly that smoking a cigar in here would be redundant."

But now, ironically, it was just her in the room. And she kind of missed Connor.

She took a seat in the Gainsborough chair behind Connor's desk and turned on the computer. He had one of those triple-screen setups that allowed him to track multiple financial markets. The way it looked you'd think he was also able to launch a missile attack. Or at least land a few jumbo jets.

The first code Nora punched in was for access to his T3 Internet connection. Next was the code for his 128-bit encrypted VPN, or virtual private network. In layman's terms, it was the ultimate secure passageway between two points via cyberspace.

Point one being Connor's computer.

Point two being the International Bank of Zurich.

It had taken Nora four months to locate the VPN code. In hindsight, she realized, it should've taken four minutes. But she never thought he'd be so obvious as to put it in his PalmPilot. Under A for "account numbers," no less.

Of course, he wasn't as obvious about spelling out which accounts went with which codes. That required a few late-night trial-and-error sessions while he was asleep in bed.

For all the complexity of tapping into Connor's Swiss bank account—and all the connotations of wealth and privilege that went with having such an account—the transaction page for the International Bank of Zurich was remarkably simple and low-key. No fancy lettering or soothing background music by Honegger.

Just three options, in plain type, alone on the screen.

DEPOSIT.

WITHDRAWAL.

TRANSFER.

Nora clicked on TRANSFER and was immediately taken to another page, which was equally simple. It listed Connor's account balance and provided a box for indicating how much money was to be transferred.

She typed the figure.

There was 4.3 million dollars in the account. She'd be taking a little less. 4.2 million, to be exact.

The only thing left to do was direct the money.

Connor wasn't the only one in their relationship to have a VPN. Nora typed in the code for her private numbered account in the Cayman Islands. Thanks to horny tax attorney Steven Keppler, it was about to be christened in grand style.

She hit the EXECUTE button and sat back in Connor's chair. A horizontal bar on the screen charted the progress of the transfer by slowly shading in. Putting her feet up on the desk, she watched it creep along.

Two minutes later, it was official. Nora Sinclair was 4.2 million dollars richer.

Her second killing of the day.

Chapter 22

SHE AWOKE THE next morning and shuffled downstairs with a big yawn to make a pot of coffee. Actually, she didn't feel too bad. Nora didn't feel much of anything.

After she downed the first cup, her thoughts turned to the day and what important things had to be done. There were phone calls to make—people who needed to know about Connor's death. And she had to check in with Jeffrey.

The first call was to Mark Tillingham. He was Connor's attorney and executor of his estate. He was also one of Connor's best friends. When Nora called, Mark was heading out the door for his Saturday-morning tennis game. She could just picture him, dressed in white, as he responded to the news with utter shock. In a way, Nora was jealous of the emotion.

Next was the immediate family. The list of whom to call, however, couldn't have been any shorter. Connor's parents were no longer alive; that left his one and only sibling—a younger sister, Elizabeth, whom he called Lizzie or sometimes Lizard.

The two were close in every way except geographically. Lizzie lived three thousand miles away, in Santa Barbara, and had her own busy career as a successful architect. She rarely made it back to the East Coast, the last time being before Nora and Connor had met.

Nora poured herself another cup of coffee and considered how best to tell a woman she'd never met, let alone spoken to, that her brother was dead at forty.

She knew she didn't *have* to make the call. She could've had Mark Tillingham do it. But Nora also knew that someone who truly loved Connor would do it herself. So after finding the phone number in his PalmPilot, she dialed.

"Hello?" came a woman's voice, groggy if not a little annoyed. It was barely past seven A.M. in California.

"Is this Elizabeth?"

"Yes."

"My name is Nora Sinclair. . . ."

Oddly, the sister didn't cry, at least not on the phone. Instead, there was a stunned silence, followed by a few softly spoken questions.

Nora told her what she'd told the police. Word for word: *her script.* "Though I guess we won't know anything for sure until the autopsy is done," she pointed out.

Again, there was the stunned silence from Lizzie. Maybe, thought Nora, it was the guilt of having not seen her brother in a long while. Or maybe it was the sudden loneliness of being the only surviving member of her family. Maybe she was in shock, as Mark Tillingham had been.

"I'll fly out tomorrow morning," said Elizabeth. "Have you made funeral plans?"

"I wanted to speak to you first. I figured—"

Elizabeth had begun to cry. "I hope this doesn't sound terrible, but that's the last thing . . . I don't think I could. . . . Would you mind taking care of it?"

"Of course not," said Nora. She was beginning to say good-bye when Elizabeth choked back sobs and asked, "How long had you been engaged to Connor?"

Nora paused. She wanted to affect a good cry herself, but thought better of it. Instead, she said solemnly, "Only a week."

"I'm sorry. Oh, I'm so sorry," said Elizabeth.

In the wake of the phone call with Elizabeth, Nora spent the afternoon concentrating on the funeral arrangements. From flowers to food, there was a lot she was able to accomplish over the phone. However, there remained some things in life—and especially in death—that were best done in person. Choosing a funeral parlor was one.

But even there Nora was able to use her skills as a decorator. She selected the casket as she would any piece of furniture for a client. For Connor, that meant a most regal burl walnut with carved ivory handles. The instant the undertaker showed it to her, Nora knew it was the one.

"Done!" she said.

Chapter 23

"NORA, I KNOW this probably isn't exactly a great time," began Mark Tillingham. "But there's something I need to discuss with you. The sooner the better."

The time was minutes before the funeral service that Tuesday morning; the place was the crowded parking lot of St. Mary's Church on Albany Post Road in Scarborough. Nora stared at Connor's attorney through black Chanel sunglasses. They matched her black Armani suit and basic black Manolos. The two of them stood under a large holly tree just beyond the gravel driveway.

"It's about Connor's sister. She's distraught, of course. She and Connor were so close. Elizabeth has some concerns about your intentions."

"My *intentions?*"

"Regarding the estate."

"What did Elizabeth say to you? No, let me guess, Mark. Elizabeth is afraid I might contest Connor's will."

"Let's call it 'a concern,'" he said. "The state doesn't recognize fiancées as having a legal claim, but that hasn't stopped some people from—"

Nora shook her head. "I won't contest, Mark. God! I have no interest in the estate. It was Connor I loved. Let me be very clear on this: I have no interest in Connor's estate. You can tell that to Lizzie."

Mark's face was a study in embarrassment. "Of course," he said. "Again, I'm sorry I had to bring this up."

"So, that's why she's been avoiding me?"

"No, I think it's more that she's upset. She and Connor were inseparable growing up. Their parents died when they were both very young."

"Out of curiosity, what did Connor leave her?"

Mark stared down at his tasseled black

loafers. "I'm not supposed to reveal information like that, Nora."

"You also are not supposed to be upsetting the woman Connor loved right before his funeral service."

His guilt clearly outweighed his professionalism. "Elizabeth basically gets two-thirds of the estate, including the house," he said in a lowered voice. "As I said, they were close."

"And the rest?"

"Two cousins in San Diego get lump sums. The rest goes to various charities."

"That's good," Nora said, softening a bit.

"Yes, it is," replied Mark. "Connor was good that way. Hell, he was good in a lot of ways."

Nora nodded. "Connor was great, Mark. We should be getting inside, shouldn't we?"

Chapter 24

IT WAS A lovely service, sad and very touching. St. Mary's, with the beautifully manicured Sleepy Hollow Country Club looming in the background, was the perfect spot.

At least that's what everyone kept telling Nora. There wasn't a receiving line, but people still made a point of coming up to her. She'd met some of Connor's friends and business associates previously; a few others she'd known about. The rest introduced themselves and fumbled with words of sympathy.

All the while—at the church as well as the

cemetery—Elizabeth Brown kept her distance. Not that Nora was necessarily eager for a détente. Actually, Connor's sister had done her a favor. She'd unwittingly bolstered the notion that the last person who'd want Connor dead was the woman poised to be worth millions by marrying him.

It was back at the house in Westchester, where people from the funeral had gathered for food and further commiserating, that Elizabeth finally went up to her.

"I noticed that you don't drink. Not even on a day like today," Elizabeth said.

Nora was holding a glass of sparkling water. "Oh, I drink. But I guess I prefer water today."

"We really haven't had much of a chance to talk, have we?" Elizabeth said. "I want to thank you for making all the arrangements. I don't think I could've done it." Tears began to well in her eyes.

"You're welcome. I suppose it made sense, given that I live here. I mean not *here* here but—"

"I know, Nora. In fact, that's something I wanted to talk to you about."

A man walked by, one of Connor's associates from Greenwich. Elizabeth paused so as not to be overheard.

"Come," said Nora. "Let's step outside for a minute."

She led Elizabeth out the front door to the large flagstone steps of the entrance. It was now just the two of them. *Time for some honesty?*

"Anyway," said Elizabeth. "I had a conversation with Mark Tillingham. It seems Connor has left me this house."

Nora's reaction was brilliant. "Really? Well, that's good. I'm glad it can stay in the family. Especially with you, Lizzie."

"Oh, that's so nice. Only the last thing I'm about to do is move here and live in it," said Elizabeth. She paused and dropped her head, unable to finish the sentence. Tears were now streaming down her cheeks. "I just couldn't."

"I understand," said Nora. "You should just put it on the market, Lizzie."

"I suppose. But I'm in no rush. Which is what I wanted to talk to you about," she said. "First, I want you to feel free to use the house for as long as you like. I know that's what Connor would've wanted."

"That's so nice of you," said Nora. "And unnecessary. I'm overcome."

"I've asked Mark to have all the expenses and upkeep paid for by the estate. It's the least we could do," Elizabeth said. "And, Nora, I want you to keep all the furnishings. That's what brought you and Connor together in the first place."

Nora smiled. Elizabeth's guilt was dripping from every word. On the heels of Connor's death, she thought his fiancée would be out for a payday. But now that she believed otherwise, her generosity was a way of admitting she was wrong. *Which she was,* thought Nora. Technically, at least.

I've already had my payday.

They stood in front of the grand house and continued to talk until Elizabeth realized the time. Her flight back to California was in less than three hours. "I'd better get going," she said. "Saddest day of my life, Nora."

Nora nodded. "Yes. Mine, too. Please keep in touch."

Elizabeth said good-bye—with a hug, no less—and walked to her rental car in the driveway. Nora watched, her feet close together, her hands clasped at her waist. Beneath her sturdy exterior, though, was a heart racing with excitement. She'd pulled it off! The murder. The money.

Nora pivoted on her Manolos to head inside the house. After two steps, she stopped. She thought she'd heard something. A noise from the hedges and evergreens. A *clicking* sound.

She looked toward the edge of the property and listened. . . . Nothing.

Probably a bird, she decided.

But as she took the last step into the house, the Nikon D1X digicam chirped a few final times from its perch among the rhododendron.

Click. Click. Click.

Nora Sinclair wasn't the only one with a grand plan.

Part Two

THE INSURANCE MAN

Chapter 25

THINGS AREN'T ALWAYS as they appear, sonny boy.

That was something my father was fond of telling me when I was growing up. Of course, he was also fond of telling me to take out the garbage, rake the leaves, shovel the snow, don't slouch, stand up straight. But in terms of leaving a meaningful impression, everything else was a distant second to his first little piece of advice.

So simple. Yet, as the years have taught me, so true.

Anyway, I was sitting in my newly acquired office, which was more like a glorified broom closet. The place was so snug, even Houdini would have complained. Up on my computer were the pictures I'd taken with my digicam. One after another. Nora Sinclair dressed in chic-chic black, head to toe. Nora at St. Mary's Church. At the Sleepy Hollow Cemetery. Back at Connor Brown's modest little estate house. The last shots were of her on the front steps, talking to the poor guy's sister, Elizabeth. Elizabeth was tall and blond and looked like a California swimmer. Nora was brunette, not quite as tall, but even more beautiful. Both were stunning, even in funeral attire. They appeared to be crying, and then they hugged.

What exactly was I looking for?

I didn't know, but the more I stared at these pictures, the more my father's words echoed in my head. *Things aren't always as they appear.*

I grabbed the phone and dialed the boss. The direct line. Two rings later . . .

"Susan," she announced briskly. No hello, no last name—just *Susan.*

"It's me. Hi. I need you to be a sounding board," I said. "So how do I sound?"

"Like you want to sell me insurance."

"Not too New York?"

"You mean, not too pushy? No."

"Good."

"But talk a little more just to make sure," she said.

I thought for a second. "Okay, so this old guy dies and goes up to heaven," I began in the same voice, which to my ear was dripping in New Yorkese. "Stop me if you've heard this one."

"I've heard this one."

"No, you haven't—trust me, you're going to laugh."

"I suppose there's always a first time."

It should be said at this point, if it isn't already obvious, that the boss and I have a certain rapport. Of course, some men have a real hang-up about reporting to a woman. When Susan took over her department, in fact, there were about four or five guys who gave her a hard time from day one.

That's why on day two she fired them all. I'm serious. So is Susan.

"Anyway, so this old guy arrives at the Pearly Gates and immediately he sees two signs," I said. "The first sign reads, MEN WHO WERE CONTROLLED BY THEIR WIVES. The old man looks and sees that this line is, like, ten miles long."

"Naturally."

"No comment. So the old man looks at the second sign. It reads, MEN WHO WERE *NOT* CONTROLLED BY THEIR WIVES. Lo and behold, there's only one guy in this line. Slowly, the old man walks over to him. 'Tell me,' he says, 'why are you standing over here?' The guy looks at him and says, 'I don't know, my wife told me to.'"

I listened, and sure enough, a slight laugh could be heard on the other end of the line.

"What I'd tell you? Next stop, Letterman."

"Mildly amusing," said Susan. "But I wouldn't quit your day job just yet."

I chuckled. "Now *that's* funny, considering this isn't even supposed to be my day job."

"Do I detect a little nervousness?"

"It's more like apprehension."

"Why? You're a natural at this stuff. You've got an—" Susan stopped mid-sentence. "Oh, I get it. It's because she's a woman, right?"

"I'm just saying, it's a little different, that's all."

"Don't worry, you'll be fine. No matter who or what Nora Sinclair turns out to be, you're the best man for the job," she said. "So, when's the big introduction?"

"Tomorrow."

"Good. Excellent. Keep me posted."

"I will," I said. "Oh, and Susan?"

"Yeah?"

"I appreciate the vote of confidence."

"Wow."

"What?"

"I'm still not used to you and humility being in the same room."

"I'm trying. Lord knows, I'm trying."

"I know you are," she said. "Good luck."

Chapter 26

THE PINE WOODS Psychiatric Facility, a New York State–run institution, was in Lafayetteville, about an hour-and-a-quarter drive heading north from Westchester. Unless, of course, you were Nora in her new Benz convertible. Zipping along the winding, forest-lined Taconic Parkway at over eighty miles an hour, she turned up at the hospital a solid fifteen minutes sooner.

Nora found a parking space and put the top up with a single press of a button. *Neat.* She did a quick check in the vanity mirror and shook her hair back into place. No touch-up on the makeup was needed. She was barely wearing any to begin with. Then, for some crazy reason, she had a thought about Connor's sister—the Ice Blonde. Something about Elizabeth bothered her. As if there hadn't been closure between them.

Nora shrugged it off. She locked up the convertible—even out here in the boonies. She was wearing a pair of jeans and a simple white button-down shirt. Clutched under her arm was a bag from a bookstore. As she walked toward the entrance of the main redbrick building, there wasn't another soul on the grounds.

She knew the routine inside by heart. A visit every month for the past fourteen years guaranteed that.

First came the obligatory check-in at the front desk. After showing a photo ID of herself, Nora signed in and was given a pass.

Next she made her way to the elevator bank, to the left of the desk. One was open and waiting.

During her first year of coming to the facility, it was the second-floor button she pushed. After twelve months, though, her mother was moved to an upper floor. Though no one ever admitted it to Nora, she knew that the higher up the room, the less likely the chance of the patient's ever being released.

Nora stepped onto the elevator and pressed eight.

The top floor.

Chapter 27

HEAD NURSE EMILY BARROWS was having one of those days. No big surprise. The computer system was down, her back was just killing her, the copy machine was out of toner, she had a splitting headache, someone on the night shift had spilled coffee on the medication log.

And it wasn't even noon yet.

Plus, for what seemed like the hundredth time—and may actually have been just that—she was breaking in a new nurse. This one was the type who smiled too much. Her name was Patsy, which unto itself was a little too happy sounding.

The two women were sitting at the nurses' station that anchored the eighth floor. One of the elevators, which were located right in front of them, opened. Emily looked up from the java-stained page of the medication log. A familiar face walked toward her.

"Hello, Emily."

"Hello, Nora. How are you?"

"How's she doing?"

"She's doing fine."

She and Nora basically had the same brief exchange every month, and it always ended the same way. Nora's mother was always the same.

Emily glanced over at Patsy. The new nurse—smiling insipidly—was watching and listening to the conversation.

"Patsy, this is Nora Sinclair," said Emily. "Her mother is Olivia in eight-oh-nine."

"Oh," said Patsy with a slight hesitation. A rookie mistake.

Nora nodded. "Nice to meet you, Patsy." She wished the new nurse good luck before starting down the long hallway.

Meanwhile, Patsy's voice dropped to a solicitous whisper. "Olivia Sinclair . . . she's the one who shot and killed her husband, right?"

Emily's whisper in reply was more matter-of-fact. "So a jury said. Long time ago."

"You don't think she did it?"

"Oh, she did it."

"I don't understand. How did she end up here?"

Emily peered down the hall. She wanted to make sure Nora was definitely out of earshot.

"From what I've been told—and keep in mind, this goes back a long way—Olivia was fine during the first years of her life sentence. A model prisoner. But then she just went bonkers."

"How so?"

"She basically lost touch with reality. Started to talk in a made-up language. Would only eat foods beginning with the letter *b*."

"The letter *b?*"

"It could've been worse. She could've chosen *x,* or something. At least with *b* she had bread, butter, bananas. . . ."

Patsy chimed in like a quiz-show contestant. "Bundt cake?"

Emily blinked a few times. "Uh . . . I suppose. Anyway, then Olivia tried to kill herself. In the wake of that, they shipped her here."

She thought for a second. "Or maybe it was the suicide attempt that happened first, and then the crazy behavior. Whatever—all I know is that twenty years later, Olivia Sinclair doesn't even know her own name."

"Wow, that's so sad," said Patsy, who, to Emily's amazement, could register concern without ever losing her smile. "What do you think happened to her?"

"No idea. It's like a mix of autism and Alzheimer's. She can still talk a little, do things on her own. Except none of it makes much sense. For example, you see the bag under Nora's arm?"

Patsy shook her head no.

"Every month Nora brings her a novel to read. But then when I see her reading it, the book is always upside down."

"Does Nora know this?"

"Yes, unfortunately."

Patsy sighed. "Well, it's good that she can be there for her mother."

"I'd agree, except for one thing," said the head nurse. "Her mother doesn't even recognize Nora."

Chapter 28

"HELLO, MOTHER. IT'S ME."

Nora walked across the small room and took her mother's hand. She gave it a squeeze but got nothing in return. Not that she expected to. Nora was used to feeling nothing on these visits.

Olivia Sinclair was lying in bed on top of the covers. She was propped up by two thin pillows. A withering frame and glassy stare. The woman was fifty-seven, but she looked eighty.

"Have you been feeling all right?" Nora watched as her mother slowly turned to her. "It's me, Nora."

"You're very pretty."

"Thank you. I had my hair done. For a funeral, of all things."

"I like to read, you know," said Olivia.

"Yes, I know." Nora reached into the bag and pulled out the latest John Grisham novel. "See, I brought you a book."

She held it out to her mother, but Olivia didn't take it. Nora placed it on the bedside table and sat down in a nearby chair.

"Are you eating enough?"

"Yes."

"What did you have for breakfast?"

"Eggs and toast."

Nora forced a smile. These were the moments that hurt the most, when it seemed that she was having an actual conversation with her mother. She knew better, though. Inevitably, almost self-destructively, she tested her mother to make sure.

"Do you know who the president is?"

"Yes, of course I do. Jimmy Carter."

There was never any point in correcting her, Nora knew. Instead, she told her mother about her work and some of the houses she'd decorated. There were updates on her girlfriends in Manhattan. Elaine was working too hard at her law firm. Allison was still a fashion barometer at *W.*

"They really care about me, Mother."

"Knock, knock," came a voice.

The door opened and Emily appeared with a tray. "It's time for your medication, Olivia." The nurse moved with a crisp, almost robotic rhythm. She poured water into a glass from a pitcher on the bedside table.

"Here you go, Olivia."

Nora's mother took the pill and washed it down without a fuss.

"Oh, is that his latest?" asked Emily, eyeing the novel on the table.

"It just came out," said Nora.

Her mother smiled. "I like to read, you know."

"Of course you do," said Emily.

Nora's mother picked up the novel. She opened to a page and began reading. Upside down.

As she was about to leave, Emily turned to Nora, who always seemed so brave, so beautiful.

"Oh, by the way," said Emily, "the singing group from the local high school is performing in the cafeteria. We're taking everyone on the wing down. You're welcome to come along, Nora."

"No, that's okay. I was about to head out. It's a busy time for me."

Emily left the room and Nora stood. She walked over to her mother and gave her a soft kiss on the forehead. "I love you," she whispered. "I wish you knew that."

Olivia Sinclair didn't say anything. She just watched as her daughter walked out the door.

Moments later, when no one was there, Olivia removed the jacket from her new novel and flipped it around. With the pages right side up and the jacket upside down, she began to read.

Chapter 29

I'D JUST CLEANED the lens of my digicam for the third time in twenty minutes.

In between, I counted the number of stitches on the leather steering wheel (312), reprogrammed the position of my driver's seat (up a scooch and angled a tad more forward), and learned once and for all the optimal pressure for the kind of tires I had on the BMW 330i (thirty PSI in the front, thirty-five in the back, said the manual in the glove compartment).

Boredom had officially set in.

Maybe I should've called her first. *No, I* decided. The introduction had to be in person. Face-to-face. Even at the risk of my butt falling asleep while waiting there in my car.

If I'd known this was going to turn into a stakeout, I would've brought doughnuts. Dunkin's, Krispy Kreme's, 7-Eleven's, anybody's.

Where is she?

Ten minutes later I watched from across Central Drive as a bright red Mercedes convertible pulled into the late Connor Brown's circular driveway. It stopped in front, and out she came.

Nora Sinclair. And I guess that I should add, *Wow.*

She bent from the waist and reached into what passed for the backseat and removed a bag of groceries. By the time she was fiddling with the keys to the house, I was halfway across the lawn.

I called out. "Excuse me . . . Uhm, *excuse me!*"

She turned around. Her all-black outfit from the funeral was now a pair of jeans and a white button-down shirt. The sunglasses were the same. The hair looked great—thick, lustrous, chestnut brown. I repeat myself, but—*wow.*

Finally I was standing right in front of her.

I cautioned myself not to overdo the accent. "Are you Nora Sinclair, by any chance?"

Sunglasses or no sunglasses, I could tell she was sizing me up. "That depends, I suppose. Who are you?"

"Oh, gosh, I'm sorry. I should've introduced myself first." I extended my hand. "I'm Craig Reynolds."

Nora shuffled the groceries in her arms and we shook. "Hello," she said, her voice still guarded. "You're Craig Reynolds— and . . . ?"

I reached into my suit jacket and clumsily removed a business card. "I'm with Centennial One Life Insurance," I said, handing her the card. She looked at it. "I'm very sorry about your loss."

She softened a bit. "Thank you."

"So, you are Nora Sinclair, right?"

"Yes, I'm Nora."

"I assume you must have been very close to Mr. Brown."

So much for her softening up to me. Her tone was wary again. "Yes, we were engaged. Now, please, what is this about?"

It was my turn to show a little confusion. "You mean, you don't know?"

"Know what?"

I paused for a moment. "About the insurance policy on Mr. Brown. One point nine million dollars, to be exact."

She stared at me blankly. I expected no less.

"Then I gather you also don't know this, Ms. Sinclair," I said. "You're listed as the sole beneficiary."

Chapter 30

NORA KEPT HER COOL incredibly well.

"What did you say your name was again?" she asked.

"Craig Reynolds . . . it's there on the card. I manage the field office here in town for Centennial One."

As Nora shifted her weight—a very well executed weight shift, I must say—and looked down at my business card again, the groceries began to slip from her grasp. I jumped forward and grabbed the bag before it could hit the ground.

"Thank you," she said while reaching to

take back the groceries. "That would've been a mess."

"Tell you what, why don't you let me carry this. I need to talk to you."

I could tell what she was thinking. A guy she'd never met before was asking his way into the house. A stranger. One bearing candy, no less. Though in my case it was a very sweet insurance payout.

She looked at my business card yet again.

"Don't worry, I've been house-trained," I joked.

She smiled slightly. "I'm sorry, I don't mean to come off as overly suspicious. It's just been—"

"A very tough time for you, yes, I can only imagine. You don't need to apologize. If you'd prefer, we can discuss the policy at a later date. You could come to my office?"

"No, that's okay. Please, come inside."

Nora started toward the house. I followed. So far, so good. I wondered if she was a good dancer. She certainly was a good *walker.*

"Vanilla hazelnut?" I asked.

She looked back over her shoulder. "Excuse me?"

I motioned toward the ground coffee peeking out from the grocery bag. "Though I recently came across some of those new-fangled crème brûlée beans, which smell awfully similar."

"No, it's vanilla hazelnut," she said. "I'm impressed."

"I would've preferred to have been blessed with a ninety-mile-an-hour fastball. Instead, I got a heightened sense of smell."

"Better than nothing."

"Ah, you're an optimist," I said.

"Not these days."

I smacked my forehead. "Damn. That was dumb of me to say. I'm really sorry."

"It's okay," she said, and almost smiled.

We walked up the front steps and went inside the house. The foyer was a lot bigger than my apartment. The chandelier over our head was at least a year's salary. The Oriental rugs, the Chinese vases. Jeez, what a spread.

"The kitchen's this way," she said, leading me around a corner. When we got there, it too was bigger than my apartment. She pointed to the granite slab of counter next to the refrigerator. "You can put the groceries there. Thanks."

I placed the bag down and started to empty it.

"You don't have to do that."

"It's the least I can do after that optimist comment."

"Really, it's okay." She walked over to me and picked up the bag of vanilla hazelnut. "Can I offer you a cup?"

"Absolutely."

I made sure it was nothing but small talk while the pot brewed. I didn't want to do too much too fast—the risk being that *she* might ask too many questions. As it was, I figured a couple were already headed my way.

"You know what I don't understand?" she said a few minutes later. We were sitting at the kitchen table, coffee mugs in hand. "Connor had plenty of money and no ex-wife or kids. Why would he bother with life insurance?"

"That's a *good* question. I think the answer lies in how this policy originated. You see, Mr. Brown didn't come to us. We went to him. Or rather, his company."

"I'm not sure I follow."

"Something Centennial One is doing more and more of is workers' compensation policies. As a way of enticing companies to insure with us, we offer the top people free term life insurance."

"That's a pretty nice perk."

"Yeah, it seems to seal the deal a lot for us."

"How much did you say Connor's policy was for?"

As if she'd forgotten.

"One point nine million," I said. "That's the maximum for his size company."

Her brow furrowed. "He really listed me as the sole beneficiary?"

"Yes, he really did."

"When was this?"

"You mean, when was the policy administered?"

She nodded.

"Fairly recently, it turns out. Five months ago."

"I suppose that would explain it. Though we'd been together at that point for only a short time."

I smiled. "He obviously had a good feeling about you from the start."

She tried to smile back, but the tears coming down her cheeks wouldn't let her. She began wiping them away while apologizing. I assured her that it was more than okay, that I understood. Actually the scene was kind of touching. *Or she's very good.*

"Connor had already given me so much,

and now *this*." She wiped away another tear. "And what I wouldn't give to have him back."

Nora took a long sip of her coffee. I did the same.

"So, what's supposed to happen? I assume I've got to sign some stuff before the payout is made, right?"

I leaned forward a bit on the table and gripped my mug with both hands. "Well, you see, that's why I'm here, Ms. Sinclair. There's a little bit of a problem."

Chapter 31

HE KIND OF *sounded* like an insurance man, but he didn't really *look* like one to Nora.

For starters, she noticed that he wasn't that bad a dresser. The tie matched the suit, and the suit had actually been in style sometime during this decade.

Another thing was that he had a nice personality. The few insurance guys she'd met before seemed to have about as much charisma as a cardboard box. In fact, all things considered, Craig Reynolds was an attractive man. Nicely put together. He also drove a pretty good car. Then again, thought

Nora, this was Briarcliff Manor, not the East Bronx. To manage the field office for a big insurance company in this neck of the woods, you'd kind of have to look the part.

Still, she wasn't about to let her guard down.

She'd been watching Craig Reynolds carefully and making mental notes—from the moment he first showed up to when he wrapped his hands around his coffee mug and announced that there was "a little bit of a problem" with Connor's policy.

"What sort of problem?" she asked.

"Ultimately, I don't think it will be much of one at all. The thing is, because of Mr. Brown's relatively young age, they've decided to investigate the claim."

"Who's *they?*"

"The home office back in Chicago. They basically call the shots."

"You don't have any say in the matter?"

"Not too much in this case. As I mentioned, Mr. Brown's policy originated in our corporate division, which is run from the home office. Who services it, however, is based on proximity to the client. Meaning, if it wasn't for the pending investigation, I'd be the one handling everything."

"So if you're not, who is?"

"I haven't been told yet, but if I had to guess, it's going to be a man by the name of John O'Hara."

"Do you know him?"

"Only by reputation."

"Uh-oh."

"What?"

"When you said that, you frowned a little."

"No, it's no big deal. Supposedly, O'Hara's a hard-ass—pardon my language—but that's par for the course with an insurance investigator. From what I can tell, this should be a routine inquiry."

As Craig Reynolds reached for his coffee again, Nora made another mental note: no wedding band.

"How do you like the vanilla hazelnut?" she asked.

"Tastes even better than it smells."

She sat back in her chair. Having already turned off her tears, she gave Craig Reynolds a pleasant smile. He came across as caring and thoughtful. Better yet, she noticed that when he smiled back at her, his cheeks produced a cute pair of dimples. *Too bad he doesn't have any money.*

Not that Nora was complaining. From

where she was sitting, Craig Reynolds the insurance man was worth $1.9 million. It was a windfall she wasn't about to turn down. The only wrinkle was the investigation. Routine as it sounded, it made her nervous.

But not overly so. She had a very good plan, and it was made to hold up to scrutiny. By the police, by the coroner's office, by the likes of anyone or anything that might stand in her way. And that certainly included an insurance investigation.

Just the same, after Craig Reynolds left the house that afternoon, she decided it might be a good idea to make herself scarce for the next few days. She was supposed to see Jeffrey that weekend anyway. Maybe she'd go up a day early and surprise him.

He was, after all, her husband.

Chapter 32

THE NEXT MORNING, a Friday, Nora walked out of the house in Westchester and popped open the trunk of her Benz convertible parked in front. In went her suitcase. The weatherman on TV had promised nothing but blue skies and sun with the temperature reaching a high of eighty. A "top-down day" if there ever was one.

Nora pressed the button on her keyless remote and watched as the roof of the car began to recede quietly. That's when another car caught her eye. *What the hell?*

Out on Central Drive, parked under towering maples and oaks, was the same BMW as the day before. And sitting in the front with his sunglasses on was the insurance man. Craig Reynolds.

What's he doing back here?

One sure way to find out. Nora started to walk straight for his car. She thought he'd been so friendly when they first met. But now, this . . . watching her from his car. It was a little creepy. Or worse, a little suspicious. Which was why she cautioned herself not to overreact.

Craig saw her coming and promptly hopped out of his Beemer. He began walking toward her in his tan summer-weight suit. He gave her a friendly wave.

They met halfway.

Nora tilted her head and smiled. "If I didn't know any better, I'd say you were spying."

"If that's the case, I probably should've chosen a better hiding place, huh?" He smiled back. "My apologies—it's not what it looks like. Actually, you can blame the Mets for this."

"An entire baseball team?"

"Yes, including the general manager. I was about to pull into your driveway when the Fan went to a commercial break, saying the club was about to make a big trade with Houston. So I pulled over to listen."

She gave him a blank look. "The Fan?"

"It's an all-sports radio station."

"I see. So you weren't spying?"

"Nope. I'm no James Bond. Just a long-suffering Mets season-ticket holder."

Nora nodded. She figured either Craig Reynolds was telling the truth or he was a born liar. "What were you coming to see me about?" she asked.

"Good news, actually. John O'Hara, that guy I told you about from the home office, has definitely been placed in charge of the investigation into Mr. Brown's death."

"I thought that wasn't supposed to be such good news."

"No, but *this* part is. I talked to him early this morning and he said he thought there wouldn't be any problems."

"That is good."

"Better yet, I got him to fast-track the thing. He gave me his hard-line spiel about not giving special treatment, but I asked him to do it since the Westchester office has been such a rainmaker for the company. Anyway, I just thought you'd want to know."

"I appreciate it, Mr. Reynolds. It's a nice surprise."

"Please, call me Craig."

"In that case, call me Nora."

"Nora it is." He glanced over her shoulder at the red convertible in the driveway, the trunk still up. "Taking a trip?"

"Yes, as a matter of fact."

"Anywhere interesting?"

"That depends on your opinion of south Florida."

"As they say, it's a nice place to visit but I wouldn't want to vote there."

She chuckled. "I'll have to use that one on my client in Palm Beach. Or maybe not."

"What line of work are you in—if you don't mind my asking?"

"I'm an interior decorator."

"No kidding. It must be fun. I mean, there aren't many jobs where you get to spend other people's money, are there?"

"No, I guess there aren't." She looked at her watch. "Whoops, somebody's running late for the airport."

"My fault. By all means, get going."

"Well, again Mr. Reyn—" She caught herself. "*Craig*. Thanks for stopping by. It was very sweet."

"No problem, Nora. I'll let you know when there's something to report on the investigation."

"I'd appreciate it."

They shook hands and Craig was about to walk away. "Oh, you know what?" he said. "It dawns on me, with you traveling, I should probably get a cell phone number."

Nora hesitated for a split second. While giving out the number was one of the last things she wanted to do, she also didn't want to appear suspicious to the insurance man.

"Sure thing," she said. "Have you got a pen?"

Chapter 33

I RANG SUSAN right after getting back into the car. My initial two encounters with Nora merited a report back to the boss.

"Is she as pretty in person?"

"*That's* what you want to know first?"

"Absolutely," said Susan. "This girl can't be doing what she might be doing without being a knockout. So, is she?"

"Is there a way to answer that while still sounding professional?"

"Yes. It's called being honest."

"Then, yeah," I said. "Nora Sinclair is a very attractive woman. *Stunning* wouldn't be too much of a reach."

"You pig."

I laughed.

"What's your sense from talking to her?" she asked.

"Too early to tell. She's either got nothing to hide or is a natural-born liar."

"I'm going to put ten bucks on the latter."

"We'll see if that's a good bet," I said.

"With you on it, I'm sure we will."

"You know, if you prop me up any more, I'm going to hit my head on the ceiling."

"That, or actually come through for me."

"Oh, I see. The guidebook says to play into my confidence."

"Trust me, there's no guidebook on how to handle you," she said. "Where are you now?"

"Outside the late Connor Brown's home."

"Did you already do the follow-up?"

"Yeah."

"How long did it take for her to see you?"

"Within minutes."

"Mets or Yankees?"

"Mets," I said. "Steinbrenner's done trading for the year. At least until the pennant stretch."

"Would she have actually known that?"

"No. But you can never be too careful."

"Amen," said Susan. "Did she believe you?"

"I'm pretty sure."

"Good. See, I knew you were the right guy for the job."

"Ouch."

"What?"

"That was my head hitting the ceiling."

"Let me know what happens next."

"You got it, boss."

"Don't be patronizing."

"Won't happen again, boss."

Susan hung up on me.

Chapter 34

NORA HADN'T DRIVEN very far before the irritating, nagging feeling got the better of her. Right in the middle of the road, alongside Trump National Golf Course, she threw the Benz into a tire-screeching, 180-degree turn—the steering wheel spinning like a carnival wheel in her hands. If she hurried, she thought, she could still catch up to him.

There's something funny about Craig Reynolds.

And it has nothing to do with his sense of humor.

Nora stepped on the gas and quickly began to retrace the route she'd taken from

Connor's house. Down one narrow tree-lined street and then another she sped, swerving to pass a sluggish Volvo along the way. A little farther down, an older lady walking her cocker spaniel administered a disapproving stare.

For a brief moment, Nora second-guessed herself. Was she just being paranoid? Was this really necessary? But the nagging feeling proved stronger than any lingering doubt. She stepped harder on the gas. She was almost there.

What the . . . ?

Nora slammed on the brakes.

She'd reached the corner of Connor's street and had to do an immediate double take. The black BMW was still there. Craig Reynolds hadn't left.

Why not? What is he doing now?

She shifted into reverse and backed in along the curb by some overgrown hedges and pine trees. They came in handy, shielding most of her car while still providing a decent view of his. From that distance, however, Craig Reynolds himself was barely a silhouette. Nora squinted. She couldn't tell for sure, but it looked as though he was talking on his cell phone.

Though not for long. Within a minute, the taillights of his BMW flared amid a sputtering of smoke from the muffler. The Insurance Man was finally leaving.

Nora had no idea where he was going, only that she had every intention of finding out. The plan to surprise Jeffrey up in Boston had been usurped by a new plan.

It was called Getting to Know the Real Craig Reynolds.

Chapter 35

OFF HE WENT.

Nora knew she couldn't follow too closely. He was familiar with her car, and the fact that it was bright red didn't help matters. *What a shame Mercedes doesn't make a camouflage-green convertible.*

VILLAGE OF BRIARCLIFF MANOR
INC. 1902

Even before she saw the sign, Nora had figured out that Craig was headed for the center of town. Lucky for her. After dealing with a couple of stop signs and merging traffic from Route 9A, she could barely keep him in sight. Had he been driving anywhere else but this peaceful burg, she probably would've lost him.

She was familiar with the small town, having been there several times with Connor. It was a mix of working class and chic, new money and no money. Rustic lantern posts dotted the main drag amid banks and specialty shops. Bluehairs shared the sidewalk with young supermoms pushing the latest and greatest in baby strollers. Amalfi's, an Italian restaurant that Connor adored, was bustling with lunchtime business.

Again, Nora thought she'd lost Craig.

She sighed with relief when she caught a glimpse of his black Beemer making a left turn far ahead. By the time she followed, he was already parked and stepping onto the curb.

She immediately pulled over and watched as he disappeared into a brick building. His office, she assumed.

Slowly she drove by. Sure enough, there was a sign above the second-floor windows. CENTENNIAL ONE LIFE INSURANCE, it read.

Well, that's a good sign, so to speak.

Nora doubled around and parked about

forty yards up from the entrance. So far, so good. Craig Reynolds seemed to be who he said he was. But she wasn't satisfied yet. Something told her there was more to him than met the eye.

She settled in for the wait, staring at the building, a two-story, nondescript rectangle. Certainly nothing flashy about it. She wasn't even sure if the bricks were real. They looked kind of phony, like that facing technique she'd seen on TV.

The wait didn't last long. Less than twenty minutes later, Craig walked out of the building and got back into his car. Nora straightened up in her seat and waited for him to pull away from the curb.

Where to now, Insurance Man? Wherever it is, you have company.

Chapter 36

THE BLUE RIBBON DINER was where. It was a few miles out of town heading east, not far from the Saw Mill River Parkway. The place had that classic, old-time diner look. Square box with chrome accents, a ribbon of windows all around.

Nora found a space off to the side in the parking lot that had a view of the front doors. She glanced at her watch—well past noon.

She'd skipped breakfast and was starving, actually. It didn't help that she was also downwind from the kitchen exhaust fan. The smell of burgers and all things fried had her rifling through her purse for a half-eaten roll of peppermint Life Savers.

About forty minutes later Craig came strolling out of the diner. As Nora watched, she recorded another impression. He was definitely an attractive man who carried himself well. There was a certain coolness. A confidence. A swagger.

The tailing resumed.

Craig ran a couple of errands and eventually returned to his office. A dozen times during the rest of the afternoon, Nora wanted to call it a day, and a dozen times she talked herself into remaining parked about a block and a half from his building. She was mainly curious about what the night would bring. *Does Craig Reynolds have a social life? Is he dating anyone? And where exactly does he call home?*

At about six, the answers started to come.

The lights went off at Centennial One Life Insurance, and out walked Craig from the building. However, there would be no bar scene, no big dinner plans, no girlfriend to meet up with. At least, not that night. Instead, he picked up a pizza and drove home.

That's when Nora discovered that Craig Reynolds was hiding something after all: he wasn't nearly as well-off as he'd have everyone believe.

By the looks of the place where he lived, he'd clearly put all his money into his car and wardrobe. The apartment in Pleasantville was a run-down unit in the middle of a bunch of other run-down units in what looked like a strip mall of housing. A few white vinyl-sided buildings with black-shuttered windows. A small patio or balcony for each unit. Not exactly impressive. *So is Craig paying alimony? Child support? What is his story anyway?*

Nora considered hanging outside the Ashford Court Gardens a little while longer. Maybe Craig had plans, only for later.

Or maybe, thought Nora, she was getting delirious from not eating all day. Looking at the pizza box balanced on Craig's hand had been enough to set off a new round of stomach growling. The peppermint Life Savers were a distant memory. It was time to get some dinner. *Maybe the Iron Horse in Pleasantville? Dining alone—how quaint.*

She drove off, satisfied with her decision

to follow Craig around. She knew that people weren't always whom they appeared to be. All she had to do was look in the mirror. Which reminded Nora of another of her mantras: Better paranoid than sorry.

Chapter 37

THE AD IN THE *Westchester Journal* said this apartment had a spectacular view. Of what, I have no idea. The front looked out on a side street in Pleasantville while the back sported a sweeping vista of a parking lot complete with the mother of all Dumpsters.

It got only worse inside.

Vinyl flooring throughout. Faux black leather armchair and a love seat that probably hadn't seen much love. If running water and electricity constitute an "updated kitchen," then, by golly, that's what I had. Otherwise, I doubt that yellow Formica countertops were somehow the rage again.

At least the beer was cold.

I put down the pizza and grabbed one out of the fridge before plopping down on the lumpy couch in the middle of my "spacious living room." It's a good thing I don't suffer from claustrophobia.

I picked up the phone and dialed. I had no doubt that Susan was still in her office.

"Did she follow you?" she asked right off the bat.

"All day long," I said.

"Did she see you go inside the apartment?"

"Yep."

"Is she still outside?"

I gave her an exaggerated yawn. "Does that mean I actually have to get off the couch and look?"

"Of course not," she said. "Take the couch with you."

I smiled to myself. I've always loved a woman who can give as good as she gets.

The window next to the couch had a ratty old roller shade that was drawn all the way. Carefully, I pulled back one of the edges and sneaked a peek.

"Hmmm," I muttered.

"What is it?"

Nora had parked about a block down the street. Her car was gone.

"I guess she'd seen enough," I said.

"That's good. She believes you."

"You know, I think she still would've believed me if I had a decent apartment. Maybe something in Chappaqua?"

"Is someone complaining?"

"It's more like an observation."

"You don't get it. This way she thinks she's got something on you," said Susan. "Dressing and driving beyond your means makes you more human."

"Whatever happened to just being nice?"

"Nora comes across as nice, doesn't she?"

"Yeah. Actually, she does."

"I rest my case."

"Did I mention the yellow Formica countertops?"

"C'mon, the place can't be that bad," Susan said.

"Easy for you to say. You don't have to live here."

"It's only temporary."

"My saving grace. Hell, that's probably the real reason for this apartment," I said. "It'll make me work faster."

"The thought did cross my mind."

"You don't miss a trick, do you?"

"Not if I can help it," she shot back. "Seriously, though, good work today."

"Thank you."

Susan gave me an end-of-the-day sigh. "Okay, it's official. Nora Sinclair has gone backstage on Craig Reynolds. Now what?"

"That's easy," I said. "Now it's my turn."

Chapter 38

THERE WAS ONLY one empty seat in the first-class cabin. Under normal circumstances, Nora would've regretted that it wasn't the one next to her. Then again, normally she didn't have such a cute guy sharing the same armrest. From the side, he kind of looked like Brad Pitt, only with no wedding ring on his finger, no Jennifer on his arm.

During takeoff Nora—sans her own wedding ring—checked out her window-seat companion with a furtive glance. She was pretty sure he was doing the same with her. *Of course he is. What man wouldn't?* When the captain turned off the FASTEN SEAT BELT sign, she knew the guy was ready to make a move.

"I'm a stacker myself," he said.

She turned with the coy pretense of just now realizing she wasn't alone. "Excuse me?"

"On the coffee table there." He smiled broadly and nodded at the *Architectural Digest* open in her lap. On the right-hand page was a picture of a spacious living room.

"See how the magazines are spread out?" he said. "Fact is, there are only two types of people in this world . . . stackers and spreaders. So which one are you?"

Nora stared him right in the eye, unblinking. As conversation starters went, she had to give him a few points for originality. "Well, that depends. Who wants to know?"

"You're absolutely right," he said with an easy laugh. "You shouldn't reveal such personal information to a complete stranger. My name's Brian Stewart."

"Nora Sinclair."

He presented his hand, strong-looking, nicely manicured, and they shook.

"Now that we know each other, Nora, I believe you owe me an answer."

"In that case, you'll be pleased to know I'm a stacker."

"Knew it."

"Oh, did you?"

"Yep." He leaned in slightly, but not *too* much. "You come across as very put together."

"That's a compliment?"

"For me, it is."

She smiled. Maybe the real Brad Pitt was better looking, but Brian Stewart certainly was charming. Reason enough to keep the conversation going for a while.

"Tell me, Brian, what's waiting for you in Boston today?"

"A dozen venture capitalists. And a pen."

"Sounds promising. I take it the pen is for your signature."

"Something like that."

Nora was expecting him to elaborate, but he didn't. She grinned. "To think I revealed myself as a *stacker,* only to have you turn bashful on me."

He shifted in his window seat, clearly amused. "For the second time, you're absolutely right. Okay, last year I sold my software company. This afternoon I'm about to launch my new one. Bor-ing."

"I don't think so. Anyway, congratulations! And those venture capitalists—they're investing in *you?*"

"The way I see it, why put up your own money when others are willing to put up theirs?"

"I couldn't agree more."

"Now what about you, Nora? What's waiting for *you* up in Boston today?"

"A client," she said. "I'm an interior decorator."

He nodded. "Is your client's home in the city?"

"It is. Except that's not the one I'm decorating. He recently built a villa down in the Cayman Islands."

"Beautiful place."

"I've yet to go myself. But I will shortly." Nora opened her mouth as if to say something else. She stopped.

"What were you going to say?" he asked.

She rolled her eyes. "It's silly, really."

"Go ahead, try me."

"It's just that when I mentioned this client to one of my girlfriends, she said the reason he was building down in the Caymans was probably so he could keep his eye on the money he was hiding from the IRS there."

She shook her head with a convincing naïveté. "I mean, I don't want to get mixed up in anything I shouldn't be."

Brian Stewart smiled with a knowing look. "It's really not as sinister as you may think. You'd be surprised at how many people have offshore accounts."

"Really?"

He leaned in closer, his face inches from hers. "Guilty as charged," he whispered. He picked up his champagne glass. "We'll make that our secret, okay?"

Nora picked up her glass, and the two of them clinked. Brian Stewart was shaping up to be someone she might want to get to know better.

"To secrets," she said.

"To stackers," he said.

Chapter 39

"WHAT CAN I GET for you?" she asked.

I looked up at the flight attendant—tired, bored to tears, trying to be nice anyway. She and her drink cart had finally made it back to me. "I'll have a Diet Coke," I said.

"Oh, I'm sorry, I ran out of those about ten rows ago."

"How about ginger ale?"

Her eyes darted around the open cans on top of the cart. "Hmmm," she muttered. She bent down and began pulling out one drawer after another. "I'm sorry, no ginger ale, either."

"Why don't we try this the other way

around," I said with a forced smile. "What do you have left?"

"Do you like tomato juice?"

Only with a lot of vodka and a celery stalk sticking out of it. "Anything else?"

"I've got one Sprite."

"Not anymore, you don't."

It took her a second to realize that was my way of saying "yes, please."

She poured about half of the Sprite and handed it over with a small bag of pretzels. As she wheeled the cart off I held up my plastic cup. If I squinted enough at the bubbles, it almost looked like the champagne Nora was probably drinking up in first class.

I popped a minipretzel into my mouth and tried to move my legs. Wishful thinking. With my tray table down, they were wedged in from every angle. Complete loss of circulation to all lower extremities was only a matter of time.

Yes, indeed. It was right about then that I realized what the common thread of this assignment was so far. In a word, *cramped.*

Cramped office, cramped apartment, cramped seat in the last row of coach that had me breathing in the odors of the cramped bathroom directly over my shoulder.

Not that all was lost.

The one good thing about tailing people on an airplane is that you never have to worry about losing them during the flight. At 35,000 feet, no one is about to slip out the side door.

I glanced up at the royal blue curtain way, way, way down the aisle. While the odds fell somewhere between slim and none that Nora would have any reason to venture back and mingle with us poor slobs in coach, I still had to stay on my toes.

Not that I could feel them anymore.

Earlier at the Westchester airport, I was sure Nora hadn't spotted me before the flight. Well, she might have seen me, but for sure, she didn't recognize me. Besides my Red Sox baseball cap, dark glasses, jogging suit, and gold chain, I'd broken out the fake mustache. Throw in a *Daily News* that was never farther away than twelve inches from my face and I'd pretty much cornered the market on incognito.

No, Nora had no idea she had company on the flight. That much I knew. Of course, what I didn't know was the question of the day.

What's in Boston?

Chapter 40

I FOLLOWED NORA and her smart little suitcase on wheels down an escalator and past the baggage claim area. As always, she looked good, front and rear view. She had this way of walking—and a great smile when she needed it. She never once looked up at a sign for directions. Safe to say, this wasn't her first trip to Logan Airport.

She walked outside and came to an abrupt stop—looking around. What for became clear after a few minutes.

It wasn't a cab and it wasn't a friend's car. It was the shuttle bus for Hertz.

As soon as she hopped on, I made a dash for the cab line.

Taxi!

"Take me to the Hertz lot!" I barked at the back of the driver's head.

He turned around, an old-salt type, his face a road map of wrinkles and creases. *"What?"*

"Take me—"

"No, I heard you just fine there, pal. What I'm saying is, they have shuttle buses for that."

"I don't like waiting."

"Neither do I." Jabbing his finger, he pointed out the back window. "You see that line of cabs behind me? I didn't wait in it for no three-dollar fare."

I looked up ahead at Nora's shuttle bus getting farther and farther away. "Okay, give me a number," I said.

"Thirty bucks. That's my final offer."

"Twenty."

"Twenty-five."

"Deal. Drive."

Chapter 41

THE GUY SPED OFF and I immediately began to work my phone. I had the number for every airline, hotel chain, and rental car company already programmed in. It was a job prerequisite.

I called Hertz. After suffering through a minute of automated prompts, I got ahold of an available agent.

"And when will you be needing the car, sir?" she asked.

"In five minutes. Maybe less."

"Oh."

She promised to do the best she could. In case it wasn't good enough, I told the driver he might be spending some more quality time with me.

Thankfully, it didn't come to that.

Nora's shuttle driver had a helium foot. With him puttering along, we actually passed the bus before we got to the lot. By the time Nora climbed into a silver Sebring convertible, I was behind the wheel of my minivan. That's right, a *minivan.* I mean, who'd ever expect to be followed by someone driving one of those?

Just the same, I was sure to keep a little distance between us. That was until Nora made it clear she was no shuttle bus driver. Formula One racer was more like it.

The more I gunned it, the faster she seemed to go. Instead of blending in with the other cars, I was forced to blow by them. So much for my inconspicuous minivan.

Shit.

A red light. I'd already sailed through an earlier one, but this one was at an intersection. Nora made it through and I didn't.

As she became a speck in the distance, I could do nothing except curse and wait. The thought of having flown all that way only to lose her was turning my stomach.

Green light!

I hit the gas and my horn at the same time, tires screeching. The game had changed to catch-up and I was in serious jeopardy of losing. I glanced down at my speedometer. Sixty, seventy, eighty miles an hour.

There! I spotted her car up ahead. I drew a sigh of relief, slowed down, and tried to pull closer. I had two lanes to work with and the traffic was cooperating. I could move back and forth without being too obvious. Things were looking up.

If only I'd been doing the same.

Chapter 42

I SHOULD'VE SEEN the split coming, where the road divided. I was too busy staring at the big Sealy mattress delivery truck ahead of me, preparing to overtake it.

Bad decision.

With my right foot pressed to the floor, I pulled up alongside the truck. It blocked my view of Nora. Edging forward, I strained my neck to see where she was.

But it was something else I saw. Big, bright yellow drums! The kind they fill with water and stack before concrete dividers so instead of going *splat,* you go *splash.*

I looked over at the delivery truck. We

were neck and neck, the driver peering down at me.

I glanced at those big yellow drums. They were getting very close, very fast.

The lanes were about to split. I was in the left one, Nora in the right. I needed to get over.

The goddamn truck!

As soon as I nosed out in front, the driver sped up. I jammed on my horn while flooring the accelerator.

Up ahead, Nora passed the yellow drums and shot off to the right.

I was still stuck in the left lane and running out of real estate. Fast.

Fuck it.

I slammed on the brakes. If I couldn't cut in front, I'd duck in from behind. All two tons of the minivan began to swerve wildly as I watched the Sealy mattress truck—an easy ten tons—start to veer. That's when I realized he wanted into my lane.

I couldn't hear the horns behind me. Or the screeching of tires. The only sound was my heart pounding as the nose of my minivan kissed the truck's back, metal against metal.

Sparks flew. I lost control of the wheel. I

spun out wildly, nearly flipping over. I would have were it not for one small detail.

Splash!

My face hit the air bag, and the yellow drums did the rest. It hurt like hell, but I knew right away. I was one lucky son of a bitch.

Traffic started to move again as I stepped out of the minivan. Like me, everyone else had survived with barely a scratch. There was water everywhere, pools of it, but that was it.

Idiot. I was furious with myself. Finally, I collected myself and made the call.

"I lost her."

"What?!" snapped Susan.

"I said—"

"I heard you. How could you lose her?"

"I had an accident."

Her register immediately shifted to concern. "Are you okay?"

"Yeah, I'm fine."

"In that case, *how the hell could you lose her?*"

"The woman drives like a maniac."

"What, and you don't?"

"I'm serious. You should've seen her."

"I'm serious, too," she barked. "You should've never lost her."

I was pleading with myself to stay calm. However, Susan wasn't exactly making it easy. As tempting as it was to grab her anger and throw it right back, I realized I'd be better off just taking it on the chin.

"You're right," I told her. "I screwed up."

She calmed down a bit. "Do you think maybe she spotted you?"

"No. It wasn't like she was trying to lose me. She just drives fast."

"How much luggage did she have?"

"A small roller. She carried it on."

"Okay, then. Cut your losses and come on back to New York. Wherever she's going, it's safe to assume she'll be returning to Connor Brown's house soon enough."

I decided that it was a good idea to change the subject. "Did we get the okay on the dig?" I asked.

"Yes, the dig is a go. The paperwork should come soon," she said. "I'll let you know."

I said good-bye, and that should have been it. But this was Susan I was talking to. In case I wasn't absolutely clear about her disappointment, she gave me one more shot.

"Have a safe flight home," she said. "Oh, and try not to screw up anything else today."

I listened as she hung up and then I shook

my head slowly. I started to pace, trying to burn off the anger. It wouldn't burn off. The more I paced, the worse I felt. The tension began working its way through my body, and before I knew it, it all collected in my fist.

Smash!

And like that, my rented minivan had one less window.

Chapter 43

NORA TOOK ANOTHER LOOK in the rearview mirror. Something had happened back there, maybe an accident.

If that's what it was, she assured herself that it was merely a coincidence and had nothing to do with the weird feeling in her stomach. The one she had had after leaving the Hertz lot. The "I'm not alone" feeling.

Now, as she arrived in the heart of Back Bay, it seemed to disappear.

The traffic on Commonwealth Avenue fell somewhere between a slow crawl and a parking lot. There was some protest march over on Newbury, and every other street was paying the price. Nora lucked out and found a spot after circling only three times.

She'd put his wedding ring on while riding the shuttle bus at the airport. After her customary look in the car's vanity mirror, she was ready to go. The suitcase came out; the convertible top went up. *It's showtime, babe.*

As usual, Jeffrey was working when she let herself in. She'd come to realize there were only three things that took him away from his writing. Food, sleep, and sex, not necessarily in that order.

Instead of calling his name, Nora quietly walked toward the back of the brownstone. Between his deep concentration and the background music, there wasn't a chance he'd hear her.

She opened the door beyond the butler's pantry and stepped out onto the private patio. With its tall fleur-de-lis trellises covered in ivy and other strategic plantings, the cozy area offered seclusion.

It took her only a minute to get ready. Reclining on a cushioned wicker chaise, she reached for her cell phone and dialed.

Seconds later she could hear the phone ringing inside.

Jeffrey finally picked up.

"Honey, it's me," she said.

"Oh, don't even tell me you're not coming."

She laughed. "Not yet I'm not."

"Wait a minute, where are you?"

"Take a peek out back."

She looked up as Jeffrey appeared in the window of his library. His strong jaw dropped, then he started to laugh, which she could clearly hear over the phone.

"Oh . . . my . . . ," he said.

Nora was naked on the chaise lounge, except for her sling-backs. She purred into the phone. "See anything you like?"

"As a matter of fact, I see a lot that I like. I don't see anything I don't like."

"Good. Don't hurt yourself running down the stairs."

"Who said anything about using the stairs?"

Jeffrey opened the window, climbed out, and shinnied down the copper-plated downspout. Very athletic, actually. All to the delight of Nora.

Whatever the world record was for a man shedding his clothes, it was promptly broken. Then Jeffrey slowly crawled up to her on the chaise lounge. He dug his hands deep into the seat cushion and wrapped his muscular arms around her back. He was a sexy man once you tore him away from his computer.

Nora closed her eyes. She kept them shut the entire time they made love. She wanted to feel something for Jeffrey. Anything. But she felt nothing.

C'mon, Nora. You know what has to be done. You've been here before.

The voice inside her head didn't sound like an old friend now. More like an unwelcome stranger, someone she almost didn't know. She tried to ignore it. It was no use. That just made it louder. More insistent. More controlling.

Jeffrey climaxed, then rolled off her, out of breath. "What a terrific surprise. You're the best."

Ask him if he's hungry, Nora.

She wanted to cry out against the little voice inside. But that would just be a waste of time. There was only one way to make it stop.

And she knew it.

"Where are you going?" Jeffrey asked.

Nora had risen from the chaise without a word. She was already heading inside the house. "The kitchen," she said over her shoulder. "I'm going to see what I can make you for dinner. I want to cook for you."

Chapter 44

OH, BROTHER—what to do, what to do? This is a disaster so far.

The Tourist sat alone in the small, dingy room with another Heineken. He'd already had four. Or was it five? At this point, keeping count didn't strike him as being very important. Neither did the Yankees game droning on his TV. Or eating the sausage-and-onion pizza getting cold on the table in front of him.

On the table were newspaper clippings about the shoot-out in New York. There were easily a dozen articles about the "Sidewalk Showdown."

The story had legs, which didn't exactly surprise the Tourist. He'd left behind a host of unanswered questions. A lot of ink was being devoted to conjecture and speculation; some of it credible, most of it wacky. The short note that came with the clippings summed it up. *The circus is in town. Keep your head down, Tourist. Will be in touch.*

He smiled and re-read the conflicting eyewitness accounts. *How was it,* wrote a columnist from the *Daily News, that the same event could be seen so differently by people who were no more than twenty feet away?*

"How indeed?" the Tourist said out loud. He sat back in his chair and put his feet up on the table. He had every confidence that his identity would remain a secret. He'd taken the necessary precautions, covered his tracks. He might as well have been a ghost.

There was only one thing bothering him now, and it bothered him a lot.

What was the list he'd copied off the flash drive all about? All those offshore accounts.

One point four.

Billion.

What about it?

Was it worth some poor schmuck's life outside Grand Central?

Apparently so.

Was it worth somebody else's life?

Like his?

Definitely not.

Was it part of a bigger picture that might make sense eventually?

Who could tell? But he sure as hell hoped so.

Chapter 45

JEFFREY PEERED ACROSS the candlelit dinner table at Nora. "Are you sure you're okay with this?"

"Of course I am," she said.

"I don't know, you seemed a little put-off when I suggested we go out instead of eating in."

"Don't be silly. This is wonderful." Nora tried to match her body language to her words. That took some serious acting. She was supposed to be back at his brownstone, busy preparing his last meal. She had made up her mind.

Now here they were at Jeffrey's favorite

restaurant. Nora had never been more on edge. She felt like a racehorse at a starting gate that refused to open.

"I love this place," said Jeffrey, looking around. They were at La Primavera in the North End of Boston. The decor was simple and elegant with white linen tablecloths, gleaming silverware, soft lighting. When you sat down it was assumed you wanted regular water, not bottled. And frankly, Nora could have cared less.

Jeffrey had the osso buco, Nora the risotto with porcini mushrooms. But she had zero appetite. The wine was a Poggio dell'Oliviera Chianti Classico, the '94 Reserve. The wine, she needed. When the plates were cleared, Nora steered the conversation to the following weekend. Her unfinished business was weighing heavily on her mind.

"You forgot," said Jeffrey. "I'm traveling, darling. That book festival down in Virginia."

"You're right, I did forget." Nora felt like screaming. "I can't believe I'm letting you loose with hundreds of your adoring female fans."

Jeffrey folded his hands in front of him and leaned on the table. "Listen, I've been doing some thinking," he said. "It's about the way we've treated our marriage. Or, really, the way I've treated it—the secrecy. I think I've been unfair to you."

"Have you sensed that it's bothering me? Because—"

"No, actually, you've been so understanding. It's made me feel worse. I mean, I've got the most wonderful wife in the world. It's time the world knew it."

Nora smiled, as she should have, but inside, the warning lights were flashing. "What about your fans?" she asked. "All those women next week in Virginia who want to see one of *People* magazine's sexiest and most eligible *bachelors?*"

"Screw 'em."

"That's kind of what they're hoping for, honey," said Nora.

Jeffrey reached for her hands, clasping them lightly. "You've been understanding and I've been incredibly selfish. But no more."

Nora sensed there was no talking him out of it. At least not right then. He was such a typical guy. He had his mind made up about what was best for *her,* and there was no changing his mind.

"Tell you what," she said. "Do your book fair, wow the ladies with your looks and charm and erudition, and then we'll talk about it when you get back."

"Sure thing," he said in a tone that suggested otherwise. "There's just one problem."

"What's that?" Nora asked. *You want to propose to me again, in the middle of this crowded restaurant?*

"Yesterday, I did an interview for *New York* magazine. I came clean and told them about you. The wedding in Cuernavaca. You should have seen the reporter, she couldn't wait to put the scoop in her article. She asked if the magazine could get shots of the two of us. I said sure."

Nora's poker face finally folded. "*You did?*"

"Yes," he said, clasping her hands tighter. "That's not a problem, is it?"

"No, it's not a problem."

Not at all, she thought. *It's a big problem.*

Chapter 46

NORA RETURNED TO Manhattan late the following afternoon. She missed her loft apartment, the comfort and quiet of it, the things she'd bought for herself over the years. She missed what she considered her *real* life.

While she drew herself a bath, she listened to her messages. She'd been checking them periodically while away. There were four new ones. The first three were work-related, bitchy clients. The final one was from Brian Stewart, her first-class companion to Boston, the Brad Pitt look-alike.

The message was short and sweet, the

kind she liked. Brian expressed how much he enjoyed meeting her and how he looked forward to seeing her again. "I should be back in the city by the end of the week and I'd love to take you out for a night on the town. It'll be fun, I promise."

If you insist, Brian.

Nora took her hot bath. Afterward, she ordered in Chinese and sorted through her mail. Before the eleven o'clock news ended, she was sound asleep on the couch, sleeping like a baby. And she slept *late.*

Just before noon the next day, Nora strolled into Hargrove & Sons on the Upper East Side. Personally, she thought the place was beyond stuffy, with many of the sales staff seemingly older than the antiques they were peddling. But the store was a favorite of her client, longtime film producer Dale Minton, and he had insisted on meeting her there.

Nora browsed on her own for a few minutes. After walking by yet another plaid sofa, she felt a tap on her shoulder.

"It *is* you, Olivia!"

The overly excited man standing before her was Steven Keppler — middle-aged, midtown tax attorney with a bad comb-over.

"Uh . . . hi," said Nora. She quickly flipped through her mental Rolodex and came up with his name. "How are you, Steven?"

"I'm great, Olivia. You know, I was calling out your name. You didn't hear me?"

She played it cool. "Oh, that's so typical of me. The more I shop, the less I can hear what's going on around me."

Steven laughed and let it go. As he launched into his "fancy meeting you here" small talk, Nora remembered his ogling tendencies. How could she forget? Sure enough, his eyes were beginning to drool. Do eyes drool? Well, Keppler's did. Meanwhile, she was keeping one eye on the entrance for Dale. This could be a disaster in the making.

"So, Olivia, are you shopping for yourself, or a client?" asked Steven.

"A client," she said, looking at her watch.

That's when she saw him. Dale Minton was waltzing through the front door that very second, looking as if he owned the place. He certainly could have, if he wanted to.

"Oh, there he is now," she said. She tried not to panic, but the image of Dale calling her Nora with Steven looking on, and vice versa, was fraying her nerves.

"I'll let you do your business," he said. "Just promise me I can take you out to dinner sometime." The guy certainly was an opportunist. He knew what she knew, that yes was a much quicker answer. No would've required making an excuse.

"Yes," said Nora. "That would be nice. Call me."

"I will. I'm on vacation beginning next week, but when I get back, I'm going to hold you to that promise."

Steven Keppler turned to go with Dale still a few feet away. It was close, but she dodged a bullet. Then . . .

"It was good seeing you, Olivia," called Steven loudly.

Nora gave him a weak smile and glanced at Dale, who looked thoroughly confused. "Did that man just call you *Olivia?*" he asked.

Nora prayed to the goddess of quick thinking. She delivered. Nora leaned into Dale with a whisper. "I met him at a party a few months back. I told him I was Olivia—for obvious reasons."

Dale nodded, no longer confused, and Nora smiled. Her two lives remained safely apart.

For now, anyway.

Chapter 47

A BLOND WOMAN drifted from one piece of old furniture to another, her eyes shielded by a pair of dark sunglasses. She was playing detective and feeling slightly ridiculous, to tell the truth. But she *needed* to watch Nora Sinclair.

Had this been anywhere but New York, she would've stood out. But this was the Upper East Side of Manhattan. Here, she blended in. Simply another browsing customer at Hargrove & Sons.

The blonde stopped at an oak hallstand with shiny brass hooks and pretended to look at the price. Her eyes and ears remained fixed on Nora.

Or was it *Olivia* Sinclair?

She didn't know what to make of the exchange with the balding guy. *Anyone who answers to two names is probably guilty of something.*

She continued to watch Nora—now joined by an older man. Just to be careful, she wandered away from them a couple of times. Still, she managed to overhear some of the conversation.

The older man was a client. Accordingly, Nora was actually an interior decorator. Her comments and suggestions, the jargon— she definitely knew how to talk the talk.

Nora's profession was never really in doubt, though. It was the rest of her life that was in question. Her two lives, her secrets. But there was no proof of anything yet. Which was why the blond woman had decided to have a look-see for herself.

"Excuse me, do you need any help? May I be of assistance in any way?"

The blonde turned to see an elderly sales clerk hovering close behind. He was wearing a bow tie, a tweed jacket, wire-rimmed eyeglasses that looked as old as he was.

"No, thank you," she said, her voice barely a whisper. "I'm just looking. But I don't see anything I like."

Chapter 48

AFTER I LOST Nora up in Boston that Saturday, the rest of the weekend could be summed up in one word: *shitty.*

On my list of spontaneous dumb things to do, squaring off with a rental-car window scored pretty high. Thankfully, I hadn't broken my hand, at least according to my extensive medical self-evaluation. The epitome of rigor, it consisted of one question: *Can you still move your fingers, you idiot?*

When Monday morning finally rolled around, I swung by Connor Brown's house to see if Nora had returned. She hadn't. After making the same trip, with the same result, in the late afternoon, I decided it was time to try her cell phone.

I took out my notepad, where I'd written the number Nora had given me, and dialed from my car.

A man answered.

"I'm sorry, I may have the wrong number," I said. "I was trying to reach Nora Sinclair."

He didn't know anyone by that name.

I hung up and checked my notepad against the log my cell phone kept of outgoing calls. Nope. I'd definitely dialed the right number. It just wasn't Nora's.

Huh.

I stared at my steering wheel for a moment before grabbing the phone again and dialing. This time a young, pleasant-sounding female voice.

"Good morning, Centennial One Life Insurance."

"Very convincing, Molly," I said.

"Really?"

"Absolutely. If I didn't know better, I'd think you had a nail file in you hand."

Molly was my new receptionist. After Nora followed me to work, it was decided that the "field office" could no longer be a one-man operation.

"Do me a favor, will you?" I asked. "Run a cell phone check on Nora."

"The number's not already in her folder?"

"It may be, but I want to make sure she hasn't changed it recently."

"Okay. Give me ten minutes."

"I'll give you five."

"Is that any way to treat your new receptionist?"

"You're right," I said. "Make it *four* minutes."

"No fair."

"Tick, tick, tick . . ."

Molly had been out of school for only two years. While still a little green, according to Susan, and prone to the occasional lapse in judgment, she was proving to be a quick study. No surprise then when she called me back in *three* minutes.

"It's still the same number we have for her," said Molly. She read it to me, and I checked it against the number Nora had given me.

I had to smile. The only difference was the last two digits. They were flip-flopped.

Interesting.

Maybe I was the one who mixed them up. Or maybe that was what Nora wanted me to think. Or, at least allow for.

"Anything else you need?" asked Molly.

"No, I'm all set. Thanks."

I said good-bye, putting down the phone in favor of my notepad. On purpose or not, Nora had managed to elude me once again. Now what?

I'd learned early in my career that sometimes there is a difference between information you have and information you can use. This was one of those times. I had Nora's correct cell phone number but had to act as though I didn't.

With my banged-up hand I wrote her a note and left it at the front door of Connor Brown's house. I was fairly sure she'd get it. The question was when.

Chapter 49

IT WAS THE NEED for closure that had Nora back in Briarcliff Manor a couple of days later. Despite Connor's sister's offering her the use of the house for as long as she wished, Nora wanted to move on. Actually, she hoped never to see the bitch from California again.

The offer she *was* going to take Elizabeth Brown up on was possession of the furniture. All 11,000 square feet of it. As the interior decorator, Nora knew what everything cost—and everything cost a lot. A small fortune, really. One she was all too pleased to pocket in the name of assuaging Lizzie's guilt, or whatever it was.

All she needed was a little help.

"Estate Treasures, can I help you?"

"Hi, it's Nora Sinclair calling. Is Harriet there?"

"Sure, Nora, hold on a second."

Nora switched ears with her cell phone. She was in the backseat of the Town Car that was taking her out to Connor's house.

Harriet got on the line. "Well, if it isn't my favorite decorator."

"I bet you say that to *every* decorator."

"As a matter of fact, I do. And wouldn't you know, they all believe me. So how's business, Nora?"

"Pretty good. That's why I'm calling."

"So when can I expect you here in the shop?"

"Actually, that's going to be my question to you, Harriet. I need you to make a house call."

"*Oy.* Where am I going? New York City, I hope. Nora? Talk to me."

"Briarcliff Manor. A client of mine recently passed away."

"I'm sorry to hear that."

"So was I," said Nora calmly. "Anyway, I

was asked to deal with his furnishings on behalf of the estate."

"You want to consign them?"

"That's what I was thinking."

"A house call, huh? How many rooms are we talking about?"

"Twenty-six."

"Oy."

"I know. That's why I called you. No one could do a better job on this than you."

"I bet you say that to all your suppliers."

"And wouldn't you know, they all believe me," said Nora.

Nora took a few minutes to discuss some of the furniture and a date for when Harriet could come and look at it. By the time she said good-bye her Town Car was pulling into Connor's driveway.

As the driver grabbed her suitcase, she got out and headed for the front door. That's when she saw the note from Craig Reynolds.

Please call me ASAP.

Chapter 50

THE BUZZ FROM my office phone was followed by Molly's voice. "It's her," she announced.

I smiled. There was only one *her* she could be talking about. Nora was back in town. It was about time.

"Here's what I want you to do, Molly," I said. "Tell Ms. Sinclair I'll be right with her. Then put her on hold and stare at your watch for forty-five seconds. After that, put her through."

"You got it."

I leaned back in my chair and gazed at the ceiling. It was composed of those white acoustic tiles that begged to have sharp pencils thrown up into them. I could've been taking the time to gather my thoughts, only that's all I'd been doing the past week. There wasn't a stray thought of mine within a hundred-mile radius.

Ring.

Thank you, Molly.

I picked up the phone and did my best impression of frenzied. "Nora, are you still there?"

"I'm still here," she said. I could tell immediately she wasn't very happy about having to wait.

"Bear with me for one more second, okay?"

I put her on hold again before she could object. Then I stared back up at the ceiling. *One one thousand, two one thousand . . .* At fifteen one thousand, I got back on the line and let out a deep breath.

"Gosh, I'm sorry to keep you waiting, Nora," I said, now doing my best impression of apologetic. "I was finishing up with another client on the other line. I take it you got my note?"

"A few minutes ago, yes. I'm here at the house now."

Time to test her lying ability. "How was your trip? Maryland, right?"

"Actually, it was Florida," she said.

No. *Actually, it was Boston,* I wanted to say, but knew I couldn't. Instead: "Oh, that's right. Wouldn't want to vote there! Was it a good trip?"

"Very much so."

"You know I tried reaching you on that cell phone number you gave me—except it turned out to be somebody else's."

"That's odd. What number were you dialing?"

"Let me check, I've got it right here."

I read it back to Nora.

"That explains it," she said. "The last two digits are eight-four, not four-eight. God, I hope it wasn't me who mixed them up. I'm sorry if I did."

Oh, she's smooth.

"That's okay. It was probably my mistake," I said. "It wouldn't be the first time I've suffered from digit dyslexia."

"In any event, we're talking now."

"Yeah, we are. Anyway, the reason I wanted to speak to you was the insurance inquiry."

"Is there news?"

"You could call it that." I hesitated before going on. "Please don't read too much into this, but I think we should discuss it in person."

"It's bad, huh?"

"That's not what I'm saying."

"Except if it was good news, you would've told me over the phone. At least admit that."

"Yes, okay, it's perhaps not the best news," I told her. "Really, though, don't read too much into it. Is there a time later today we could meet?"

"I suppose I could come by your office around four."

And I suppose you won't need directions, Nora, given that you've already staked the place out.

"Four's good—great, actually. Only we might want to do it someplace else besides here. There's a crew here painting. The fumes are pretty bad," I lied. "Tell you what, do you know where the Blue Ribbon Diner is?"

"Sure, just outside of town. I've been there."

I know.

"Good," I said. "I'll meet you inside at four for a cup of coffee. Or given the time, should I say high tea?"

"Not if we're talking about the same diner."

I laughed and agreed that we should stick to coffee.

"See you at four, then," she said.

You can count on it, Nora.

Chapter 51

THE BLUE RIBBON wasn't going to win first place for anything in the categories of food, decor, and service, but as suburban diners went, it was pretty decent. The eggs were never runny, the ketchup bottles were almost always filled, and the waitresses—while hardly a threat to win any congeniality contests—were nonetheless professional. They got your order mostly right and were quick on the coffee refills.

When I walked in a few minutes shy of four, the host gave me a nod of recognition. In my short time in the area, the Blue Ribbon had become my go-to eating place. Though

I was sure there were better haunts around, I didn't care enough to go find them.

"Actually, there's going to be two of us," I told the host, who'd automatically grabbed a lone menu upon seeing me. He was Greek and wore a stained black vest over a wrinkled white shirt. A walking cliché, yes, but the good kind, as far as I was concerned.

Nora arrived a couple of minutes later. I waved from my seat, which was in a red-upholstered booth by the back. She was wearing a dark skirt, cream-colored blouse that looked like silk, and heels. *For me, Nora? You shouldn't have.* As it was postlunch and predinner, the diner was only half filled. She spotted me easily.

Nora walked over, and we shook hands and said our hellos. I thanked her for coming. I also noticed that she smelled nice. *Watch it, Craig.*

As Nora took a seat, a waitress immediately appeared at the table. In a small bit of mirth amid her otherwise all-business demeanor, her name tag read, HEY, MISS.

The two of us ordered coffee, and I tacked on a slice of apple pie. My waistline didn't need it, but I figured it was a good strategic move. I mean, how can you *not* trust a guy who orders apple pie?

To look at Nora as the waitress left was to know I should keep the small talk to an absolute minimum. Her body language spoke loud and clear. Tight, controlled, on edge. She was there to hear some bad news and had no interest in prolonging the suspense.

So I cut to the chase.

"I feel awful," I said. "All along I've been talking about this inquiry like it was totally routine and nothing to worry about. Then the other day . . ." My voice trailed off as I shook my head, exasperated.

"What? The other day *what?*"

"It's this goddamn O'Hara!" I said. I didn't scream it, though my volume was enough to turn a head or two at other tables. I took it down a notch. "I don't know why they let a guy like that be in charge of investigations. It's just not necessary."

Nora looked at me, waiting, which I could tell, she wasn't used to doing.

"He's apparently contacted the FBI," I said.

She squinted. "I don't understand."

"Neither do I, Nora. O'Hara's got to be the most suspicious guy I've ever met. As far as he's concerned, the whole world is a conspiracy. O'Hara can definitely be a head case."

"Great." Nora leaned back in the booth, her shoulders slouched. Her green eyes blinked in confusion. I almost felt sorry for her. "The FBI? What does that mean?"

"Something that no one who's suffering a loss should ever have to endure," I said. Then came a short, sweet dramatic pause. "I'm afraid your fiancé's body is going to be exhumed."

"What?"

"I know, it's terrible, and if there was anything I could do about it, I would. I can't, though. For whatever reason, this idiot O'Hara refuses to accept that a forty-year-old guy can naturally have a heart attack. He wants more tests performed."

"But there was an autopsy."

"I know . . . I know."

"This O'Hara guy doesn't believe the results?"

"It's not so much that, Nora. What he wants are more thorough tests. General

autopsies are . . . well, they're general; they
don't always uncover certain things."

"What do you mean? What *things?*"

Nora's question hung in the air as the
waitress returned. As she put down our coffee and my apple pie, I watched Nora get
more and more worked up. Her emotions
struck me as genuine. It was the motivation
that seemed less clear. Was she the grieving
fiancée, or the murderous woman grappling
with the sudden risk of being exposed?

The waitress left.

"What things?" I said, repeating her question. "Any number of things, I suppose. For
instance, and I'm only speaking hypotheti-
cally, if Connor was an abuser of drugs, or
perhaps there was some preexisting medical condition that went unreported on the
insurance application—both these things
could possibly void the policy."

"Neither was the case."

"You know that, and to be perfectly candid
and off the record, I know that. Unfortunately, John O'Hara doesn't."

Nora pulled back the paper lid on one of
those oversize thimbles of half-and-half. She
dumped it in her coffee. Added two sugars.

"You know what?" she said. "Tell O'Hara he can keep the money. I don't want it."

"I wish it were that simple, Nora. Centennial One actually has a legal obligation to pay off the policy, barring any discrepancies. Strange as it may sound, you don't have a choice in this matter."

She lowered her elbows onto the table. Then her head dropped into her hands. When she lifted it back up I could see a tear rolling down her cheek. She whispered: "You're literally going to dig up Connor's coffin? That's what you're going to do?"

"I'm so sorry," I said, and actually I did feel bad. What if she was innocent? "You can see why I didn't want to have this conversation over the phone. The only thing I can tell you is that if I were O'Hara, I'd never do something like this."

As I said those words, watching as she dried her eyes with her napkin, I couldn't help thinking about my father and his words.

Things aren't always as they appear.

I still couldn't tell if Nora's tears were real or fake, but this much I did know. She'd come to despise John O'Hara. And the more she hated him, the more I could gain her trust.

Pretty ironic, I had to admit.

For John O'Hara wasn't out in Chicago at the home office of Centennial One Life Insurance.

Instead, John O'Hara was sitting in a booth at the Blue Ribbon Diner, eating a slice of apple pie and answering to the name of Craig Reynolds.

And insurance wasn't exactly my game.

Part Three

VERY DANGEROUS GAMES

Chapter 52

SUSAN WAS BARKING in my ear. She was pissed. *"What do you mean, you told her we were exhuming Brown's body?"*

"Trust me, it's to our advantage," I said. "More than ever, Nora thinks I'm on her side. Plus, you told me yourself that digging up the body poses a risk. She could find out on her own."

"I said it poses a *small* risk."

"And what I'm saying is that we just turned it around to our advantage."

"*We* didn't do anything, O'Hara. You did this on your own without discussing it with me first."

"So I winged it a bit."

"No, you winged it a lot. That's your trade-mark, isn't it? That's what gets you in trouble," she groused. "There's a reason we have a game plan, and that's so we both know what the other is doing."

"C'mon, Susan, at least agree this plays into our favor."

"That's not the point. I need you to be a team player, understand? You're not the undercover cop anymore."

I hesitated, but then said, "You're right. I'm the undercover federal agent."

"Not for long if you call any more audibles like that. I don't like cowboys."

Neither of us said anything for a few seconds. I broke the silence. "You know, I liked it better when you were building me up."

Susan managed a small, frustrated laugh.

"Tell me, genius," she said, "now that Nora knows we're about to dig up her fiancé, what's your next move?"

"That's easy," I answered. "We wait for the results. If our lab says foul play, we've got our killer."

"You'll still need evidence that she did it."

"Which happens to be a lot easier to find when you know what you're looking for."

"What if the lab doesn't find anything?"

"Then I tell Nora the good news and work that much harder to trip her up."

"You're forgetting one thing."

"What's that?"

"She might actually be innocent."

"This coming from someone who thinks everyone's guilty."

"I'm just saying . . ."

"No, I understand. Anything's possible. But the woman has been involved with at least two dead guys in two different states. If it's a coincidence, then Nora Sinclair has had some serious bad luck with men."

"Silly me," she said. "Let's strap her to the electric chair."

"There we go, much better. I thought you were someone else for a second."

"Speaking of which, what are the odds Nora develops eyes for your alter ego?"

"Nah. Craig Reynolds isn't in her league," I said. "He doesn't make enough money."

"You never know. You've been telling me how much she thinks you're on her side. Based on that, she might want to slum it for a change."

"Then I've got *just* the apartment. Perfect for slumming."

"You're not going to start on that again, are you?"

"No, but if I end up spending too much more time in that dump, I'm going to put in for hazard pay."

"O'Hara, should that turn out to be the hardest part of this assignment, you'll be a lucky man."

Chapter 53

NORA GENTLY PUSHED through the door of her mother's room at the Pine Woods Psychiatric Facility and tried her best to smile. She was in a horrible mood and she knew it. So did anyone else who came into contact with her—Emily Barrows and that new nurse, Patsy, being the most recent, when she had arrived on the psych ward.

For a little while, she pretended as if she had never met Craig Reynolds for coffee the day before. She acted as if he never told her that Connor's body was going to be exhumed.

"Hello, Mother."

Olivia Sinclair was sitting on top of the covers in her yellow nightgown. She glanced at Nora with a blank smile. "Oh, hello."

The clouds that were hanging low for most of the day had begun to clear. Sunlight now sliced its way into the room through the horizontal blinds. Nora grabbed the chair in the corner and pulled it to the bed.

"You're looking well, Mother."

Any daughter would've said that. The difference with Nora was that she actually believed it. She no longer used her eyes to see her mother. Only her memories. If anything, it was force of habit. After Olivia was sent off to prison, Nora was never allowed to visit. As she grew up, her mother stayed frozen in time. Nora went through a series of foster homes, and her *idea* of Olivia was one of the only constants in her life.

"I like to read, you know."

Oh, shit. "I know you do, Mother. I'm afraid I forgot to get you a book this time. Things have been . . . well, they've been—"

A lawn mower started up on the grounds outside. The raw churning of the motor penetrated the room and gave Nora a jolt. She suddenly felt paralyzed and out of breath. The only thing working was her tears. Her facade crumbled, and the outside world came pouring in. She wiped her eyes.

"I'm sorry, Mother."

For the first time, Nora told her mother about a recurring dream of watching Olivia shoot her father. How vivid in her mind the night remained. What was said, what everyone was wearing, even the smell of sulfur.

What does it matter? She doesn't even know who I am.

Nora grabbed a tissue from the bedside table. It was as if the dam had burst. Her tears. Her emotions. Everything pouring out. She was losing control. There was an overwhelming compulsion to talk to someone.

Nora drew the deepest breath, coaxing her lungs to expand. Finally exhaling, she closed her eyes and spoke. "I've done some terrible things, Mother. I need to tell you about them."

Nora opened her eyes, the truth on the tip of her tongue. But that's where it stayed. Something awful was happening to her mother.

Springing from her chair, Nora ran to the door. She burst out into the hallway and screamed, "Help! Hurry! I need help! My mother is dying!"

Chapter 54

NURSE BARROWS'S EYES left the page of the medication log, her head whipping in the direction of the scream. She recognized Nora's voice right away.

Hurriedly navigating the corner of the nurses' station, she yelled out for Patsy, who was in the supply room.

Reaching the hallway, Emily saw Nora frantically waving her arms. There were about thirty yards separating her and Olivia Sinclair's room, and Emily began covering them faster than her chunky frame should've allowed.

"What is it?" Emily yelled out. "What happened?"

"I don't know," cried Nora. "She's —"

Emily ran right by her and into the room. What she saw was a scene straight out of *The Exorcist*. Olivia Sinclair was convulsing on the bed, her body fully extended while her arms and legs trembled and twitched with spasms. The rattling of the metal-frame bed was now a near deafening noise.

But for all that was happening—including Nora's complete state of panic—Emily Barrows instantly became calm. She glanced over her shoulder to see Patsy just arriving at the doorway.

"Give me a hand," she said to the younger nurse.

Patsy joined her with quick, nervous steps.

"Is this your first seizure?" Emily asked.

Patsy nodded.

"All right, here's what you do. First, you roll her on her side so in case she vomits, she won't choke on it," said Emily. She folded her arms and nodded at Patsy, who again seemed frozen. "Don't just stand there, dear."

Sputtering into action, Patsy lifted Olivia onto her side. "Okay, what now?"

"Now you wait."

"For what?"

"For it to stop."

"You mean, this is all I do?"

"Exactly. Don't try to restrain her in any way. Simply keep track of the clock. Nine times out of ten it won't last more than five minutes. If it does, we call for a doctor."

Nora stood there, her shock doubled by the fact that Emily had turned her mother's seizure into a teaching lesson. "There's got to be something more you can do!"

"There really isn't, Nora. Trust me, it looks a lot worse than it is."

"What about her tongue?! Isn't there a chance she can swallow her tongue?!"

Emily shook her head, trying to remain patient. "That's a myth," she said. "It's not even a possibility."

Nora was still not satisfied. She was about to insist on getting a doctor when suddenly everything stopped. The bed, the noise . . . her mother's convulsions.

The room fell silent. Emily eased Olivia over onto her back again, propping her head on the thin pillows. Nora rushed over and grasped her mother's hand, giving it a squeeze.

For the first time she could remember, she actually felt a squeeze back.

"Everything's okay, Mother," said Nora softly. "Everything's okay."

"There, there," whispered Nurse Barrows, and she had a calming hand on Nora's shoulder. "I know you thought she was dying, but trust me, dear, you'll know when somebody's dying. You'll know."

Chapter 55

SIX FEET UNDER?

I really don't know where that expression came from. Definitely not from the Sleepy Hollow Cemetery at the Old Dutch Church in Westchester County. With six feet of soil dug up next to Connor Brown's tombstone, there was no sign of a coffin. Only when the dirt pile was twice as high did I finally hear the flattened *thud* of shovel hitting wood.

At least I wasn't doing the digging in this famous old cemetery, where Washington Irving and several Rockefeller ancestors are supposedly buried.

"They should've called that TV series

Twelve Feet Under," I said to the chain-smoking cop standing alongside me. I guess he didn't get HBO, because he didn't get the joke. Of course, the cop's blank stare might have just been the humorless combination of fatigue and resentment.

My objective was to get in and get out as quickly and discreetly as possible. That meant a pared-down crew, no loud machinery, and a two A.M. start time. Broad daylight and a big production was the last thing I wanted.

In addition to the stone-faced cop, I had three workers from the cemetery. After setting up a couple of small floodlights, they dug for about an hour. The only other person with us was a driver from the FBI's pathology lab. He looked barely old enough to have his license.

I glanced again at the cop next to me. "Talk about your graveyard shift, huh?"

I got no laugh or chuckle in return. *Be that way,* I thought.

So I turned my attention back to the gaping hole in the ground. Standing on top of Connor Brown's half-exposed coffin were the three guys from the cemetery. They were about to secure straps around the handles, which didn't look sturdy enough to me.

"You sure those things are going to hold all that weight?" I asked.

All three looked up. "Should," said the tallest one, who was under five foot six. His English was okay, though. The other two were fluent only in nodding.

The straps were tied and the three guys climbed out of the hole in the ground. They lifted an aluminum frame with a crank attached to it, straddling it over the pit before hooking up the other end of the straps.

There was a sudden noise.

What the hell was that?

No one actually said those words and yet our collective looks made it clear we were thinking the same thing. It sounded like twigs snapping, footsteps maybe. *The Headless Horseman out for a late-night ride?*

We all froze and listened for it again. Above us the thick oak branches swayed, creaking and moaning. But the noise didn't return.

The three cemetery guys—not quite as spooked as the rest of us—got back to work and started to crank.

Slowly, Connor Brown's coffin began to rise.

Almost on cue the wind picked up even

more. There was a sudden chill in the air that raced up my spine. I wasn't terribly religious but I couldn't help wondering about what we were doing. Disrupting the dead. Toying with the order of things.

I was getting a bad feeling about this.

Snap!

The sound ripped through the wind, echoing in the night. *Not twigs.* This was ten times louder. The handles on one side of the coffin had splintered, forcing the hinges open with a horrific nails-on-blackboard screech. Out spilled the contents in a slow-motion roll. The corpse of Connor Brown.

"Jesus fucking Christ!" the cop beside me yelled.

We rushed to the edge of the pit and were met with a putrid smell. My gag reflex kicked in, seizing my throat, and I had to step back—but not before catching a glimpse. A decomposing face; white, stringy flesh; eyeballs bulging in hollowed-out sockets, glazed over but staring right up at me.

The cemetery guys were cursing in a mix of Spanish and English as the kid from the pathology lab just shook his head. Next to me was the cop. Puking.

"What the hell do we do now?" I asked.

The answer came in the shape of a ladder. The diggers had to go back down into the hole. The only way to get the body up now was to carry it.

"Please, we need help," said the cemetery crew spokesman.

It was the easiest decision I'd ever made.

I turned to the cop, who was still bent over and coughing up the last remnants of his dinner. He looked back at me with the most incredulous, pale face. "Me?" he gasped. "Down there?"

My smile said it all.

Sorry, pal, but you should've laughed at the G-man's jokes.

Chapter 56

NORA WASN'T SURE if she'd been spotted, but there was no doubt they'd heard
something. The twig snapping beneath her
feet as she tried to get closer sounded like a
firecracker.

When they all turned to look, she dropped
to the ground behind the closest headstone.
She pulled her knees tight against her chest
and held her breath. It was a good time to
wonder if she'd taken too much of a risk
being there.

But Nora knew she couldn't stay away.

She had to see this, disturbing and
macabre as it was. Connor's body being

taken back from the earth—were they really going through with it?

Yes, they were.

Nora shuddered. According to legend, a witch was buried out there in an unmarked plot. Even with a sweater on, she could feel the cold granite slab against her back. Slowly, she took a peek around the head-stone. *Phew!* They had gone back to work. Straps had been hooked up to some con-traption over Connor's grave. They were beginning to raise his coffin.

She watched in disbelief. With each turn of the crank, she became more upset. Everything had been going so smoothly. There was no cause for concern. She was free and clear. And now this.

Who the hell does this O'Hara guy think he is? Asshole! Fucker!

That prompted another question. *Where the hell is he?*

Nora thought for sure that by following Craig Reynolds that night, she'd get her first glimpse of O'Hara. It was the main reason she was there.

But he wasn't one of the three workmen with the shovels. He surely wasn't the cop. Besides Craig, that left only one other man—and he was barely a man. *There's no way that kid is John O'Hara,* thought Nora.

Right then the top of the coffin rose above the ground. At the sight of it, she turned away, unable to watch. Her back pressed hard against the gravestone again, she could hear her heart pounding.

That was nothing compared to what she heard next.

A horrific snapping—and it came right from Connor's grave. Every muscle in Nora's body tensed. She didn't know what had happened, and part of her wanted it to stay that way.

But she had to look.

So she peeked around the gravestone.

Her eyes went wide and her mouth dropped. She nearly screamed. One side of Connor's coffin was dangling, the lid wide open. Her mind filled in the rest, and as she watched the policeman vomit, she wanted to do the same.

In fact, she was sure she would've if not for another instinct taking over.

Run!

Chapter 57

THE NEXT DAY Nora drove back to Manhattan and directly to the Bliss spa in her SoHo neighborhood. She had a carrot-and-sesame body buff as well as a hot oil massage. That was followed by a manicure and pedicure. Usually nothing relaxed Nora more than a little *blissful* pampering.

But three hours and four hundred dollars later, she was no better off. The previous night still weighed on her mind. It was late afternoon and the thought of spending the evening alone was giving her chills.

She considered calling Elaine and Allison. Maybe they'd be up for a last-minute get-together. As Nora reached for her cell phone, though, she changed her mind.

She had another idea. Maybe a better way to distract herself. Instead of dwelling on what was, she'd focus on what might be. Her on-deck circle. *Batter up, Brian Stewart.*

Nora called the wealthy software magnate she'd met on the plane and asked if he had plans for the evening.

"Nothing I can't cancel," he quickly replied. "Give me two shakes of a lamb's tail." When he called back after clearing his schedule, he was ready to fill it again. All with Nora.

"I hope you don't have to be up too early tomorrow morning," he warned with a laugh. Excitedly, he outlined what was in store.

Cocktails at the King Cole Bar.

Then dinner at Vong.

Topped off by dancing in the West Village at Lotus.

Nora couldn't have been more pleased. After spending time in a graveyard, a night on the town seemed just right.

Chapter 58

OVER A BOTTLE of Perrier-Jouët at the King Cole Bar, Brian Stewart regaled her with funny stories from his childhood. Nora listened and laughed. At the same time, she couldn't help notice how a lot of them involved his family. The way Brian talked, she could tell how close they were. It made her jealous. In all her years shuttling from one foster care home to another, she was lucky if anyone even remembered her birthday.

Not that she was about to tell Brian any of that.

By this point in her life, Nora had perfected a made-up story of her upbringing. The

architect father. The schoolteacher mother.
The three of them living blissfully in the
rolling hills of Litchfield, Connecticut. The
more people she told, the more she was
able to forget the truth. One day, she hoped,
it would be as if her mother never really
killed her father while Nora watched.

Over dinner at Vong, Brian switched to
wine and Nora to Pellegrino. As they ate and
drank, the two of them became increasingly
cozy with each other. She was actually able
to look at him without thinking of Brad Pitt.
Brian was handsome enough in his own
right.

Not to mention fun to be with, which
wasn't always the case with rich men. More
times than not, the wealthy ones she met
turned out to be exceedingly boring and
incredibly full of themselves. Rich *and* exciting ones were hard to find. Which made
Nora all the happier that she'd met Brian.

The feeling seemed mutual.

The way things were going, it looked as if
they wouldn't make it to Lotus for dancing.
She tried to picture his apartment. Surely it
would be huge, probably a penthouse.
Maybe some kind of interesting loft space.
She'd find out soon enough.

"Are you having a good time?" he asked.

"The best."

He smiled. Except it wasn't exactly a happy smile. Something was bothering him and he looked nervous.

Nora inched forward in her seat. "What's wrong?"

He fidgeted with his dessert spoon, almost as if he were working up his nerve. Apparently, he was. "There's something I have to tell you," he said. "I have a confession to make."

"Damn, you're married."

"No, I'm not married, Nora."

"Then, what is it?" she asked.

His dessert spoon was getting a real workout now. "It's something else I'm not," he said. He finally put down the spoon and took a deep breath. "What I'm trying to say is that I'm not really a rich software developer."

The words hung in the air, as did the silence that followed them. Nora was speechless. Brian's face was red, and it wasn't from the alcohol. His admission had sobered them both up.

"I'm telling you this because I couldn't lie to you anymore," he said.

"Why did you lie in the first place?"

"I was afraid you wouldn't have been interested in me."

Nora blinked. "What do you really do?" she asked.

"I'm an advertising copywriter."

"Ah, you lie for a living. So, there were no venture capitalists waiting for you in Boston?"

"No, just a client. Gillette."

She shook her head. "Let me get this straight—you thought the only way I'd like you was if you were rich?"

"I guess I did."

"Or was it because you thought that was the only way I'd *sleep* with you for one night—as in tonight?"

"That's not true."

She shot him a dubious look. *"Really?"*

"Okay, it's a little bit true," he admitted. "At least at first. Like I said, though, I couldn't lie to you anymore."

"Is *anything* that you've told me true?"

"Yes. Everything, as a matter of fact. Everything except the part about being fabulously wealthy. I'm sorry I lied," he said. "Can you forgive me?"

Nora paused, if only for effect, before reaching over and taking his hand. "Yes," she said. "I can forgive you. I do forgive you, Brian."

A few minutes later, when all seemed well again, she excused herself from the table to use the ladies' room. It was in the front of the restaurant. As she walked by it and headed out the door to hail a cab home, Nora wondered briefly how long it would take Brian to realize she wasn't coming back.

Chapter 59

THE TALL BLOND woman quickly turned her face away as Nora walked by. They were so close, she could feel the heat of the other woman's body. This was a dangerous moment. No, this was a *mistake* on her part.

The blonde had been sitting at the bar at Vong, sipping a martini and watching Nora the entire time. She was sure she'd been witnessing a date—probably a first one, given the body language. She couldn't hear the conversation, but it was clear they were getting along.

Which made Nora's sudden exit all the more puzzling.

Minutes passed. The blonde stabbed at the olive in her martini with a toothpick, her mind allowing for the various possibilities. Nora leaving momentarily to make a call, for instance. More plausible was her going out for a quick smoke. Then again, she'd yet to see Nora with a cigarette in her hand.

The woman looked back over at the table where Nora's date sat, waiting. *He certainly is a good-looking guy,* she thought. *He kind of looks like* —

"Excuse me," came a voice over her shoulder.

She turned to see a middle-aged man with salt-and-pepper hair. He was wearing a turtleneck, sport coat, and way too much aftershave.

She glanced up at him, not saying any-thing, waiting.

He put his hand on the empty stool next to her. "Is this seat taken?"

"I don't believe so."

He flashed a cheesy grin and sat down. "Hard to believe there could be a vacancy next to such a very pretty woman," he said while positioning his forearm on the bar. He leaned into her. "Can I buy you another drink?"

"I haven't finished this one yet."

"That's okay, I'll wait," he said, nodding confidently. "All night, if I have to."

The blonde threw him a flirtatious smile and then lifted her martini. She poured it over his head.

"There, all done," she said.

She got up and walked away. But not toward the door. Convinced that Nora wasn't returning, she headed for the table where her date remained sitting alone.

"Excuse me, are you waiting for Nora Sinclair?"

He looked at her, a little puzzled. "Uh . . . yes, actually, I am."

"I'm afraid she's not coming back."

"What do you mean?"

"I just saw her walk out of the restaurant."

More puzzled, he peered over his shoulder toward the exit, his eyes scanning. He started to get up.

"Don't bother," she said. "It's been a good five minutes now."

He sat back down. "I don't understand. Are you a friend of hers, or something?"

"No, I wouldn't say that." She slid into the chair that had been Nora's. "Do you mind if I ask you a couple of questions, though?"

Chapter 60

NORA NEEDED TO GET out of New York for at least a few days. Fortunately, she had somewhere she could go.

The traffic was light heading due north on I-95. About half an hour south of Boston, though, that all changed. A jackknifed tractor trailer had backed everything up for miles, and Nora was reminded why she always chose to fly.

Still, she didn't care.

After the cemetery and her dinner with Brian Stewart—the Don Juan wannabe with no real dinero—what Nora wanted was a little stability in her life. Wheels to the ground. Taking the day to drive up to Boston was good for her. So was spending the night with her hubby.

"Boy, did I ever miss you!" Jeffrey said, greeting her in the foyer of the Back Bay brownstone. He held her in his arms, kissing her lips, then her cheeks, her neck, and starting all over again.

"I'm almost tempted to believe you," teased Nora. "Here I thought you'd forget all about me after your book festival and those adoring Virginia women."

"How could I forget about *this,* and *these,* and *this?*" asked Jeffrey.

"I couldn't agree more," said Nora.

They continued to kiss and kid each other all the way up the stairs and into the master bedroom. Their clothes littered on the floor and their bodies sweating, they made love that afternoon and again in the early evening. The farthest either of them strayed from bed was when Jeffrey ran to meet the delivery guy with their Vietnamese takeout.

They ate wakame salads, Cuu Long chicken, and lemongrass beef while cuddling and watching *North by Northwest.* Nora adored Hitchcock, who was one of the kinkiest bastards ever. By the time Cary

Grant was dangling off Mount Rushmore, though, Jeffrey was asleep.

Then Nora waited patiently. When she finally heard that little nose-whistling sound he made, she slid out of bed and down the hall. Into the library and behind the computer.

Everything went very smoothly indeed. Nora got into his offshore account easily, took the tour, and saw what Jeffrey had put away for a rainy day. Nearly $6 million.

The moment of truth was fast approaching, certainly faster than the arrival of that *New York* magazine photographer.

But first things first. A few loose ends that needed tying in Briarcliff Manor. All having to do with a certain insurance man and some test results. What would old Alfie Hitchcock have done with that? *He certainly would have raised some hackles with that scene at the cemetery,* Nora thought, and couldn't hold back a smile.

Chapter 61

THE TOURIST—ah, the poor Tourist—was feeling restless and frustrated and bent out of shape. There were at least a hundred other places he'd rather have been, but this place—his temporary home away from home—was where he *needed* to be.

He still hadn't figured out the list of off-shore accounts. Obviously, the people in the file were evading taxes, right? But *who* were they? What was the price of admission to the list? And why had the file been worth someone's life?

He'd already read the newspaper, and finished off a fat Nelson DeMille novel about

Vietnam. Now he was sitting on the couch, reading the latest issue of *Sports Illustrated.* While he was in the middle of an article on the Boston Red Sox's fading pennant hopes for the year, the silence of the living room was broken.

Someone was at the door.

Quietly, he grabbed the Beretta by his side and stood. He walked to the window, pulling back the drawn shade for a peek at the front stoop. To make things worse, it was pouring outside, turning everything to mud.

Standing there was some guy with a flat, square box in his hand. Behind him, in the driveway, was a Toyota Camry with the engine running.

The Tourist smiled. *Dinner is served.*

Tucking the gun behind his back and underneath his shirt, he opened the door and greeted yet another delivery guy from Pepe's House of Pizza. He'd already ordered half a dozen times from there since he arrived.

"Sausage and onion?" asked the delivery guy. He looked college-aged, maybe a little older. Tough to tell under the brim of his Yankees baseball cap.

"Yep. How much?"

"Sixteen-fifty."

"You'd think I'd know that by now," the Tourist muttered to himself. He reached into his trouser pocket. His hand came up empty. "Wait a minute, let me get my wallet." He was about to turn around when he noticed that the delivery guy was being rained on. "Why don't you come on in," he offered.

"Thanks, I appreciate it."

The guy stepped inside while the Tourist headed toward the kitchen for his wallet. "It looks pretty wet out there," he said over his shoulder.

"Yeah. Wet means we're busier than usual."

"I bet. Why go out for dinner in the rain when you can have someone bring it to you, right?"

The Tourist returned with a twenty in his hand. "Here you go," he said. "Call it even."

The delivery guy handed over the pizza and took the twenty. "Thanks, I appreciate it." He reached inside his raincoat and smiled. "Only we're not quite even yet."

The Tourist frantically swung a hand behind his back, but it was too late, too slow. His gun was a distant second to the one pointed at his chest.

"Don't move!" said the pizza guy. He walked around and relieved the Tourist of the Beretta tucked into his jeans. "Now place both hands against the wall."

"Who are you?"

"I'm the guy who's gonna make you wish you'd ordered Chinese, *O'Hara*."

Chapter 62

FEELING INCREDIBLY STUPID, John O'Hara, the Tourist, allowed himself to be patted down. He couldn't believe he'd been suckered by this kid, this young pup, this whelp.

"Okay, turn around slowly."

O'Hara did a 180. Very slowly.

"Now, where is it?" the guy asked. "The suitcase. What's inside. Whatever you've got."

"I don't know. Honest, man."

"Bullshit. *Man.*"

"Hey, I'm telling you the truth. I handed it off as soon as I got it. A garage in New York."

The delivery guy pressed the barrel of his gun to O'Hara's forehead. Hard, so it hurt. "Then I guess there's nothing left to talk about."

"You kill me and you're dead within twenty-four hours. *You. Personally.* That's the way it works."

"I don't think so," Pizza Guy said, and cocked the gun.

O'Hara tried to read the kid's eyes. He didn't like what he saw. Coldness and confidence. This guy probably worked for the file's original seller. Maybe he *was* the seller. "Okay, okay, hold on. I know where it is."

"Where?"

"I have it here. I had it all the time."

"Show me."

O'Hara led him down the hallway to the bedroom. He could hear the faint sound of a neighbor's stereo. Thought about screaming for help. "Under the bed," he said. "I'll get it. It's in my duffel bag."

"You just stay where you are. I'll look under the bed for both of us."

The delivery guy bent down to take a peek. Sure enough, there was a black duffel. He grinned. "You don't know what it is, do you?"

"What makes you say that?"

"Because if you did, I don't think you'd be sleeping here with it."

"Then I guess I should be happy to give it back to you."

"That's right. Now, pull it out. Nice and easy."

"What's your part in this? You the seller? Or are you another messenger?"

"Just pull out the bag. I'm a messenger, by the way. Like my friend. Guy you shot at Grand Central Station. He was like a brother to me."

The Tourist knelt and slowly began to reach under the bed.

"Keep one hand on top of the bed," said Pizza Guy.

"Whatever you say." With his left hand perched on the bedsheets, the right disappeared, looking for the duffel bag.

And the gun taped to the side.

"You got it?" asked the delivery guy. "Don't fuck with me."

"Yeah, I got it. Relax a little, huh? We're both pros, right?"

"One of us seems to be."

O'Hara swung out his arm and fired two shots, the bullets ripping through the guy's chest. He fell to the floor, dead. Actually, there were *two* of the dead guy in the double-mirrored closet door, which was doubly creepy.

O'Hara checked for ID. He wasn't surprised that he didn't find any. Not even a wallet.

He went out to the kitchen and made the requisite phone call. They'd come and remove the body, even clean up the bloodstains on the carpet. They were very efficient. Until then, there was only one thing to do.

He opened the pizza box and grabbed a slice of sausage and onion. *The first bite is always the best.* And now, as he chewed his food, came the questions for the ages, the only ones that counted. Who had sent Pizza Guy after him? Who knew he was there? Who wanted him dead?

And how could he use any of this to his advantage in the future?

Oh yeah, and did he have a future?

Chapter 63

"WHAT HAVE YOU been up to, O'Hara?"

"Oh, this and that. You know me, I keep myself busy. How about our little test on the late Connor Brown?"

"Nothing . . . nada . . . zip," said Susan, disappointed.

After two days of waiting at my temporary apartment, I got a call from her late in the afternoon. Connor Brown's second autopsy report had just landed on her desk. Susan told me that the more comprehensive tests showed basically the same result. The guy died of cardiac arrest. No sign of foul play. Nothing. Nada. Zip.

"Was there *anything* this time around that the first autopsy didn't show?" I asked.

"Only a pretty nasty ulcer," she said. "Of course, with a guy working in finance who dies of a heart attack at forty, there's no real big surprise there."

"No, I suppose not. That was it, nothing else?"

"Oh, you mean, besides the abrasions from the body falling out of the coffin?"

"Shit, the kid from the pathology lab squealed, didn't he?"

"No, actually it was the cop who's still throwing up three days later, thanks to you."

I found myself smiling at an old image in my memory file.

"It was a dirty job and somebody had to help do it."

"Somebody besides you, naturally."

"Hey, the guy didn't laugh at my jokes."

"Say no more."

"So, I guess it's time to give Nora a call."

"I had a thought on that," she said. "Maybe you should stall on the test results, see if she starts to get shaky."

"Were it anybody else, I'd say yes. Not with Nora, though. The only thing she'd get is more suspicious. I'm afraid she'd pull back."

"You sure about that?"

"Sure as I can be. I think if there's a break to be had with her, it comes when she believes everything is hunky-dory."

"As in, the money is on its way?"

"Right. Let her know for a fact she's about to become one point nine million dollars richer."

"That would make me feel hunky-dory."

"You and me both."

"This means you're going to have to work faster," Susan said. "As excuses go, 'the check is in the mail' buys you only so much time."

"Shouldn't be a problem. Craig Reynolds has built up a lot of goodwill with her. Even more so when I call with the good news."

"Just remember one thing," said Susan. There's always "one thing" more with her.

"What's that? Today's 'one thing more'?"

"While you're working to get Nora to drop her guard, make sure you don't drop yours."

Chapter 64

I DIDN'T WASTE any time. After I hung up with Susan I dialed Nora on her cell. She didn't answer. I left a message and was sure to mention I had some good news for her.

Nora didn't waste any time, either. She called me back almost immediately. "I could use some good news," she said.

"I thought you probably could. That's why I called you right away."

"Is it regarding . . ." Her voiced trailed off.

"Yes, the results came back from the second autopsy," I said. "While I'm not sure if 'good news' is the way to put it, you'll be glad to know all the follow-up tests confirmed the conclusion of the original autopsy."

She didn't say anything.

"Nora, are you there?"

"I'm here," she said before another patch of silence. "You're right. 'Good news' isn't really the way to describe it."

"How about 'relieved'?"

"Maybe that's it," she answered, her voice starting to choke up. "Now Connor can finally rest in peace." Nora began to cry softly, and I must admit that she sounded convincing. With a last sniffle, she apologized.

"No need to be sorry. I know how hard this has been for you. Well, I guess I don't."

"It's just that I still can't get the thought out of my mind. Actually digging up a coffin."

"It was easily one of the most unpleasant experiences I've had on this job," I said.

"Does that mean you were there?"

The truth will set you free. "I'm afraid so."

"What about the guy responsible for all this?"

"You mean that psycho O'Hara?"

"Yes, something tells me he'd actually enjoy being on hand."

"Maybe," I said. "But he's still back in

Chicago. Between you and me, he's not the type to get his hands dirty. The good news, though—and I think we can rightly think of *this* as good news—is that O'Hara is finally ready to put an end to his little inquisition."

"He's no longer suspicious, I take it?"

"Oh, he'll always be suspicious," I said. "Of everyone and everything around him. In this case, however, I think even he realizes the facts are what they are. Centennial One will make the payout. One point nine million dollars to the penny."

"When will it happen?"

"There's some processing—you know, routine paper shuffling. I'd say I'll have a check for you in a week. Does that sound okay?"

"More than okay. Is there anything I need to do in the meantime? Anything to fill out?"

"There's a release form to sign, but you do that once you have the money in hand. Other than that, there's only one thing you have to do."

"What's that?" she asked.

"Allow me to buy you lunch, Nora. For everything I've put you through, it's the least I could do."

"That's really not necessary. Besides, it

wasn't *you* who put me through anything. You've been very sweet. I mean it, Craig."

"You know something, you're right," I said with a laugh. "If there was ever a meal that should be expensed to the company, this is it."

"Amen," she said with a laugh of her own. The free and easy kind. Relaxed. Uninhibited.

Music to my ears.

Like the sound of someone's guard beginning to drop.

Chapter 65

AT LUNCHTIME SUSAN walked into Angelo's, one of the oldest and best restaurants in Little Italy and not that far from the FBI offices. Dr. Donald Marcuse was waiting for her at a secluded booth in back.

"Susan. Such an honor. Imagine, getting you out of the office."

Susan found herself smiling. Donald Marcuse always knew how to put her at ease: sarcasm. He was mainly a forensic psychiatrist, who often worked with the Bureau, but she'd seen him for about six months after the breakup of her marriage.

"Your hair looks great, by the way," he said.

She was wearing it in a short bob these days and had started to touch up the brown lately, which just killed her, slayed her.

"Just for informational purposes," Susan said, "not that I really give a shit, but is that considered a sexist remark these days?"

The doctor shrugged. "Here's my theory: if a woman can say it, then so can a man. I don't know if the theory holds up to scrutiny."

"Probably not. It sounds too logical."

They ordered lunch, then talked about current affairs and the wicked ways of New York until Susan glanced at her watch.

"Enough fun for the day, huh?" Marcuse said, and smiled pleasantly. "What's really on your mind?"

For the next few minutes, Susan told the psychiatrist what she knew about Nora Sinclair. Then she asked him to fill in as many blanks as he possibly could. She wanted to know what had turned Nora into a killer and what kind of killer she was.

As was her style, Susan took notes as Marcuse talked. She would review the notes back in her office and possibly share them with O'Hara.

According to Marcuse, a "black widow" was a woman who systematically murdered spouses, sexual partners, and occasionally other family members. An alternative to the "widow" was a "for-profit crime" killer. With this type of killer, everything was just business. The primary motive was profit.

"Almost all female serial killers kill for profit," said Marcuse, and he would know.

The doctor continued, pleasantly and matter-of-factly. Nora probably had a firmly implanted belief that men are not to be trusted. Possibly she was hurt herself.

Even more likely, her mother was hurt by a man, or men, when Nora was young.

"Maybe Nora was abused as a child. Most of my peers would say so. I don't much care for that kind of easy answer myself. Takes all the fun out of it."

Donald Marcuse finally stopped talking about Nora and looked at Susan. "She's gotten under your skin, hasn't she? It's not like you."

Susan looked up from her notes. "She's so dangerous, Donald. I don't give a shit if she was abused. She's pretty and charming, and she's a murderer. And she isn't going to stop."

Chapter 66

THE PHONE IN THE Westchester house rang the next morning at about eleven. Nora picked up, thinking Craig was confirming their lunch date for later that afternoon.

She was wrong.

"Nora, is that you?"

"It is. Who's this?"

"Elizabeth," she said. "Elizabeth Brown."

Shit. Connor's sister was calling from Santa Barbara and Nora immediately felt a little dumb that she didn't recognize her voice. After all, technically speaking, she was her houseguest.

The concern, however, was short-lived.

Elizabeth's guilt-induced sweetness picked up where it had left off. She couldn't have sounded nicer.

"I've been worried about you," she said. "Are you doing okay?"

Nora smiled to herself. "Thank you, Elizabeth. I'm holding up. I really appreciate your checking in. You know, at first I was a little wary about staying here. Of course, I don't want to overstay my welcome."

"Oh, please, I hope you're not thinking that's why I called," she said. "Nothing could be further from my mind."

"Are you sure?"

"Positive. Besides, I wouldn't have the time to deal with selling the house even if I wanted to."

"I take it you're busy with work."

"Yes. I've got two buildings that I designed in construction right now and a third about to break ground."

"The glamorous life of an architect, huh?"

"I wish," she said with a sigh. "No, I'm afraid I'm somewhat of a cliché when it comes to how many hours I've been putting in. Maybe it's just the best way for me to keep my mind off Connor."

"I know," said Nora. "I've taken on three

more clients recently—three more than my schedule can actually accommodate."

The two continued to talk for a few minutes. There was nothing forced about the conversation. No hesitation. Every sentence seemed to flow naturally.

"You know, this is a shame," said Elizabeth.

"What's that?"

"The circumstances under which we've gotten to know each other. We have a lot in common on our own."

"You're right, we do."

"Maybe if your travels bring you out this way, we can get together for lunch, or something. Or if I come back to New York?"

"I'd like that," said Nora. "I'd like that a lot. It's a date."

In your dreams, Lizzie.

Chapter 67

A LITTLE BEFORE twelve-thirty, I pulled into Connor Brown's driveway—that's how I always thought of the place: *Connor Brown's house.* Before I even came to a stop Nora was walking out the front door.

She was wearing a light summer dress, sleeveless with a red and green floral pattern. It showed off her tan nicely, not to mention her legs. She got in my car and announced that she was starving.

"That makes two of us," I said.

We drove over to a restaurant called Le Jardin du Roi in the town of Chappaqua. It was upscale without being overly fancy, and

I guess the mix of white linens and wooden beams qualified it as suburban chic. We took a table for two in the far corner.

It was a half-business, half-ladies-who-lunch crowd. With me in my suit and Nora in her blousy summer dress, we looked to have both halves covered. Nora was without a doubt the most attractive of the women in the restaurant, though—and the head turning done by all the other men in suits confirmed it.

A waiter came over. "Can I bring you both anything to drink?"

Nora leaned in across the table. "Will you get in trouble if we have wine?" she asked.

"Depends on how much," I replied, cracking a smile. When she smiled back I assured her, "No, I won't be breaking any company rules."

"Good." She picked up the wine menu and handed it to me.

"No, go ahead," I said. "You decide."

"If you insist."

"Would you like a minute?" asked the waiter.

"No, that won't be necessary," said Nora. She pulled the wine list toward her and immediately ran her index finger down the page, stopping midway.

"The Châteauneuf-du-Pape," she announced. It was a decision made in less than six seconds.

"A woman who knows what she wants," I said as the waiter nodded and walked off.

Nora shrugged. "At least when it comes to wine."

"I was thinking more generally."

She shot me a curious look. "What do you mean?"

"Take your career, for instance. I get the distinct impression you knew from an early age that you wanted to be an interior decorator."

"Not true."

"You mean you weren't always changing the furniture around in your Barbie Dream House?"

She laughed, and seemed to be having a good time so far. "Okay, true," she said. "What about you, though? Did you always know what you wanted to do?"

"No, I only sold lemonade at my lemonade stand. No insurance policies."

"Maybe that's what I'm really asking," she said. "Don't take this the wrong way, but with you I get the opposite impression: that you were maybe cut out for something else."

"Like what? Give me an example. How do you see me, Nora? What should I be doing?"

"I don't know. Something . . ."

"More exciting?"

"I wasn't going to say that."

"Yes, you were—and it's okay. I'm not insulted."

"You shouldn't be. In fact, you should take it as a compliment."

I chuckled. "Now you're pushing your luck."

"No, I'm serious. You have a certain way about you, a kind of inner strength. And you're funny."

I was spared from having to respond by our waiter returning with the wine. As he opened the bottle, Nora and I exchanged a few glances over our menus. Was she flirting with me?

No, Einstein, we're flirting with each other.

With a swirl and a sip, Nora okayed the Châteauneuf-du-Pape. The waiter poured. When he left, she proposed a toast. "To Craig Reynolds. For being so incredibly nice to me throughout this entire ordeal."

I thanked her and we clinked glasses, our eyes locked on each other.

And little did I know that the real ordeal was just beginning.

Chapter 68

THE BUSINESS SUITS had left. So had the ladies who lunch. There were only two holdouts from the afternoon crowd at Le Jardin. Nora and moi. The house pâté and the hearts of palm salad, the roasted salmon and the coquilles St. Jacques—most of it was devoured, though at a leisurely pace. All that remained on our table in the corner were the last sips of wine.

From our *third* bottle of Châteauneuf-du-Pape.

Mind you, it wasn't part of my original plan to drink half a vineyard at lunch. Once we got going, though, the plan was revised and then revised again. Alcohol, after all, makes a great truth serum. What better way to find out something about Nora that I wasn't supposed to? The more we talked, the better my chances. At least, that was the story I kept telling myself.

Eventually I glanced over my shoulder at the waitstaff, who were setting the tables for dinner. A busboy was lazily sweeping a broom near the bar. I turned back to Nora. "You know, there's a fine line between lingering and loitering, and I think we've officially crossed it."

She looked around to see what I was talking about. "You're right," she said with an embarrassed smile. "We'd better get out of here before he sweeps us out with the breadcrumbs."

I signaled for the check from our much-relieved waiter. The 30 percent tip I left meant a relatively guilt-free departure for the two of us—if not exactly a sober one. I expected as much from Nora. After all, she was thin as a rail. But despite having about eighty pounds on her, I was feeling the effects, too.

"Why don't we walk for a bit," I said as we stepped outside.

I was reassured when she agreed. Drinking on the job is one thing. Drinking and driving is another. A little fresh air and I knew I'd be all right.

"Maybe we'll see the Clintons," Nora chirped. "They live right up the street."

I decided to lay off that one. Too easy. We strolled the sidewalk along the various storefronts. I stopped at a window of an embroidery place called the Silver Needle.

"This reminds me of my mother," I said. "She loves to knit."

"What kind of things does she make?" asked Nora, who was a surprisingly good listener, not as into herself as I would have expected.

"The usual. Afghans, scarves, sweaters. Actually, I remember this one Christmas back in my high school days when she knitted me *two* sweaters: one red, the other blue."

"That's sweet."

"Yeah, but you don't know my mother," I said with a finger raised. "For Christmas dinner I show up at the table wearing the red sweater—and what does she say to me? 'What's wrong, you don't like the blue one?'"

Nora gave me a push on the shoulder. "You're making that up!"

Yes, I was.

"No, it's true," I said. We started walking again. "What about your mother? Is she a knitter?"

Nora suddenly looked uncomfortable. "My mother . . . she passed away some years ago."

"I'm sorry."

"It's okay. She was a great mom while I had her."

We continued to walk, only now in silence.

I shook my head. "See what I've done?"

"What?"

"I've taken a perfectly good time and spoiled it."

"Don't be silly," Nora said with a wave of her hand. "This is still a perfectly good time. In fact, it's one of the best times I've had in a while. I needed this."

"Aw, you're just saying that to make me feel better."

"No, I'm saying it because it's *you* who makes me feel better. As you might imagine, these last couple of weeks have been awful. Then, out of nowhere, you come along."

"Yeah, except I was making things even tougher for you."

"At first, yes," she said. "However, it turns out you were a blessing in disguise."

I tried not to flinch at the irony of that last word as we stopped at an intersection and waited to cross. The afternoon sun was beginning to dip below the trees. Nora folded her arms against her chest with a slight shudder. She seemed vulnerable, actually.

"Here," I said. I had removed my suit jacket and I draped it over her shoulders. As she pulled the lapels together our hands touched briefly. In front of us the WALK sign flashed, but we didn't move a step. Instead, we stood there, perfectly still, looking at each other.

"I don't want this to end," she said. Then Nora leaned in close, her voice dropping to a whisper. "Let's go somewhere, okay?"

Chapter 69

I DIDN'T HAVE to be Johnny Casanova to figure out what she meant. *Let's go somewhere.* Even Johnny Knucklehead could've gotten the not-so-subtle hint. Nora wasn't talking about getting a cup of coffee to clear our heads.

No, the only thing not obvious to me at that moment was the following: *How was Johnny O'Hara going to respond?*

All through lunch I didn't mind that Nora and I were getting cozy with each other, flirting, whatever it was we were doing. In fact, that was kind of the idea. Now suddenly things had gotten a little *too* cozy.

Could she be interested in me? Of course, it wasn't really me. It was Craig Reynolds, the insurance man.

Maybe it was the wine she'd had. Or maybe it was something else, something I wasn't seeing. An angle she was playing. One thing was for sure. It wasn't my money she was after.

Selling life insurance isn't usually recognized as a rich guy's game. Even the best at it are no match for the likes of a Connor Brown, hedge-fund manager and financial guru. Besides, Nora had seen where I was living as Craig. She already knew the BMW and the fancy suits were a front. Yet, despite all that, she said what she said.

Let's go somewhere.

I stood there, staring deep into her green eyes on the corner of that intersection in downtown Chappaqua. The chance to go in any direction.

"Follow me," I said.

We walked back to my car parked outside the restaurant. I opened the passenger-side door for her.

"Where are you taking me?" she asked.

"You'll see."

I walked around and got behind the wheel. We strapped on our seat belts and I started the engine, giving it a few extra revs while still in park. Then I kicked it into drive.

Chapter 70

NORA CAUGHT ON a mile or so before we got there.

"You're taking me home, aren't you?"

I turned to her with a slow nod. "I'm sorry," I said.

"That makes two of us. You're right, though. Must have been the wine. I'm so embarrassed."

My tone, my body language—I made it look as though this was an easy decision, that the thought of being with her never really entered my mind. If only that were true.

Nora was an absolutely beautiful woman who'd presented me with an amazing offer. It took every ounce of willpower to remind myself why I was with her in the first place.

Still, there was no denying some chemistry, a connection between us. Something I was convinced she couldn't fake. And even if she could, why bother?

We drove the last stretch of road to "Connor's house" in silence. The one time I glanced over at her, I couldn't help notice that her dress was riding up her leg. Tanned thighs, slender, firm, giving me a reminder of just what I was passing up.

I pulled into the circular driveway and came to a pebble-crushing stop. That's when she let me off the hook.

"I understand," she said. "It probably wouldn't have been the best thing for us to do. Not under the circumstances."

"Probably not."

"Thanks for lunch. I had a wonderful time." She leaned over and gave me a soft peck on the cheek. I could feel her hair brush against my face. I could smell her perfume, very nice, a hint of citrus.

"I'll . . . um . . ." I cleared my throat. "I'll let

you know when the paperwork on the insurance money has been taken care of, okay?"

"Sure, Craig. You've been great."

Nora stepped out of the car and walked slowly up the front steps. *And out of my life?* I waited for her as she took the house keys out of her purse. I looked away for a few seconds to fiddle with the radio dial. When I looked back she was still trying to get the door open.

I put down the window. "Everything all right?"

She turned back to me, shaking her head with a frustrated sigh. "The damn key's stuck. This is getting more embarrassing by the second."

"Hold on."

I got out of the car to take a look. Sure enough, there was the key sticking halfway out of the lock.

Stuck, however, it wasn't.

As soon as I gripped it, the rest of the key slid smoothly into the cylinder. I turned around and there was Nora, inches away.

"My hero," she said, pressing her body up against mine. Her legs were very firm. Her breasts, very soft. She wrapped her arms around me and began kissing my lower lip gently. "I fibbed. I don't really think this is a bad idea."

That's when instinct took over and my willpower completely failed.

I kissed Nora back.

Chapter 71

LIKE A CRASHING WAVE, the two of us spilled into the foyer of the house. I kicked the front door closed behind us. *What are you doing, O'Hara?*

There was still time to stop it. A chance to pull away. All I had to do was quit kissing Nora.

But I couldn't stop. She felt so soft, so damn good in my arms. She smelled delicious: her body, her hair. Her green eyes were amazing up close.

Nora took my hand and guided it up her dress along the inside of her thighs. Her breath caught. When I reached the smooth silk of her panties she held me tighter, her hips starting to move with my touch. She began to moan, and it had to be real, had to be. Why fake it with me?

Off went my shirt. Down went my pants. We stopped the kissing for just a moment—only long enough to lift Nora's dress over her head. "Fuck me," she said, slightly out of breath. Just like that. Except she made it sound sexy and irresistible.

Nora pulled us both to the floor and straddled me. She pushed aside her panties, took me in her hand, and guided me inside her. Even in the heat of the moment a funny line ran through my head: *You're fucked, O'Hara.*

I was dizzy. The whole room was spinning. The room? We were in the marble foyer of Connor Brown's house, the man she'd been engaged to. The man she may have killed. It couldn't get any more screwed-up than that, I thought.

Think again. The next thing I knew, I heard a ringing down by my feet. It took me a moment to figure out what it was.

My cell phone.

Christ. I knew who it was. Susan! She was checking in. Talk about incredible timing.

"Don't even think about getting that," said Nora.

Don't worry, I won't.

The ringing stopped as we kept going, never breaking stride. We were in rhythm, incredibly in sync. She swept her beautiful brown hair down across my face. She was on top; then she was on the bottom; she was on her hands and knees, the delicate curve of her back belying the deep moans that asked for more until the foyer echoed with the two of us climaxing.

For a good couple of minutes, if not more, the two of us just stared up at the ceiling, saying nothing, getting our breathing under control.

Finally, I blinked. "The key was stuck?"

"Hey, you're the one who fell for it."

"I did, didn't I?" I said. Then we were laughing, really laughing, as though it was the funniest thing that had ever happened to either of us. Nora had a great laugh when she let herself go. You wanted to laugh along with her.

"Are you hungry?" she asked. "Steak? We have Kobe. Or how does an omelet sound?"

"And she cooks, too."

"I'll take that as a yes. If you want, there's

a shower in the guest room. It's up the stairs, your first right."

"That would be great."

She rolled on her side and kissed me. "Not as great as you, Craig Reynolds."

Chapter 72

I STEPPED OUT of the shower and wiped the back of my hand on the fogged-up mirror until I could see myself staring back. I shook my head. Shook it a second time.

Well, you've really done it now, O'Hara.

Undercover work requires a certain amount of room to maneuver—but this was stretching the limits. I'd gone way beyond the call of duty, only not in the way where they give you a medal at the Hoover Building in Washington.

From here on out, it was going to be very, very tricky.

"Craig, are you okay?"

Nora was calling me from the bottom of the stairs. I opened the door to the bathroom. "The shower was great. I'm coming."

"Good," she said. "Because your omelet's going to be ready in a flash."

I combed my hair straight back, put my clothes back on, and loped downstairs to join Nora in the kitchen. Oh man, she was quite the sight, decked out in only her bra, panties, and a spatula. What a spectacular-looking body, and with a great smile.

I noticed there was only one place setting on the table. "You're not having anything?" I asked.

"No, I've been nibbling a little bit on the ham." She raised a bottle of water. "And I've got my usual. Watching the waistline."

"I was watching it for you. You don't have any reason to worry."

I sat down and watched as she tended to the skillet on the stove. *Staring* was more like it. She was as stunning from the back as from the front. And as for that waistline—"What waistline?"

Cool it, O'Hara.

But honestly, I couldn't. It was a weird feeling, and it immediately had me thinking about someone I used to know. A narcotics officer, a friend. He was a really good guy, a good cop. At least, he was until he made a fatal mistake. He foolishly sampled the goods and got addicted.

The lesson was hard to miss. Even after my shower I thought I could still smell Nora on my skin. I could still taste her. And all I could think about was how I wanted more of her. I didn't know how I could stop myself.

"Here you go," she said.

I gazed down at the big, fluffy western omelet she'd put in front of me. "Looks delicious." And I was hungry, maybe because I'd burned off lunch back in the foyer.

I picked up my fork and took a bite. "Spectacular."

She cocked her head. "You wouldn't lie to me, would you?"

"Who, me?"

"Yes, *you,* Craig Reynolds." Nora leaned over and ran a hand through my hair. "You want a beer, or something?"

"How about some water." The last thing I needed was more alcohol.

She went to the cabinet for a glass while I continued on her omelet. Truth be told, it really was delicious.

"Can you stay the night?" she asked, returning with my water. "*Please* stay."

The question surprised me, though it probably shouldn't have. I started to look around the kitchen, all the more aware of whose house I was in. The place was professional-grade everything—beautiful, actually—top-drawer in every nook and cranny. Viking, Traulsen, Miele, Gaggia—the best brands in the world.

Nora glanced in the direction of the foyer. Her sundress was still lying on the marble floor.

"I think it's a little late to be weirded out," she said.

She was right, and I was about to admit as much—when my stomach suddenly felt very strange.

Chapter 73

"WHAT'S WRONG?" NORA ASKED.

"I don't know," I said. "Out of nowhere I'm starting to feel . . ."

Like I'm going to vomit all over the kitchen.

I sprung out of my chair and raced for the bathroom, barely making it to the toilet in time. I dropped to my knees and heaved violently. Up came the omelet. Most of lunch as well.

"Craig, are you all right?" she asked from behind the bathroom door.

No, I wasn't. I'd been hit by a tidal wave of nausea and I was reeling. My vision was blurred. All I could do was hold on tight and hope for it to pass.

If that cop from the cemetery could see me now.

"Craig? You're scaring me."

I was too busy retching to respond to anything she was saying. I was too dizzy and weak.

"Can I get you something?" she asked.

With my arms wrapped around the porcelain, I was faced with a horrible fear: what if this never passes? That's how bad I felt, how awful and terrified.

"Craig, please say something."

The next moment, however, it did pass. Oddly. Luckily. As fast as it came, it seemed to disappear. Just like that.

"I'm okay," I said, as much surprised as relieved. "I'm okay now. I'll be out in a minute."

I lumbered over to the sink, rinsed my mouth, and splashed some cold water on my face. Again I was staring at myself in the mirror. It had to be food poisoning, right?

But there was no escaping another possibility—I was suffering from pure, unadulterated anxiety on the heels of having fucked up very badly. Simply put, the omelet didn't mix very well with the huge and unforgiving pit in my stomach.

Jesus, O'Hara. Get a grip!

I returned to the kitchen and a very confused Nora. "You scared the hell out of me," she said.

"Sorry. That was bizarre." I struggled to offer up a believable explanation. "Maybe it was a bad egg."

"Could be. Oh, I feel just terrible. Oh, Craig. You're feeling better now, though?"

I nodded.

"You sure? Don't try to be a hero."

"Yes."

"Now *I'm* the one really feeling awful," she said. "You'll never eat anything I cook for you again."

"Don't be silly, it wasn't your fault."

Her lower lip curled down. She seemed hurt and *frightened.* I went over and put my arms around her. "I'd kiss you but—"

She broke into a smile. "I think I can dig you up a toothbrush," she said. "On one condition."

"What's that?"

"You agree to spend the night here. Once again—with feeling—*pretty please?*"

Maybe if she hadn't been wearing only her

bra and panties. Maybe if I hadn't been hold-ing her at that moment. Maybe then I could've said no. Maybe, but I doubt it.

"On one condition of my own," I said.

"I know what you're going to say and I wouldn't think of it."

Which meant we slept far away from the master bedroom that evening. Not that we actually did much sleeping. I promised myself it would be only this one night. The next day I'd put an end to it. I'd figure out some other way to be close to her without being intimate.

Yet deep down I sensed what was hap-pening. I could feel it everywhere.

I was hooked on Nora.

Chapter 74

THE SOUND OF the doorbell chiming downstairs made for a rude awakening the next morning.

Nora sprung right up in bed. "Who could that be *this* early?"

I looked at my watch. "Shit."

"What?"

"It's not that early. It's almost nine-thirty."

Her reaction was a frisky grin that somehow managed to be wholesome and sexy at the same time. "I guess we really tired each other out."

"Go ahead and laugh, I was supposed to be at my office an hour ago."

"Don't worry, I'll write you a note."

The doorbell rang again. This time, repeatedly. It sounded like wind chimes during a hurricane.

"Whoever it is, I'll get rid of them," Nora said. Beautifully naked, she climbed out of bed and went to the window. She peeked through the curtain. "Damn, I forgot."

"Forgot what?"

"It's Harriet."

I didn't know who Harriet was, but it didn't matter. All I knew was that I didn't want her or anybody else at the door—not with me on the other side of it. "You can get rid of her, right?"

"Actually, I can't. She's doing me a big favor."

"What if she sees me here with you?"

"That won't happen. I asked her to look at the furniture for her consignment store. Just hang out; I'll make sure we stay clear of this room. It won't take long."

John O'Hara didn't really have a problem with that; Craig Reynolds, on the other hand, had a job to get to. "Nora, I'm already late for work as it is," I said. "There's got to be a way I can slip out a back door, or something."

"She's already seen your car. If it's gone

when she's leaving, she'll ask me about it. Neither of us wants that."

I took a deep breath and let it out. "How long is this going to take?"

"I told you, it won't take long." She unlocked the window and opened it. "Sorry, Harriet, I'll be right there," she called down. "Great *hat,* sweetie."

Nora spun and, with a running start, jumped back into bed with me. "Now about your going to work today, you," she said, her hand reaching beneath the sheet. "I don't think it's a good idea."

"Oh, you don't, do you?"

"Absolutely not. I think you should play hooky so we can have some fun. What do you think?"

It didn't matter what I said. Nora's hand under the sheet could already tell what I thought.

"I suppose I could take a day off."

"That's the spirit."

"What should we do?"

Nora glanced down at the sheet covering me. "Well, I'll tell you. It looks like someone wants to go camping."

She hopped back out of the bed. *Very limber. Must work out a lot.*

"Wait, you can't leave me *now*," I said.

"I have to. Harriet's waiting and I've got to go put some clothes on." She glanced down at the sheet again, the same frisky grin on her face. "Hold that thought," she said.

Chapter 75

I LAY IN BED, staring up at the ceiling, *holding the thought,* as it were. This was probably a maid's or nanny's bedroom, and it was still a lot nicer than mine. I finally began plotting out the rest of the day, like where Nora and I might go. More important, how I'd navigate our budding relationship, or whatever was going on between us.

She certainly knew how to get what she wanted. The question remained: Was it me she wanted? And what did I want out of this? To prove Nora innocent?

I told myself to snap the hell out of it. The

only question that *really* mattered was whether she had anything to do with the death of Connor Brown—and the disappearance of his money. That was my job, getting the answer.

I closed my eyes. Seconds later they popped open.

I jumped out of bed and ran to my suit hanging over a chair. I grabbed the ringing phone out of my pants pocket and checked the number to see what I already knew. *It was Susan!*

I couldn't blow her off twice, could I? She knew that I always kept the phone with me and that I would never be out of range.

Be yourself, O'Hara.

"Hello?"

"Why are you whispering?" she asked.

"I'm at a golf tournament."

"Ha-ha. Where are you really?"

"The Briarcliff Manor library."

"I believe that even less."

"Except it happens to be true," I said. "I'm brushing up on my life insurance jargon."

"Why?"

"Nora's been asking a lot of questions. She's very sharp. I don't know if she's testing me or just curious. Either way, I need to know what I'm talking about."

"When's the last time you had contact with her?"

Something told me "all night long" wasn't the best answer to that question.

"Yesterday," I said. "Craig Reynolds took her to lunch to apologize for all the hassles John O'Hara put her through."

"Good move, slick. You obviously told her about the payout coming, right?"

"Yes, and she seemed relieved. That's when she started to ask some of the questions, though."

"You think she suspects you?"

"It's hard to tell with her."

"You've got to get her to open up to you."

I swallowed hard on that one. "Here's a thought: what if Craig Reynolds follows up on the lunch by asking her out to dinner?"

"You mean, like a *date?*"

"I wouldn't pose it quite that way. Her fiancé just died. But, yes, *like a date.* You said you wanted her to open up more."

"I don't know," said Susan.

"Right, neither do I. I'm running out of options, though, not to mention time."

"What if she says no?"

I laughed. "You underestimate the O'Hara charm."

"Hardly. It's why you're working this case, pal. But as you said yourself, Nora doesn't seem like the type to fall for an insurance man."

I bit my tongue. "Personally, I'd thought you'd be more concerned about Nora saying yes."

"Trust me, I am," she said. "But I think you have a point. It's probably our best shot."

I was about to agree when outside the bedroom I could hear voices. Nora and Harriet coming up the stairs, talking.

"Damn."

"What is it?"

"I've got to hang up," I said. "I'm getting the evil eye from a librarian."

"All right, get going. But listen—be careful, O'Hara."

"You're right. This looks like a really bad-ass librarian."

"Very funny."

I hung up, got back into bed, and resumed staring at the ceiling. I hated having to lie to Susan, but I hardly had a choice. She wanted to know if I thought Nora suspected something. Now I was wondering the same thing about *her.* Could she tell I was lying?

Susan was one of the least gullible people I'd ever known. That's why she was the boss.

Chapter 76

NORA RETURNED, all bright smiles and full of pep. Hard to resist. She jumped up on the bed and kissed my chest, my cheek, my lips. She rolled her eyes and made a funny face that could have won my heart under normal circumstances, which these certainly weren't.

"Did you miss me?"

"Terribly," I said. "How'd things go with Harriet?"

"Wonderfully. I told you it wouldn't take long. I'm good. You wouldn't believe how good I am."

"Yes, only you weren't the one stuck in this room."

"Oh, you poor thing," she said, teasing me. "You need some fresh air. All the more reason why you can't go to work today."

"You're not going to take no for an answer, are you?"

"As a matter of fact . . . no."

I nodded at my coat and trousers draped on the chair. "Okay, but are you sure you want to spend two days in a row with me in those clothes?"

She shrugged. "I've taken them off you once. I won't mind doing it again."

We showered, dressed, and took her car out for a spin. The Benz.

"So, where are we going?" I asked.

Nora slid on her sunglasses. "I've got it under control."

She drove first to a gourmet market in town called Villarina's. I, naturally, acted as if I'd been there before. As we walked in she asked me whether there was anything I didn't eat. "Besides my omelets."

"I'm not a big fan of sardines," I said. "Other than that, go for it."

She ordered a small feast. Various cheeses, roasted peppers, a pasta salad, olives, dried meats, some French bread. I offered to pay. Reaching for her purse, she said she'd hear nothing of it.

Next stop was a liquor store.

"How about we go with white today? I prefer pinot grigio, myself," she said.

She checked to see what was already chilled and pulled out a bottle of Tieffenbrunner. We were all set for our picnic.

More so when Nora showed me the blanket in the trunk. Cashmere, with a Polo logo. She'd packed it while I was in the shower.

We drove to nearby Pocantico Lake and found a patch of grass that offered some privacy, not to mention gorgeous views of the Rockefeller estate with all its expensive hills and dales and whatnot.

"See, doesn't this beat going to work?" she said after we plopped down on the blanket.

But I *was* at work. As we talked over the food and wine, I was doing my subtle best to get something from Nora that would point to her involvement in Connor Brown's death—and the transfer of his money that had started this whole investigation.

Trying to gauge her computer literacy, I casually referred to the firewalls built into a new web program I was using at the office.

When she nodded I tacked on, "To think, only a year ago I thought a firewall had to do with asbestos."

"You and me both. I only know what it is from one of my former clients. He was some big Internet guy."

"One of those dot-com millionaires, huh? Jesus, what do they do with that kind of money?"

Nora made another funny face.

"Lucky for me, a lot of redecorating. You can't imagine."

"Very true. Though I can imagine the taxes these guys must pay."

"I know. Of course, I guess they have their ways of minimizing them," she said.

"You mean like loopholes? What?"

She looked at me for a moment. "Yeah, like loopholes." There was a slight squint in her eyes. Hesitation bordering on suspicion. Enough to make me back off.

So for the rest of the afternoon, I played it cool . . . like a guy enjoying an unexpected day off from work, with a beautiful woman he couldn't get enough of.

Chapter 77

GO HOME, O'HARA. Run away, you idiot.

But I didn't run.

After the picnic, we caught a movie at the art-house cinema in Pleasantville. That was Nora's idea as well. *Rear Window* was playing at the Jacob Burns, and she told me it was one of her all-time favorites. "I love Hitchcock. Do you know why, Craig? He's funny, and he also gets the dark side of life. It's like two great flicks for the price of one."

By the time the movie was over, we'd filled up so much on popcorn that we decided to pass on the dinner Nora had planned at the nearby Iron Horse Grill. I stood in the town parking lot with her as if the two of us were in high school again, unsure of how our date should end.

Not Nora. "Let's go to your place," she said.

I regarded her for a moment, fixing on her expression. She'd already seen "my place," run-down shoebox that it was. Was she playing me, wondering how I'd react? Or did she really not care how I lived?

"My place, huh?"

"Is that all right?"

"Sure," I said. "I've got to warn you, though, it may not be what you're expecting."

"What would that be? What am I expecting?"

"Let's just say it's a far cry from what you're used to."

Nora looked me in the eye then. "Craig, I like you. That's what this is about. Just you and me. Okay?"

I nodded. "Okay."

"Can I trust you? I want to."

"Yeah, of course you can trust me. I'm your insurance guy."

With that, we drove to my place. Nora didn't bat a pretty eyelash when she saw it—for the second time. Ashford Court Gardens, my home sweet home.

Hand in hand, we ventured inside.

"I should point out, the maid is on strike," I said with a grin. "Unbearable work conditions, she claims."

Nora looked around at my less-than-tidy surroundings. "That's okay," she said. "It tells me you're not seeing anybody else. I kind of like it, actually."

I offered her a beer and she accepted. Handing it to her in the kitchen, I was sure to make fun of the yellow Formica countertops before she did.

She took a swig and put down her red leather purse. "Well, aren't you going to show me around?"

"You're pretty much looking at it," I said.

"You do have a bedroom, don't you?"

I'd told myself this had to stop right here, right now. Of course, if I'd really meant it, we never would've been standing in my kitchen. I would've said something back at the movie theater, a pretense of wanting to "slow things down."

Instead, we were already starting to kiss as we headed to my bedroom. I was about to get between the sheets with Nora again. Talk about giving new meaning to *undercover agent.*

But I was actually planning to turn it to my advantage. And I thought I knew right where to start.

Chapter 78

"HOW'D YOU GET into her purse without her knowing?" Susan asked.

Well, you see, boss, after Nora and I had wild, crazy sex in my bachelor digs, I waited until she fell asleep. Then I slipped out to the kitchen and rummaged through her bag.

On second thought . . .

"I have my ways," I simply said. "Isn't that why you chose me for this?"

"Let's just say you have a track record, O'Hara. And you were available."

I was in the office behind my desk the next day, giving Susan an update over the phone on what we'd last discussed: my "dinner date" with Nora. Susan's main concern was that I might be coming on too strong—that I might scare Nora off.

Ha.

Once I assured Susan that wasn't the case, her attention fell on what I'd found in Nora's purse.

"What's the shyster's name again?" asked Susan.

"Steven A. Keppler."

"And he's a tax attorney in New York City?"

"That's what his card said."

"How soon can you talk to him?"

"That's the thing. I called and Keppler's away on vacation until next week."

"Of course, he may not know anything."

"Or he may know everything. I'm an optimist, remember?"

"He'll claim client privilege if indeed that's what Nora is."

"He probably will."

"What will you do then?"

"Like I said, I have my ways."

"I know, that's what scares me," she said. "Remember, you've got to be careful with lawyers. Some of them, believe it or not, actually know the law."

"Funny how that works, huh?"

"You'll keep me informed? You *will* keep me informed."

"I always do."

Hanging up with Susan, I pushed my office chair back and took a deep breath. I felt restless and out of sorts. My computer was in screen-saver mode, and with the heel of my shoe I hit the space bar on the keyboard. The monitor lit. I pulled up my chair and clicked open the file I had on Nora. I started to browse through the pictures I'd first taken of her with the digicam after Connor Brown's funeral.

I stopped on the last one and studied it.

It was the shot of her talking with Connor's sister, Elizabeth, on the front steps. Nora was dressed in black, with the same pair of sunglasses she wore with me on our picnic. Elizabeth Brown was almost as good-looking, only she was a California blonde—an architect, according to my notes.

I leaned forward and stared at the photograph closely. On the surface there was nothing unusual about what I was looking at. But that was the thing. *Perception versus reality.* Either Nora had nothing to hide . . . or she had everyone fooled. The police.

Friends. Elizabeth Brown. *Christ.* Could she really be standing there and calmly talking to the sister of the man she'd murdered?

Was Nora that convincing? That conniving? What made her so dangerous was that I couldn't tell for sure. Not even now.

All I knew was one thing: I couldn't wait to see her again.

I closed the file, telling myself I was out of control. I had to do something. I was standing way too close to the flame, the heat was getting to be too much. I needed to get away. *Cool it, O'Hara.* At least for a few days.

I had an idea then. Maybe a way of getting my priorities back in order.

I dialed Susan again and told her what I wanted to do.

"I need a couple of days off."

Chapter 79

NORA STEPPED OFF the elevator on the eighth floor of the Pine Woods Psychiatric Facility. She took a swig of water, finished it off, and tossed the empty bottle in a trash barrel. As she always did, she walked to the nurses' station. Except no one was there that afternoon. Not Emily. Or Patsy. *What an apt name that is.* Not anyone.

"Hello?" she called out.

There was no response, just the echo of her own voice.

Nora hesitated for a moment before deciding to continue on down the hallway. It wasn't as if she had to sign in after all these years.

"Hello, Mother."

Olivia Sinclair turned to her daughter, who was standing in the doorway. "Hello," she replied with her usual blank smile.

Nora gave her a kiss on the cheek and pulled up a chair. "Are you feeling all right?"

"I like to read, you know."

"You do," said Nora. She placed her purse down on the floor and reached into the plastic bag she had with her. Out came a copy of Patricia Cornwell's latest novel. "Here you go. I didn't forget this time."

Olivia Sinclair took the book and slowly ran the palm of her hand over the cover. With her index finger she traced the embossed lettering of the title.

"You're looking a lot better, Mother. Do you realize how much you scared me last time?"

Nora watched as her mother's gaze remained on the novel's shiny cover. *Of course she doesn't realize anything.* The walls she'd built around her world were too thick.

But that fact, usually the cause for Nora's pain every time she visited, was now cause for relief. From the moment her mother suffered the seizure, she worried that she'd been responsible. Her tears, her emotions, the sudden compulsion to admit her sins—everything she had no business bringing with her into that room—had triggered the reaction. The more Nora thought about it, the more she was convinced that's what had happened.

Not now, though.

To look at her mother—so removed, so totally oblivious—was to know that the incident had nothing to do with her. Strange as it seemed, the idea that she could've been responsible for the seizure would have been reason for hope.

"I think you're going to enjoy that book, Mother. Kay Scarpetta. You'll let me know next time, okay?"

"I like to read, you know."

Nora smiled. For the remainder of her visit she spoke only of positive things, fun things. Occasionally her mother looked at her, but most of the time she stared at the turned-off television.

"Okay, I think I'm going to be leaving now," Nora said after about an hour.

She watched as her mother picked up the plastic cup sitting on the bedside table. It was empty.

"Do you want some water?" asked Nora.

Her mother nodded as Nora stood and reached for the pitcher.

"Whoops, that's empty, too." Nora took the pitcher and headed for the bathroom. "I'll be right back."

Her mother nodded again.

Then she waited. As soon as she heard the sound of the faucet, Olivia reached beneath the bedcover for the letter she'd written. It explained so many things she'd wanted to tell her daughter for so many years but knew she couldn't.

Now she felt she had to tell Nora the truth.

Olivia swung her bare feet off the bed and reached down to Nora's open purse, the letter clutched tightly in her hand. She let it fall inside. After all this time, it was as simple as letting go.

Chapter 80

"THERE YOU ARE!"

A startled Emily Barrows looked up from her seat at the nurses' station to see Nora standing in front of her, looking gorgeous as ever, of course. She hadn't heard her footsteps. She was too engrossed in her book.

"Oh, hi, Nora."

"I didn't see you when I got here."

"Sorry, dear. I must have been in the bathroom," said Emily. "It's just me here this afternoon."

"What happened to that other nurse—the one you were training?"

"You mean Patsy? She called in sick

today." Emily nodded at the open book in front of her. "Thankfully, it's been a quiet one."

"What are you reading?"

Emily held up the cover. *A Time for Mercy,* by Jeffrey Walker. Nora smiled. "He's good."

"The best."

"Not too hard on the eyes, either, huh?"

"If you're into tall and ruggedly handsome, I suppose."

Emily watched as Nora laughed. This was definitely not the tight, dour woman who'd shown up last time. If anything, she seemed in a better mood than she'd ever been.

"Did you have a nice visit with your mother, Nora? Seems like it."

"Yes, I did. It was certainly better than the last time I was here." Nora tucked her hair behind her ears. "That reminds me," she said. "I want to apologize for my behavior that day. I was very emotional. You, on the other hand, calmly took care of things. You were great. Thank you, Emily."

"You're welcome, but that's what I'm here for."

"Well, I'm glad you were here *that* day." Nora glanced down at Emily's book. "Tell you what, when his next one comes out I'll get you an autographed copy."

"Really?"

"Sure. I happen to know Mr. Walker. I did some work with him."

Emily's smile was radiant. "Oh God, that would make my day all right. My week!"

"It's the least I could do." Nora flashed a warm smile. "After all, what are friends for?"

Figure of speech or not, Emily knew that it was a nice thing to say. Nora finally waved good-bye and headed for the elevator bank.

After Emily watched her hit the DOWN button, she returned to her Jeffrey Walker novel. Only when she heard the closing elevator doors did she look back up. That's when she saw it.

Nora's purse was on the counter.

Emily figured that she'd realize she'd left it by the time she reached the lobby. Just the same, she called down to security. Hanging up the phone, she resumed her reading. But before she could finish a sentence, her eyes went back to the beautiful and expensive-looking purse.

She noticed it was open.

Chapter 81

ELAINE AND ALLISON could hardly believe their ears. They weren't used to Nora talking about another man—not since her husband, Tom, had died suddenly.

But that's what their good friend was doing as they ate dinner amid the exposed brick walls of the Mercer Kitchen in SoHo that night. In fact, talking didn't begin to describe it. *Gushing* was more like it. This was so not Nora.

"There's this incredible energy with him, just beneath the surface. This quiet confidence I just love. He's down-to-earth, but he's special."

"Wow. Who knew insurance guys could be so sexy?" joked Elaine.

"Certainly not me," said Nora. "But Craig, well, he *shouldn't* be an insurance man."

"More important, how does he *dress?*" asked Allison, ever the fashion editor.

"Nice suits, but nothing stuffy. He likes to go open collar. I don't think I've seen him in a tie."

"Okay, let's cut to the chase," said Elaine with a wave of her hand. "How is your fella in bed?"

Allison rolled her eyes. "Elaine!"

"What? We tell each other everything."

"Yeah, but they just met. How do you know they've even had sex yet?" Allison turned to Nora with a sneaky grin.

"We've had sex."

Elaine and Allison leaned forward on their elbows. "*And?*" they both asked simultaneously.

Nora, in complete control of the moment, took a slow sip of her cosmopolitan. "The sex was okay. . . . No, I'm kidding. It was incredible."

The three of them laughed like teenagers.

"I am so jealous," said Elaine.

Nora got a little serious suddenly, and it

surprised even her. "I don't feel alone when I'm with him. I haven't felt like that in a long time. I think . . . I think we're a lot alike."

Elaine turned to Allison. "Maybe we've been looking in the wrong place. A city of a million single men and she meets Mr. Incredible out in the 'burbs."

"You didn't tell us, what were you doing there in the first place?" asked Allison.

"I've got a client in Briarcliff Manor," said Nora. "I was in Chappaqua at an antiques store and there he was, looking for old fly-fishing rods. He collects them."

"And the rest is history," said Allison.

"She *reeled* him in from there," added Elaine. "I repeat, I am *so* jealous!"

She wasn't really and Nora knew it. The only thing Elaine was, was happy—happy that her friend, who hadn't seemed able to get on with her life, had met someone. And Allison was equally happy for Nora.

"So when do we meet this Craig?" she asked.

"Yeah," said Elaine. "When do we get to meet Mr. Incredible?"

Chapter 82

NORA RETURNED TO her loft after dinner with one thing on her mind: Craig. All that talk about their sex life had her wishing she were with him now. She'd have to settle for hearing his voice. After changing into her pajamas, she climbed into bed and dialed his number.

It rang five times before he picked up.

"Did I wake you?"

"Not at all," he said. "I was in the other room, reading."

"Anything good?"

"Unfortunately, no. It's all work stuff."

"Sounds boring."

"It is. All the more reason I'm glad you called."

"Do you miss me?"

"More than you know."

"Ditto for me," she said. "I wish I were there with you. I have a feeling you wouldn't be doing any reading."

"Oh yeah? What would I be doing?"

"You'd be holding me."

"Anything else?"

Nora breathed into the phone. "Kissing me."

"Kissing you where?"

"On the lips."

"Soft or hard?"

"First soft, then hard."

"Where are my hands?" he asked.

"Different interesting places."

"Where exactly?"

"My breasts. For starters."

"Hmmmm. Good start, as I remember. Where else?"

"My inner thighs."

"Ooh, I like that."

"Wait . . . they're moving higher. Slowly. You tease."

"I like that even more."

Nora bit her lower lip. "So do I, actually."

"Can you feel me?" he whispered.

"Yes."

"Am I inside you?"

Click.

"What was that?" he asked.

"Shit, it's the other line."

"Ignore it."

Nora looked at her caller ID. "I can't, it's one of my girlfriends."

"*Now* we're talking," he said with a laugh.

"Very funny. Hold on a second, okay? I had dinner with her earlier and if I don't answer, she'll be worried."

She clicked over to the other line. "Elaine?"

"You weren't asleep yet, were you?" she asked.

"No, I was *very* wide awake."

"Wait, you sound out of breath."

"I'm on the other line."

"Don't tell me . . . Craig?"

"Yes."

"And I beeped right in the middle of it, didn't I?"

"It's okay."

"Call waiting interruptus. I'm sorry."

"Don't be."

"I just wanted to tell you again how ecstatic I am for you, honey. Now get back to whatever you two were doing."

"I think I will."

"*Soooo* jealous!"

Click.

"You still there?" asked Nora.

"I'm here," he said.

"So, where were we?"

"We were at the point where I definitely wasn't going to be able to sleep tonight."

"Me, either. Tomorrow I'm driving out there for the real thing."

Nora waited for him to say something. Instead, there was silence. *What is he thinking?*

"I can't tomorrow," he said finally.

"Why not?"

"I've got this thing I've got to attend in Chicago at the home office. In fact, that's what I was doing the reading for."

"What kind of thing? You can't just blow it off?"

"I would, it's a seminar. Only I'm one of the featured speakers."

"Oh," she said, deflated. "Poo."

"I'll be back in a couple of days."

"Will you call me from Chicago?"

"You know it. Maybe we can even pick up where we left off."

"Maybe, if you're a good boy."

"Oh, I'll be good, all right," he said. "You don't have to worry about me."

Chapter 83

BUT NORA *DID* WORRY.

All night long, in fact. She'd said she
wasn't going to be able to sleep much, and
she was right. What she wanted—what she
longed for—was to know if Craig had been
telling her the truth. It was the way he talked
about his seminar. She'd felt the same
inkling of doubt when they'd first met.
Something not quite right.

The next morning Nora awoke at dawn.
No shower. No makeup. No time to waste. In
an old sweatshirt and a baseball cap pulled
down over her eyes, she drove north to

Westchester. The first stop was Connor's house in Briarcliff Manor.

There, she made a switch, dropping off the red Benz convertible for one of the two other cars collecting dust in the garage. A green Jaguar XJR.

This way, Craig wouldn't recognize her. Plus, she liked the Jag almost as much as the Benz.

Twenty minutes later she was parked down the street from Craig's apartment, waiting with a large cup of Starbucks coffee in her lap. She sipped and watched.

The first time she'd followed him, she hadn't known what to expect. This time was different. He'd told her he had a noon flight out of town.

About ten the paint-chipped front door opened, and out he came. Bright yellow T-shirt, tan sport jacket—he looked good. The timing made sense if he was driving to the airport. Better yet, he was carrying a suitcase.

She felt relieved.

Then Nora watched as Craig climbed into his black Beemer. His combed-back hair was still wet from a shower. His good looks seemed so effortless, she thought. She missed him, and he hadn't even left town yet.

He backed out of the short driveway and turned in Nora's direction. Hurriedly, she ducked down in the front seat, waiting for him to pass. The green Jaguar was just another parked car along the curb, albeit the nicest one.

She'd follow him for a few miles until it was crystal-clear he was headed to the airport. Everything would be okay. *Better* than okay. He'd call later that night from Chicago and she'd tell him how much she missed him, which wouldn't be hard to do. She'd joke with him about having an AT&T orgasm.

Nora smiled at the thought. *What is going on with me?* she wondered.

She was tailing Craig from about a hundred yards as he headed southeast toward the Westchester airport. It was a route she knew well. Along the way she chided herself. "Better paranoid than sorry" was her favorite mantra, but she felt she'd gone a bit overboard this time.

She'd had these same doubts about Craig before, but like the first time, following him was turning up nothing.

Nothing, that is, until he put his blinker on.

Chapter 84

THERE WERE A LOT of ways to get to the Westchester airport, but unfortunately, this wasn't one of them. The road didn't even qualify as the scenic route. When Craig signaled and made the turn, Nora knew right away: he had another destination in mind.

She didn't want to jump to conclusions. There was such a thing as a "good" lie, and she held out hope. Maybe he was surprising her with something.

Miles later, when she saw a sign announcing Greenwich, Connecticut, straight ahead, she thought of her favorite jewelry shop there, Betteridge. She tried to picture Craig presenting her with a small box topped with a bow, telling her that he made up the trip to Chicago so he could surprise her with a gift, a little white lie.

But Greenwich came and went.

And with it, so did much of Nora's hope. She still didn't want to jump to conclusions, but she was as close to the edge of anger as someone could get. Anger, hurt, a lot of mixed emotions—and none of them good.

That's when Craig entered the town of Riverside, Connecticut. The way he was driving, it was pretty clear that he was familiar with the area. Why was that? Eventually he turned down a dead-end street.

Nora stayed by the corner, finally easing to a stop. She looked around. The houses weren't huge or anything, but they were well maintained. A far cry from his apartment in Westchester.

So what is Craig doing out here in Connecticut? Why the suitcase? Why lie to me?

About midway down the street his BMW pulled into a driveway past a red mailbox. Nora watched intently as he got out of his car, her eyes straining to cover the distance.

He stretched, then walked up the front

steps of the house, a white Colonial with forest green shutters.

Before he could knock, the door swung open and out ran two young boys.

They jumped into his arms and he hugged and kissed them in a way that instantly ruled out uncle, cousin, or volunteer Big Brother. Craig Reynolds was definitely their father.

Does that mean he's . . . married?

Nora's eyes shot to the front doorway at the sight of someone else. Her heart pounded and she wanted to throw up. But as quick as Nora saw the woman standing there, she realized she couldn't be looking at Mrs. Craig Reynolds. Not unless he had a thing for foreign-grandmother types. This woman had *nanny* written all over her.

Then someone else caught Nora's eye. Leaning out of the far window on the second floor was another woman—attractive in a suburban kind of way. She was waving down to Craig. Something different written all over her.

Wife.

Nora threw her head back against the seat of the Jaguar and cursed like crazy. Every four-letter word in the book. "You fucking liar, cheat, scum, Craig!"

Nora kept watching as he herded the two boys inside; she couldn't take her eyes off them. She was trying to sort everything out. There was still a part that didn't make sense: why did he have an apartment in Westchester if he lived out here?

No sooner did she finish mulling the question than the front door opened again. Craig and the two boys came out, laughing and trading playful arm slaps, and now his sons each had a knapsack. Craig had a large duffel bag. They all piled into the BMW. They were leaving. To go where?

Nora glanced up at the DEAD END road sign in front of her. She shifted into drive. She couldn't have Craig pass a parked green Jaguar for a second time that morning.

Turning into the next street over, she sat there and stewed for a few minutes, figuring out what to do next. She couldn't care less where Craig was taking his kids. It sure wasn't a seminar in Chicago, with him as the featured speaker. What else was there to know besides that he was cheating on his wife?

Nothing.

She decided she'd drive back to Westchester. Later, at some point, Craig would call her. That would be interesting, wouldn't it?

But before getting back on the road, Nora couldn't help herself. She had to take one last look at his cute little house in the subs. A closer look. It was almost as if she couldn't believe what she'd seen in the past few minutes. Craig was sure something else, wasn't he? Actually, he was more like her than she could have dreamed. Maybe that was the attraction?

She turned down Craig's street and slowly approached the driveway. Suddenly she slammed the brakes. And stared. On the side of his red mailbox a name was stenciled, faded but still legible.

Nora *really* couldn't believe what she was seeing.

The name on the mailbox was O'HARA.

Chapter 85

FUELED BY RAGE, betrayal, maybe even a little heartbreak, Nora drove like a demon back to Westchester. She was out of her mind and seething with contempt.

But she was also besieged by unanswered questions, dangerous ones. Why the setup by O'Hara? Was there really an insurance policy? And what about the sex—how did it factor in? The only thing she knew for sure was that she'd been lied to, and by an expert.

How about that, sweetheart? Lied to by a pro.

She arrived back at the Westchester

house and went on a rampage, breaking expensive things left and right. She upended a table and ripped down a painting. She hurled a Baccarat vase against the wall. Shards of glass were everywhere.

Then it was Nora who got smashed.

She drank more than half a bottle of vodka, mumbling to herself the entire time until her words became one big slur. She vowed revenge, but the planning and plotting would have to wait. By midafternoon she was passed out on the sofa in the living room.

She didn't wake until the following morning. The hangover was almost a blessing, wicked as it was. It immediately took her mind off of what had made her drink in the first place.

Not for long. Simply by brewing coffee, her wrath returned. It was the smell. Vanilla hazelnut. The same coffee she'd shared with Craig after he first introduced himself.

Only it wasn't Craig. It was *never* Craig.

The hangover eventually eased. With a clearer mind, she came back to those unanswered questions. First and foremost, why was O'Hara posing as someone else?

Forget about the insurance policy, does the Centennial One company even exist?

After seeing the office in town, she took for granted that it did. Now all bets were off. Nora picked up the phone. She dialed information in Chicago, asking for Centennial's supposed home office.

"Please hold for the number," said the operator.

But Nora wasn't convinced that proved anything. She wrote it down and dialed.

"Good morning, Centennial One Life Insurance," said a woman with a pleasant-sounding voice.

"Yes, may I speak with John O'Hara, please?"

"I'm sorry, Mr. O'Hara is traveling."

"Can I have his voice mail?"

"Unfortunately, the voice mail system is down right now," said the woman.

"How convenient."

"Excuse me?"

"Never mind."

"If you'd like, I can take a message."

"No, that's okay." Nora was about to hang up. "I'm sorry, what's your name?"

"It's Susan."

"Actually, Susan, I do have another question. Can you tell me if a Craig Reynolds is still employed with your company?"

"Hold on, let me check the directory. Reynolds, you said, right?"

"Yes."

"Oh, here he is. Mr. Reynolds is with one of our offices in New York. Briarcliff Manor, to be exact. Would you like the number?"

"Sure."

Nora took it down. "Thanks, Susan."

"You're quite welcome, Ms. —" She paused. "I'm sorry, what did you say your name was again?"

"I didn't."

Nora hung up. She immediately went to her purse and retrieved the business card "Craig" had given her. Sure enough, the numbers matched.

"Oh, you're good, O'Hara," she mumbled to herself as she grabbed the car keys.

But the honeymoon's over.

Part Four

TILL DEATH DO US PART

Chapter 86

NORA KEPT JABBING a finger at the SEEK button on the radio, jumping from one station to another all the way to Briarcliff Manor. There wasn't a single song she wanted to hear, most of it rap crap that made her want to scream. Finally, that's what she did! She was anxious and fidgety, and not just from all the coffee she had drunk. Thinking about O'Hara had left her wired.

When her cell phone rang she nearly drove off the road.

It's him.

Her first thought was to call him out right there, a few choice words to let him know she knew who he really was. But as she reached for the phone, she decided no. O'Hara wasn't getting off that easy.

Nora glanced at the caller ID. In the glare of the sun, she couldn't make out the number. Still, she was certain it was him.

"Hello?"

"Where have you been?"

So much for certainties. The slightly annoyed voice on the cell belonged to Jeffrey. She hadn't returned his calls the past two days.

"I'm so sorry, honey, I've been meaning to call you," she said. "You beat me to it."

He instantly warmed. "Jeez, I was getting worried, hon. I couldn't imagine where you were."

An excuse was needed, a good one. "It's that same damn client of mine—the client from hell. You know, the same one who threatened to fire me if I didn't personally pick out fabrics with her?"

"How could I forget—she cost me a weekend with you."

Nora stayed silent, ominously so.

"Oh, no," he said. "Don't tell me."

"I'm going to try to get out of it."

"What's she demanding this time?"

"She wants me at her house in East Hampton to look at the new conservatory. She *is* a good client, one of my first."

"It's already Friday, Nora. When will you know?"

He's mad. He calls me Nora only when he's pissed.

"I'll call you this afternoon. Believe me, the thought of spending another weekend with this woman is killing me. I *miss* you."

"Actually, you do sound stressed, sweetie. Is everything else all right?"

"Yes, everything's fine." The image of O'Hara flashed in her head. "Sometimes one person can just put you on edge, you know?"

"All the more reason to be with the one person who can make it all better," said Jeffrey. "Call me later? I love you."

Nora agreed and said good-bye, ending the call with an "I love you, too."

She was satisfied with her on-the-spot Jeffrey Maintenance—but just barely. It was getting harder to keep track of her lies, which meant risk. Nevertheless, she wasn't about to commit to Jeffrey for the weekend without having a better bead on O'Hara and what he was up to.

A minute later she arrived in the village

center. She miraculously found a parking space, then stepped out and looked up at the sign above the second-floor windows.

"Centennial One Life Insurance."

She read the name slowly, as if she'd somehow missed something the first time. She wasn't taking anything for granted.

Not anymore, O'Hara.

Chapter 87

"HI, CAN I help you?"

Through her sunglasses, Nora stared at the cheerful young woman sitting behind the desk: mid-twenties, intelligent eyes. *Overqualified for this job.*

"Yes, I'm here to see Craig Reynolds. Is he in?"

She watched as the young woman hesitated ever so slightly. *She has to be in on the charade. Not a bad actress, really.*

"I'm sorry, Mr. Reynolds isn't here right now."

Nora glanced at her watch. "Is he at lunch? Maybe at Amalfi's?"

"Actually, he's traveling today."

"Do you know when he's expected back?"

"Monday, I believe," said the young woman. "Did you have an appointment to see him? Would you like to set one up?"

"No. Craig said I should just drop by. Maybe you can help me, though. I'm looking to get a copy of an insurance policy."

There was that slight hesitation again, a little dart of the eyes. Otherwise, the girl was excellent in her role.

"Is it your policy?" she asked.

"No, but I'm the beneficiary."

"I see." The young woman shook her head. "Unfortunately, I'm only able to give out a copy to the actual policyholder."

Nora glanced down at the nameplate on the desk. "Molly, is it?"

"Yes."

"Well, you see, Molly, that's going to be a little difficult in this case. Reason being, the *actual* policyholder is dead."

"Oh, God, I'm sorry."

"Yes, I am, too. He was my fiancé."

A look of recognition came over Molly's face. "You're Ms. Sinclair, aren't you?"

"How did you know?"

Molly glanced over her shoulder as if to

underscore the smallness of the office. "It's just a two-person operation here. So I'm familiar with your case. Again, I'm terribly sorry."

Nora removed her sunglasses and stared directly into Molly's eyes. "I suppose it wouldn't be a problem, then, to give me a copy of the policy, right?"

Molly blinked a couple of times before breaking into a smile. "Of course not. Let me see if I can locate it back in Mr. Reynolds's office."

As she got up and headed into a back room, Nora glanced around. It *was* a small office and it had all the appearances of being legitimate. There were files lying about and printed pamphlets. Still, there was something not quite right. Namely, Molly. For someone who purported to know everything going on in the office, she was winging it a little too much.

Just then she returned from the back office . . . empty-handed, shaking her head.

"I apologize, Ms. Sinclair, I can't seem to find the policy," she said.

Nora tapped her forehead. "You know what? I just realized something. Craig told me it was up at the home office in Hartford."

"He did? Oh, well, that's where it must be."

She studied Molly for a second. The young woman had winged it one too many times. Apparently her "boss" had neglected to tell her that the home office for Centennial One Life Insurance was supposed to be in *Chicago*.

Nora slid her sunglasses back on. "In that case, why don't I wait until Monday, when Craig gets back."

"I'll tell him you stopped by, though, okay?"

I'm sure you will, Molly.

Nora returned to her car and immediately took out her cell phone. The ripple effect O'Hara was having on her life suddenly felt more like an undertow. Nora pressed 2 on her speed dial. That's what it was all about from here on out. *Speed.* She had to work fast and tie up all the loose ends.

"Hello?"

"Great news, honey," she said.

"You got out of it?"

"I did. So I'm all yours this weekend."

"Fantastic!" said Jeffrey. "I'm dying to see you."

Chapter 88

IT WAS EERILY QUIET as the three of us walked toward our very special campsite for the evening. This was going to be great. It was going to be *perfect.*

"Are we gonna get in trouble, Daddy?"

I looked back at Max, the younger of my two boys. At the age of six, he was just beginning to grasp the notion of accountability. Meanwhile, it was his father who perhaps needed the refresher course. Though not in this particular instance.

"No, we've got special permission to be here tonight," I explained.

"Yeah, dumbhead," blurted John Jr. "Dad

wouldn't take us here without asking first. Right, Dad?"

At the age of nine, John Jr. had long since discovered the obnoxious joy of being the older brother.

"Cool it, J.J.," I told him. "Max asked a good, smart question. You did, Max."

"Yeah!" said Max. "Smart!"

I smiled to myself and picked up the pace. "C'mon, guys, we're almost there."

On some of our past trips together, I'd taken them to Bear Mountain and the Mohawk Trail. I'd even taken the boys out to Yellowstone for a week. Now I felt the need to do something really different. Or maybe it was guilt about Nora that I was trying to ease. Either way, I had one night with the boys and I was determined to make it a great one.

I turned to them as we came to a dead stop. "So, what do you guys think?"

Max and John Jr. stared with wide eyes and dropped jaws. For once, they were speechless . . . and I was loving it. There aren't that many campsites in the Bronx, but I was pretty sure I'd found the best.

"Welcome to Yankee Stadium, boys."

The two of them immediately dropped

their knapsacks and sprinted for the field. It was late afternoon and there wasn't a soul around. Nobody but us. Derek Jeter and company were in the middle of a West Coast road trip and we had the place to ourselves. The House That Ruth Built! Just lock up when you leave, said my friend in the front office. He could do worse than to have an FBI guy in his debt.

I opened up my duffel and broke out all the necessary equipment. Bats, gloves, caps, jerseys, about a dozen scuffed-up balls.

"All right, who wants to hit first?"

"Me, me, me!"

"No, me, me, me!"

Until the very last rays of sunlight slanted behind the massive scoreboard and soaring stands, my two sons and I had the time of our lives in Yankee Stadium.

"Do we really get to sleep here?" asked John Jr. in amazement.

"Of course we do, dumbhead!" chirped Max, turning the tables on his older brother. "Daddy said so."

"That's right, I did." I walked over to the duffel and grabbed the tent kit. "Now which way should we face?"

I had one finger pointing toward center field, and another in the direction of home plate.

"Tell you what, we'll compromise and face third base. That's where my favorite Yankee played when I was growing up."

"Yeah, mine too," yelled John Jr. "A-Rod!"

The boys and I set up our pup tent. Actually, I set it up as Max and John Jr. continued to run amok on the infield dirt. They were still bursting at the seams with excitement, and it was incredible to watch them. Maybe I was finally getting my priorities in order.

Chapter 89

THEY EMBRACED AND KISSED like a couple of overheated teenagers in the foyer of the house in Back Bay. Nora had just arrived.

"What a treat," said Jeffrey, holding her tight in his arms, stroking her hair. "I've got you for an entire long weekend. Imagine that."

"Don't be sarcastic, now. I feel bad, though, about keeping you from your novel," she said. "I know how close you are to being done."

"Actually, I'm not close at all."

She looked at him, confused, and then he broke into a grin.

"You finished?"

"Yesterday, after a marathon all-night session. I must have been channeling my frustration over not hearing from you."

"See?" she said with a playful poke at his chest. "I should leave you hanging more often."

"Funny you should say that."

"What do you mean?"

"The hanging part. I changed the ending; that's how my main character dies now."

"Really. Let me read it."

"I will, except first I want to show you something. Come."

"Yes, master. Anywhere."

He took her hand and led her upstairs. They passed his library, heading toward the master bedroom.

"If you're about to show me what I think you're going to show me, I've already seen it," she quipped.

He laughed. "Such a one-track mind!"

Steps before the doorway to the bedroom he stopped and turned. "Now close your eyes," he whispered.

Nora obliged and he guided her into the room.

"Okay, you can open your eyes now," he said.

Nora did. Her reaction was immediate. "Omigod."

She looked at Jeffrey and then back above the fireplace again. She walked toward it, slowly. An oil painting—*of her.*

"Well?"

"It's beautiful," she said before realizing how that might sound, since it was her portrait. "I mean—"

"No, it's beautiful, all right." He wrapped his arms around her from behind, rested his head on hers. "How could it not be?"

She continued to stare, and finally tears welled in her eyes. He really did love her, didn't he? The painting represented how he felt, how he saw her.

Jeffrey gave her another squeeze. "See, it wasn't a mattress. It was a canvas." He glanced over his shoulder at the mahogany four-poster. "Of course, now that we're up here . . ."

Nora turned around to face him. "You really know how to get a girl into bed, don't you?"

He flashed a grin. "Whatever it takes."

"I love it."

"And I love you."

They kissed and undressed, making their way toward the bed. He lifted her gently, a feather in his strong arms. He laid her down on top of the duvet and paused before joining her. His eyes unblinking, he simply wanted to enjoy the view. And Nora let him. He deserved to look at her naked; he was so good to her.

They made love slowly at first. Then feverishly, holding nothing back. Their legs and arms intertwined like a fuse. Until, finally, they exploded. At least Jeffrey did—and Nora played her part to perfection, at least as good as Meg Ryan in *When Harry Met Sally,* though not to comic effect.

A minute passed as they embraced, neither saying a word. With a deep exhale, Jeffrey finally rolled to one side. "I'm hungry," he said. "How about you?"

Nora propped up her head with the pillow. She couldn't help seeing her portrait on the wall, and for a moment she stared into her own eyes. She wondered if there was any woman in the world quite like her.

"Yes," Nora finally answered, softly. "I'm hungry, too."

Chapter 90

NORA WAS STANDING over the polished stainless-steel Viking stovetop, looking like a dream, when Jeffrey joined her in the kitchen. "You were right," he said. "A shower did feel good."

"See, I told you. Nora knows best."

He peeked over her shoulder at the skillet. "Are you sure there's nothing I can do in here?"

"Not a thing, darling. I've got everything under control."

She reached for the spatula. There really was nothing he could do, was there? She'd made up her mind. As he sat down she gave his omelet one last flip.

There's no turning back. I have to do this. Tonight's the night.

"Oh, I forgot to tell you," he said. "That magazine photographer is coming up next weekend. He'll be here Saturday afternoon to take the shots of us for the article."

"I guess that means you've thought it through and made your decision?"

"About telling the world what a truly lucky guy I am? Yes. Jeffrey Walker and Nora Sinclair are a blissfully married couple. If anything, I feel even more strongly about going public."

She stifled a laugh.

"What?"

"You make it sound like a stock offering," she said. "Like business." Nora turned back to the burner and scooped up Jeffrey's omelet, putting it on a plate.

For a silent minute she sat at the table with him and watched as he swallowed bite after bite. He looked happy and content. And why not?

"So tell me more about the novel," she eventually said. "It ends with a hanging?"

He nodded. "I've written guillotines, sword

duels, and firing squads, but never a good old-fashioned hanging." Suddenly he lifted his hands up to his neck and made a choking noise before giving way to a laugh.

Nora tried her best to smile, too.

"You know, Nora, we should talk about—"

"What's wrong?"

Jeffrey slowly opened his eyes. "Nothing," he said with a catch in his throat. He cleared it. "What was I saying? Oh, yeah . . . we should talk about the—"

Again he stopped. Nora watched his face carefully. The drug was having some effect, but she worried she'd measured short on the dosage. *He should be further along by now. Something must be wrong.*

"What *was* I saying?" he asked, his voice straining for composure.

No sooner did he ask the question than he began to teeter in his chair. Then he started to sound like a broken record. "We should talk about . . . talk about . . . the honeymoon." He grabbed his stomach, gasping in pain. He looked helplessly into Nora's eyes.

She stood and went to the sink, filling a glass with water. With her back turned, she quickly poured in the powder, a heaping overdose of neostigmine, or, as her first husband, Tom the cardiologist, liked to call it . . . *the kicker.* Combined with the chloroquine phosphate Nora had mixed with the omelet, it would speed up the respiratory collapse and, ultimately, the cardiac failure. All while being completely absorbed into his system.

"Here, take this," she said to Jeffrey, handing him the glass.

He coughed and sputtered. "Wha—what's this?" he asked, barely able to focus on the fizzy concoction.

"Just drink it," Nora said. "It will take care of everything. Plop, plop. Fizz, fizz."

Chapter 91

HE WANTED ANSWERS; he needed to make the right connection. He had to make sense out of the puzzle pieces.

Suddenly this was very personal with O'Hara—the Tourist.

The mysterious file he'd rescued outside Grand Central Station.

The list of names, addresses, bank accounts, amounts.

A pizza delivery guy who had tried to kill him.

But who was behind that? The original seller, the blackmailer?

His own people?

What did they want? Did they know he'd copied the file? Did they only suspect it? Or were they simply taking out insurance in case he had?

They don't trust me. I don't trust them.

Isn't that cozy and nice.

Way of the world these days.

So anyway, every free moment he got—like after his big day with the boys in Yankee Stadium—he worked with the names on the file, trying to figure it out. The truth, though, was that he wasn't exactly a genius at this sort of thing.

He'd gotten *this* far, though.

All the individuals in the file were keeping money illegally in offshore bank accounts.

Over a billion dollars.

He had contacted a few of the banks on the list, but that probably wasn't the way in.

He'd called the homes of a few of the tainted individuals. But that was a bad way to go, too. What did he expect them to admit to?

Then late on Sunday night, he was reading the *New York Times,* the Style section. For other reasons, actually. Nora Sinclair reasons. Things he could talk to her about.

And there it was!

Pow!

Bingo!

Three, four, five, nine, eleven names from "the list," all of them at the same bigwig party held at the Waldorf-Astoria.

And he finally got it—the blackmail, the scam, the panic about it, even why he'd been called in to make sure everything went just right. And then, why somebody might want to kill him, just because he *might* know something.

Which, as it turned out now, he definitely did.

O'Hara knew a lot more than he wanted to.

About *both* of his undercover cases.

Chapter 92

CHOP, CHOP, O'HARA. Get a move on. Susan wanted an arrest, and that meant I was in hurry-up mode and presumably it would be okay if I bent a few rules. At least, that was my interpretation. Of course, sometimes I hear what I want to hear.

Sitting in a chair opposite Steven Keppler, I couldn't help noticing a few things right away. First, the attorney had a really bad comb-over. Way too much surface area for way too little hair. Second, Nora's tax guy was nervous.

Of course, a lot of people get nervous around an FBI agent—most of them for no reason.

I dispensed with any small talk and pulled a photograph out of my suit jacket. It was a print of one of the digitals I'd taken that first day in Westchester.

"Do you recognize this woman?" I asked, holding it up to him.

He leaned over his desk and answered quickly. "No, I don't believe so."

I extended my arm so he could see better. "Here, take a closer look. Please."

He took the picture and did a B-movie actor's job of studying it: furrowed brow, prolonged squint, finally an exaggerated shrug and a head shake. "No, she doesn't look familiar," he said. "Pretty lady, though."

Steven Keppler handed back the picture, and I scratched my chin. "That's really odd," I said.

"Why is that?"

"How this pretty woman would have your business card and not know you."

He shifted uncomfortably in his chair. "Perhaps someone gave it to her," he said.

"Sure, I suppose. Except that wouldn't explain why this woman would tell me she knew you."

Keppler went to his tie with one hand while simultaneously adjusting his comb-over with the other. His fidget factor was now officially off the charts.

"Let me take another look at the picture. May I?"

I handed it to him and watched, certain I was about to see some more classic bad acting. Sure enough.

"Oh, wait a minute! I think I do know who this is." He tapped the photograph a few times with his forefinger. "Simpson . . . Singleton?"

"Sinclair," I said.

"Of course, Olivia Sinclair."

"Actually, it's *Nora*."

He shook his head. "No, I'm pretty sure her name is Olivia."

This coming from a guy who a minute ago claimed he didn't know who she was.

"I take it she's a client, then?" I asked. "Pretty, as you say. I'm surprised you didn't remember."

"I did some work for her, yes."

"What kind of work?"

"Agent O'Hara, you know I can't divulge that."

"Sure you can."

"You know what I mean."

"Do I? The only thing I know is that you've

claimed not to recognize one of your own clients, who happens to be the subject of my investigation. In other words, you've lied to a federal agent."

"Need I remind you that you're talking to an attorney?"

"Need I remind *you* that I can be back here in an hour with a search warrant to turn your office upside down."

I stared at Keppler, expecting him to cut his losses and fold. Instead, the guy showed some real spunk. Actually, he went on the offensive.

"Your absurd threats might work in some quarters," he said with a raised chin, "but I protect the privacy of my clients. You may leave now."

I stood from my chair.

"You're right," I said with a deep sigh. "You're entitled to your client privilege and I'm way out of line. I apologize." I reached into my jacket. "Listen, here's my card. If you change your mind or if you'd like to arrange for police protection, give my office a call."

His face soured. "Police protection? Are you telling me this woman's dangerous? Olivia Sinclair? What exactly is she being investigated for?"

"I'm afraid I can't tell you that, Mr. Keppler. But, hey, I'm sure if she entrusted you with her business, she must be convinced that you'd never divulge anything about your dealings."

His voice notched up an octave. "Wait a minute—where is Olivia Sinclair now? I mean, you're following her, right?"

"That's the thing," I said. "We were, but we don't know where she is now. Mr. Keppler, I can't tell you everything about this case, but I will tell you this. It involves murder. And possibly more than just one."

So much for the lawyer's spunk and his protection of his client's privacy. When he was finally able to put a few words together, he asked me to sit down again.

"With pleasure," I said.

Chapter 93

THE BOOK ON Jeffrey was closed. His numbered account was all but cleaned out, and there wasn't a hint of suspicion from any of the authorities. The photographer from *New York* magazine never got his shots, and the interview itself was scrapped. All in all, Nora knew she should've been pleased with the way things had gone in Boston. But as she returned to New York, she knew that everything was wrong.

She was thinking about O'Hara.

She paused before reaching for her cell phone. She cautioned herself: she couldn't let on what she knew.

Finally she dialed and hit SEND.

"Hello?" *Well, well, it's the bad boy himself.*

"Is this my phone-sex partner?" Nora asked.

He let go with a chuckle. "Mom, is that you?"

In spite of everything, she laughed.

"Oh, that's gross."

"I was going for funny."

"So, Mr. Craig Reynolds, why didn't you call me from Chicago? Too busy?"

"I know. I'm sorry," he said. "I got caught up with the seminar."

"That must have been some seminar. You were good, huh? Showed your stuff?"

"You have no idea."

Nora suppressed a snicker. *I've got more of an idea than you think, John O'Hara.*

"Listen," he continued, "I'll make it up to you."

"Yes, you will. What are you doing tonight?"

"The same thing I was doing all afternoon. Work."

"I thought that's what your trip was for."

"Believe it or not, I have to write a report on the seminar. I'm up to my ears in it as—"

"Bullshit!" Nora interrupted. "I can see you

right now. You're watching television. Looks like a baseball game, if I'm not mistaken."

He was two words shy of speechless. "What the . . ."

"Look out your window, Craig. See the red Benz? See the beautiful girl in the front seat? She's waving to you. *Hi there, Craig.*"

Nora watched as O'Hara appeared in the window, looking as stunned as he sounded. "How long have you been there?" he asked.

"Long enough to catch you in a lie. Baseball? You choose baseball over me?"

"I was taking a break from my report. That's all."

"Sure you were. So, can Craig come out and play, or what?"

"Why don't you come inside?"

"I'd rather we go for a drive," she said.

"Where to?"

"It's a surprise. Now turn off your *work.*"

"Speaking of work . . ." He stopped her.

"What is it?"

"I'm afraid the circumstances of our relationship have been starting to get to me," he said. "You're technically a client, Nora."

"It's a little late for technicalities, don't you think?"

He didn't say anything, so Nora pressed

on. "C'mon, Craig, you know you want to be with me—and I want to be with you. It's really pretty simple."

"I've just been thinking about it."

"And I've been thinking about you. I don't know what it is exactly, but you're not like anyone I've ever met," she said. "I feel like I can tell you anything."

There was a pause on the line.

He sighed. "A drive, huh?"

Chapter 94

I WASN'T REALLY in the mood for a moon-lit ride, but there I was anyway. Just me and Nora Sinclair.

The convertible top was down and the night air whipped by, cool and crisp. The road, the signs—everything a blur. Nora was turn-ing the backcountry roads of Westchester into her own personal autobahn, and I was just along for the ride.

What the hell am I doing?

That was the immediate question. Too bad I didn't have an answer.

The information so generously supplied to me by attorney Steven Keppler of the bad comb-over had been handed off to Susan. She'd given it to the computer wizards at the Bureau, who were going to hack their way into Nora's offshore account and trace her deposits and transfers. All of them. Who knew how many there were? They'd be keeping a particular eye out for anything involving one Connor Brown. Both before and after he died. Give them twenty-four hours, Susan said. Thirty-six, max.

In the meantime, all I had to do was one thing: stay away from Nora.

Yet there she was, sitting right next to me, more beautiful, more alluring, more intoxicating than ever. Was this one last hurrah?

Was it denial?

Or temporary insanity?

Was there a part of me hoping the computer wizards wouldn't find a link, wouldn't find a thing? That maybe she was innocent? Or did I want her to get away with murder?

I turned toward her. "I'm sorry. . . . What?"

She was saying something, but I couldn't hear her over the roaring engine of the Benz, and the even louder noise inside my head.

She tried again. "I said, 'Aren't you glad you came?'"

"I don't know yet," I replied in a near holler. "I still don't know where we're going."

"I told you, it's a surprise."

"I don't like surprises."

"No," she said. "You just don't like it when you're not in control. That's good to know."

Before I could say anything back, she barreled into a sharp turn, her foot nowhere near the brake. The tires screeched as the convertible lurched and seemed to have thoughts of flipping over.

Nora tilted her head back and laughed into the wind. "Don't you feel alive?!" she shouted.

Chapter 95

IT TOOK A red light for her to finally slow down.

After driving a little more than half an hour, we came upon the small town of Putnam Lake. There was one intersection, and we were the only car stopped at it. It was a little before nine. I remember every detail.

"Are we almost there?" I asked.

"Almost," she said. "You're going to like this, Craig. Relax."

I glanced to my right while she fidgeted with the radio. There was an old man at a Mobil station, wearing a UConn cap, filling up his Jeep Cherokee. For a second our eyes met. He kind of looked like my father. *Things aren't always as they appear.*

The light flashed green and Nora gunned it again.

"You in a hurry?"

"Yep. I'm a little horny, actually. I missed you. Miss me?"

We drove a few miles without saying anything, the blaring radio competing with all eight cylinders. I could barely make out the song, but then it clicked for me—"Hotel California." The way Nora was driving, it should've been "Life in the Fast Lane."

We turned again.

There was no street sign I could see, and the road was narrow and dark. I looked up at the sky. Whatever light had been shining from the crescent moon was now obscured by the towering trees. We were officially in the woods.

"I'm going to rule out Disneyland," I said.

She laughed. "That'll be our next trip."

"You do know where we're going, though, right?"

"Does someone not trust me?"

"I was just asking."

"Sure you were." She paused. "I was right, by the way."

"About what?"

"You really don't like it when you're not in control."

A minute later the paved road ended, but we kept going. There was nothing except dirt and loose rocks under the tires, the road even more narrow. The convertible made for a lousy SUV, and as it rattled along I turned to give Nora a silent, sideways stare.

"It's only a little farther," she said, her smile unchanged.

Sure enough, within a few hundred yards we came to a clearing. I tried to make out the silhouette before me. Some kind of small house—and behind it, a lake or pond.

Nora pulled up close to the front steps and shifted into park. "Isn't this incredibly romantic?"

"Whose place is it?" I asked.

"Mine."

I looked at the cabin. My eyes were beginning to adjust, and combined with the high beams of the Benz, I could make out the long, thick logs of the frame. It was rustic but well kept, though not a place I'd expected Nora to own.

"Surprise!" she said. "It's a nice surprise,

no? Don't you like my little home on the water?"

"I do. What's not to like?"

She cut the engine and we stepped outside. It was a beautiful spot all right, just about perfect. But for what?

"You know, I didn't exactly pack a toothbrush," I said.

"Don't worry, I've got it all covered. I've got *you* covered, Craig."

She pressed her remote and the car trunk opened, right on cue. What little "cargo area" the convertible offered was loaded. Not an extra square centimeter to be had.

"You did come prepared," I said, staring down at a duffel and small cooler. *Prepared for what?*

"All the fixings for a terrific late supper. Plus a few odds and ends—including, yes, a spare toothbrush for you. So what are you waiting for?"

Back up, I wanted to say.

I grabbed the duffel and cooler, and we climbed a set of old wooden stairs. Once inside, I shook my head and smiled. From the outside, the cabin looked like Abe Lincoln's childhood home. On the inside, it was a spread from a designer magazine. I should've known.

"This place belonged to a former client," Nora said as we unpacked the food. "I knew he liked the decorating job I did. I was stunned when he left it to me."

She walked over and wrapped her arms around me. As always, she smelled great, felt even better. "Enough about the past, though. Let's talk about the future, as in what we should do first. Make love, or make dinner?"

"Hmm, that's a tough one," I said straight-faced.

Of course, it wasn't supposed to be. She knew it and I knew it. What she didn't know was that I was actually telling the truth. Sooner or later, the sex had to end.

You can't keep doing this, O'Hara. Stop!

It was easier said than done. Her body pressed against mine. My thoughts raced, the temptation too much to bear.

"Call me crazy, but I haven't eaten anything since this morning," I said.

"Okay, you're crazy, but we'll eat first. There's just one teensy problem."

"What's that?"

She turned and looked at the stove. It was

a wood-burning one, and there was no wood. "Outside around back. There's a shed about fifty yards away. Could you do the honors?"

I grabbed a flashlight from the hallstand by the front door and walked out toward the shed. Even with the flashlight it was dark out there. I don't spook easily, but I heard a loud rustling in the bushes along the way and I wasn't thinking Bambi.

Where the hell is the shed?

Should I be out here like this?

I finally found it and piled wood in my arms, enough to last the night. Then I started back toward the cabin. As I said—*spooky.* Maybe it was the old man I'd seen back at the gas station in town. Whatever it was, I couldn't help thinking about my father again. *Things aren't always as they appear.*

Chapter 96

I RETURNED WITH my arms full of wood and got the stove going. Then I asked Nora what else I could do to help.

"Absolutely nothing," she said with a kiss to my cheek. "I'll handle everything from here."

I left Nora to herself in the small kitchen and relaxed on the living-room sofa with the only reading matter there, a four-year-old issue of *Field & Stream.* In the middle of a deadly article on salmon fishing at Sheen Falls Lodge in Ireland, Nora called out, "Dinner's served."

I returned to the kitchen and sat down to

pan-seared scallops, wild rice, and a romaine and radicchio salad. To drink, a bottle of pinot grigio. Very *Gourmet* magazine.

Nora raised her glass and toasted. "Here's to a memorable night."

"To a memorable night," I echoed.

We clinked glasses and started to eat. She asked me what I'd been reading and I told her about the salmon article.

"Do you like fishing?" she asked.

"Love it," I said, telling a little white lie, then found myself *elaborating* on it. Story of my relationship with Nora. "Let me tell you, when you finally reel in that big fish—the one you've been waiting for—it makes it all worthwhile."

"Where do you like to go?"

"Hmmm. There are some good lakes and streams right in the area. Trust me, you can catch a big one around here. But nothing compares with the islands. Jamaica, St. Thomas, the Caymans. I assume you've been down there?"

"I have. Actually, I was in the Caymans not too long ago."

"Vacation?"

"A little business."

"Oh?"

"I was decorating a beach house for some financier type. Gorgeous place on the water."

"Interesting," I said, nodding. I took another bite of the scallops. "By the way, this is delicious."

"I'm glad." She reached out and laid her hand on top of mine. "So, are you having a good time?"

"I am."

"Good, because I was a little worried— what you said earlier about my being your client."

"It really has more to do with the context," I said. "Let's face it, if it wasn't for Connor's death, we wouldn't be here."

"That's true, I can't deny it. But . . ." Her voice trailed off.

"What were you going to say?"

"Something I probably shouldn't."

"It's okay," I told her. I glanced around and smiled. "Ain't nobody here but us."

She half smiled back. "I don't want this to sound insensitive, but if there's one thing I've learned in my profession, it's that you can fall in love with more than one house. Isn't it naive to think the same wouldn't hold true for people?"

I looked deeply into her eyes. Where was

she going with this? What was she trying to tell me?

"Is that what this is, Nora? Love?"

She held my stare. "I think it is," she said. "I think I'm falling in love with you. Is that a bad thing?"

I listened to her say the words and I swallowed hard. And then it was as if everything about the strange night exploded in my stomach.

I suddenly felt sick. A reaction to what she'd said?

Keep it together, O'Hara.

I thought about what had happened the last time she cooked for me. How could I blame this on a bad scallop?

So I said nothing. I hoped it would pass. It had to.

But it didn't.

Then, before I knew it, I couldn't speak at all. I couldn't breathe.

Chapter 97

NORA SAT AND WATCHED as O'Hara top-
pled helplessly off the chair and cracked
open his skull on the hardwood floor, the
blood instantly spilling out from above his
right eye. It was a nasty gash, yet he didn't
seem to notice. Clearly he was more concerned with what was going on inside him.

They always were.

Still, of all the men—including Jeffrey,
Connor, and her first husband, Tom
Hollis—this was proving the hardest. Her
attraction to the man she knew as Craig
Reynolds had been real, the chemistry
always there. His wit, charm, his looks. The

cleverness, so much like her own. He was the best in all ways, and already she was missing him, regretting it had to come to this.

But it did have to come to this.

He was writhing and choking on his own vomit. Then he tried to stand but couldn't make it to his feet. The initial drug wasn't going to kill him, just set the table. But now she worried she'd used too much.

She told herself to *say* something, to act concerned. She was supposed to be the innocent bystander who didn't know what was happening. Her panic had to seem real to him. "Let me get you something. Let me help."

She hurried to the sink and filled a glass with water. From a vial in her pocket, she poured in the powder. Tiny bubbles shot to the surface, like champagne. Nora turned from the sink—and he was gone.

Where'd he go?

He couldn't have gotten very far. She took two steps and heard the slam of the door down the hall, the lock turning. He'd made it to the bathroom.

Nora ran down the hall, glass in hand. "Honey, are you okay?" she called. "Craig?"

She could hear him retching, poor guy. As

horrible as it sounded, it was a good sign. He was ready for the bubbly. Now if she could just get him to open the door.

She knocked gently. "Honey, I have something for you. It will make you feel better. I know you don't think so, but it will."

When he didn't answer, she called out again. When that didn't work, she pounded on the door.

"Please, you've got to trust me."

Finally, in between heaves, he yelled back, "Yeah, right!"

"Seriously, Craig, let me help you," she said. "All you have to do is drink this. The pain will disappear."

"Not a fucking chance!"

Nora fumed. *So, that's how you want to play it, huh?* So be it.

"Are you sure?" she asked. "Are you sure you don't want to open the door . . . *O'Hara?*"

She listened to the silence that followed, imagining his complete surprise. Oh, how she wished she could have seen the look on his face.

She taunted him from her side of the door. "That is your real name, isn't it? *John O'Hara?*"

That ended his silence. "Yes," he hollered

back in anger. "As in Agent John O'Hara with the FBI."

Nora's eyes went wide, her suspicions realized. Of all things, however, she started to laugh. "Really? I'm impressed. See, I said you were cut out for something better than insurance! I think—"

He cut her off, his voice gaining strength. "It's over, Nora. I know too much—and I'm going to live to tell about it. You killed Connor for his money, just like your first husband."

"You're a liar!" she screamed.

"You're the liar, Nora. Or is it *Olivia?* Either way, kiss all your money in the Caymans good-bye. But don't worry—where you're going, the room and board are free."

"I'm not going anywhere, you asshole! But you are!"

"We'll see about that. If you'll excuse me, I've got a call to make."

Nora listened to the three high-pitched tones coming from inside the bathroom. He was calling 911.

Again she started to laugh. "You idiot. We're in the middle of nowhere—there's no cell phone service out here!"

Now it was his turn to laugh. "That's what you think, *honey.*"

Chapter 98

I WAS SPRAWLED on the bathroom floor, covered in blood and vomit and some other fluids from my body that were clearly never supposed to see the light of day.

But suddenly I was happy as a pig in shit.

It didn't matter that I was still aching up and down, inside and out. *I was alive.*

And on the phone.

"Nine-one-one emergency . . ."

The satellites had hooked me up. Help would be on the way in minutes. All I had to do was tell them where the hell I was.

I spoke to the female operator. "My name

is Agent John O'Hara with the FBI and I'm—"

Being shot at!

I heard the gun blast and watched wood splinter off the bathroom door. A bullet whizzed by my ear and shattered the tile on the wall behind me. It happened in an instant, but it felt like slow-motion.

Until the second shot came. The only thing that one felt like was agony. I'd been lucky on the first. Not so, the next. The shot tagged me in the shoulder, ripping straight through and out. My eyes went to the hole in my shirt as blood began to spurt.

Fuck me, I'm hit.

The phone dropped from my hand, and for a split second I froze. Were it for a *full* second I would've been dead.

Instead, instinct took over. I rolled to my left, away from the door, out of the line of fire.

Nora's third shot exploded through the door and took apart the tile on the wall where I'd been a second before. It would've caught me smack in the chest.

"How do you like that, O'Hara?!" she yelled. "That's *my* insurance policy!"

I said nothing. To talk was to invite another bullet. I waited for Nora to say something more, but she said nothing.

The only sound was the muffled, tinlike voice of the 911 operator coming through my phone lying on the floor.

"Sir? Are you there? What's happening?"

Or something to that effect. I couldn't tell for sure. I didn't care. The only thing that mattered at that moment wasn't the phone.

Slowly I pulled in my left leg and raised the cuff on my pants. I hadn't packed a toothbrush for the night, but I was packing something else.

I undid the holster and removed the Beretta 9 mm. If Nora had thoughts of storming in, I'd be ready for her.

I gripped the gun in both hands and waited.

Where are you, Nora—love of my life?

Chapter 99

EVERYTHING WAS SILENT in the cabin, including my phone. Nine-one-one had my name, and though I hadn't given my location, the satellites would. Assuming the operator did the right thing. *She alerts her supervisor, supervisor alerts the Bureau, Bureau gets the coordinates pulsing from my GPS-equipped phone, and the closest police unit is dispatched. Sounds so simple.*

I just had to make sure I was still breathing when they got here.

It raised the question *Why didn't I fire back at Nora?*

I knew why. I just didn't know what to do with the answer.

I tried to get up off the bathroom floor without making any noise. The excruciating pain in my shoulder didn't exactly cooperate. I tiptoed to the door and slumped against the wall. One hand held the gun; the other reached for the lock on the knob. I turned it slowly.

I took a deep breath and blinked several times. I didn't know if Nora was still on the other side of the door, but I had to find out. My one advantage—the door opened away from me, toward the hallway.

Three.

Two.

One.

With everything I had left, I shouldered the door. It flew open.

I barreled out, low and tight to the ground. Gun drawn. I swung my arms left and right, looking for any movement. I lined up a lamp. Then I nearly took out my own reflection in a mirror down the hall.

No Nora.

I stepped sideways down the hall in the direction of the kitchen. "You're not the only one with a gun," I called out. "I don't want to kill you."

Nothing from her.

I came to the living-room doorway. Gave it a fast peek-a-boo look.

No movement. No Nora.

The kitchen was a few steps away. I could hear something. A creaking. Footsteps. She was there, waiting for me.

I opened my mouth to say something. But I didn't speak a word. The dizziness hit me so fast. I reached for the wall, tried to steady myself. My knees were rubber.

I could still hear the creaking. Was she coming? I raised my arm and pointed the gun. The barrel was shaking. More creaking. It was getting louder.

Christ, O'Hara!

That's when I put it together. The creaking was actually crackling. What gave it away was an awful smell. Something was burning.

I edged to the corner of the kitchen doorway. Chanced a quick peek. I saw the pot on the stove, and smoke. The leftover rice had been simmering on the burner. Now it was burning up.

I exhaled. Then I jumped!

It was the sound of a door slamming. *Outside.* Nora getting away?

I hobbled out the cabin as the engine of the Benz roared. My first step down the old wooden stairs missed. I went flying forward. Landed on my side. Knocked the wind out of me; pain like I couldn't believe.

Nora shifted into gear as I scrambled to my feet. For a second she glanced over her shoulder—our eyes met.

"Nora. Stop!"

"Yeah, sure, O'Hara. Stop in the name of love?"

I lifted my arm, but it was shaking. I took aim at the rear of the convertible, what I could see in the moonlight.

"Nora!" I yelled again.

She was on the edge of the clearing, about to disappear down the dirt road. I finally squeezed the trigger, squeezed it again once more for good luck.

Then everything went black.

Chapter 100

THAT BURNED WILD RICE on the stove was like potpourri compared with the smelling salts.

When I jerked my head and opened my eyes, I was staring up from the ground at two local cops. The older one was applying a makeshift pressure bandage to my shoulder while the younger one—twenty-two, if a day—gazed down at me in disbelief. I didn't have to be a mind reader to know what he was thinking.

What the hell happened to you, buddy?

But I had my own question first. "Did you get her?" I asked with a woozy drawl.

"No," said the older cop. "Though we're not exactly sure who we're looking for. The only thing we have is a name. As far as what she looks like and what she's driving, we don't know a thing."

Slowly I told them. A full description of Nora, the red Benz convertible, her address in Briarcliff Manor. Or at least Connor Brown's. Regardless, it was highly unlikely she was headed back there. She wouldn't dare, would she?

The younger cop got on his radio and relayed the information. He also checked on the ambulance, *my* ambulance.

"They should've been here by now," he said.

"I've never been a high priority," I quipped.

Meanwhile, his partner finished applying the bandage. "There, that should hold until the paramedics."

I thanked him. I thanked them both. Suddenly it dawned on me that they looked like father and son. I asked, and sure enough, they were. Officers Will and Mitch Cravens, respectively. If there was a better example of the halcyon days of life in a small town, I'd yet to see it.

I started to get up.

"Whoa, whoa, whoa," I heard in unison. All I had to do was lie there and relax, they said.

"I need my phone."

"Where is it?" asked Mitch Cravens. "I'll get it."

"It's somewhere in the bathroom. You need to turn off the stove as well," I said.

Mitch nodded at his father. "I'll be right back."

As he headed inside I remembered Nora telling me she owned the cabin, that it was left to her by a former client. "Hey, Will, there's a chance you even know Nora," I said. "This is her cabin. It was given to her by a former client who passed away."

"Is that what she told you?"

The way he asked, I knew what was coming next.

"Did she mention the name of her supposed client?" he asked.

"No. She did have the keys, though."

Will shook his head. "This place belongs to a guy named Dave Hale. While he may or may not have been a client of hers, I assure you he's very much alive."

"Is he rich by any chance?"

He shrugged. "I assume so. I've only met

him a couple of times. He lives in Manhattan. Why? Do you think he's in danger?"

"Prior to tonight, probably," I said. "I think he's safe now."

Mitch returned from inside the cabin, my phone in hand. "Found it."

I took it and flipped it open. I was about to dial Susan when it rang. She beat me to it.

"Hello?"

"You fucked with the wrong girl," came her voice. "You messed up so badly, O'Hara."

I figured wrong.

She didn't sound hysterical. Instead, she was completely calm. *Too* calm. And for the first time, I was afraid of Nora Sinclair.

"Now I'm going to hurt you where you live, O'Hara . . . for real," she said. "Can you say *Riverside?*"

Click.

The phone dropped from my hand. I pulled myself up on wobbly legs. The two cops went to grab me.

"What is it?" asked the son, Mitch.

"My family," I said. "She's going after my family."

Chapter 101

THEY UNDERSTOOD IMMEDIATELY. Any cops might have, but Officers Will and Mitch Cravens—father and son—understood a little more. There was no waiting around for the ambulance. I'd sooner bleed to death than waste another minute out in the middle of the woods.

I crumpled into the backseat of their patrol car. Mitch and his young reflexes drove with the sirens blaring as Will radioed ahead to have the police in Riverside rush to the house. Meanwhile, I called there on my phone.

"C'mon, c'mon, c'mon," I muttered while the line rang.

And rang and rang.

"Shit! Nobody's answering!"

The answering machine finally picked up, and I left a frantic message about going over to the neighbors' and waiting for the police to arrive.

My mind raced with horrible, dreadful thoughts. Was Nora already there? And how did she know where *there* was?

Will was off the radio. He turned to me. "The Riverside police will be at your house in minutes." He nodded at my phone. "No luck getting through?"

"No," I said.

"Is there a cell phone?"

"I'm about to try."

I hit my speed dial, only to hear the call go right into voice mail. I left the same message with the same ominous intro. It was like in the movies. *It's John. If you and the boys are in the house, get out right now! If you're on your way home—don't go there.*

I leaned back my head and let out a frustrated yell. I suddenly felt dizzy again. I tried to get myself to calm down and not think the worst. It wasn't possible.

"Faster, guys!"

We were already doing over eighty. We'd cut across the border to Connecticut and were making a beeline south for Riverside. I was feeling completely helpless when I had an idea. *Call Nora.*

Maybe that's what she wanted. Maybe—hopefully—her threat was nothing more than that, the only intention being to scare the hell out of me and keep the game going. I'd call her and she'd laugh wickedly. Riverside was just a decoy. She was miles in the opposite direction.

If only.

I dialed her number.

Ten rings in a row.

No voice mail.

No Nora.

The police radio kicked in with a burst of static. We were being patched through to a patrolman in Riverside. He was outside the house. The doors were locked, some lights were on; as far as he could tell, no one was around.

I looked at my watch. 9:10. They should've been there. The boys' bedtime was nine.

Will flipped the transmitter onto speaker. "No sign of forced entry?"

"Negative," we heard.

"Have you checked with the neighbors?" asked Mitch as he slowed to take a sharp turn. The front and rear left tires screeched in stereo.

"She probably would've gone to the Picottes directly across the street," I added. "Mike and Margi Picotte. Friends of ours."

"We're checking there now," said the patrolman. "How far are you guys from here?"

"Ten minutes," said Will.

"Agent O'Hara, are you there?" asked the patrolman.

"Right here," I said.

"I'd like to dismantle the lock on one of the doors to the house. If that's okay? Just to make sure no one's inside."

"Absolutely," I said. "Take an ax to it."

"Roger that."

His voice cut off with another burst of static. Outside the cruiser, the siren blared into the night. Inside, it was silence. Small-town cops Will and Mitch Cravens and me.

I caught Mitch's eye in the rearview mirror. "I know, I know," he said. "*Faster.*"

Chapter 102

MITCH GUNNED IT and turned ten minutes of driving into five. We arrived in front of my house with a fifty-foot skid. The street was aglow with police patrol lights, the red and blue twirling all around and up into the night. Pockets of neighbors stood and watched from their lawns, wondering what was going on at the O'Hara house.

At that moment, not much.

I hurried through the open front door to find four cops talking in the foyer. They'd just completed a room-to-room search.

"Empty," one of them told me.

I went into the kitchen. There were a few

dishes in the sink, a roll of Saran Wrap on the counter. *They've eaten dinner.* I checked the phone on the wall by the refrigerator. The message light was blinking, but there was only one message. Mine.

All the cops, including Will and Mitch, had gathered in the adjoining den. I went over to them.

"We need a plan," I said. "I don't have one, either. I'm not at my best right now."

A small dark-haired officer named Nicolo took the lead. He was very organized and said there was already an all-points bulletin out for Nora's red Mercedes in the entire Tri-State area. Airport security had been noti-fied. He was in the middle of telling me he wanted to use the house as a "command center" when I realized something.

The red Mercedes . . . a car . . . the ga-rage. I hadn't looked to see if the minivan was missing.

I had taken two steps when over my shoulder the room let out a collective sigh of relief. I turned to look at what they were seeing.

There, standing in the kitchen's entrance, were Max and John Jr., followed by their mother. They all had ice cream cones. Baskin-Robbins from in town.

Their jaws had already dropped at the sight of the police. When they saw me, and how beat-up I looked, those same jaws just about hit the floor.

I rushed over to hug everybody. I was so caught up in the moment that I didn't even hear the phone ring.

Mitch Cravens did. He walked over and was about to pick it up when his father stopped him. Will Cravens put his index finger to his mouth for quiet. Then he hit the speakerphone.

"Good, I have an audience," came her voice.

Every head in the room whipped around. Nora did indeed have an audience. Complete, undivided attention, especially mine.

But I wasn't the one she was calling this time.

"I know you're there, Mrs. O'Hara," she said in that same calm tone. "I just wanted to let you know something. I've been fucking your husband. Enjoy the rest of your evening."

Nora hung up.

The room was deathly silent as I looked

my wife in the eye. Actually, my *ex*-wife for the past two years.

She shook her head. "And you wonder why we got a divorce, you prick!"

Part Five

ESCAPE

Chapter **103**

THIS WAS IT. Simple as that. *The end.*

"Hey, I didn't recognize you without your trusty backpack, Fitzgerald," said the Tourist.

"Very funny, O'Hara. I didn't get to thank you for saving my bacon at Grand Central. So, thanks. I think I could have handled him, but maybe not."

The Tourist was meeting the Girl with the Backpack at a table in the food court at La Guardia Airport. The blackmailer, the seller, was due any minute. If things went right.

"This is crazy, huh? You think he'll show? The seller?" she asked.

O'Hara sipped his supersize Coke from

McDonald's. "Only if he wants his money, which I'll bet he does. Two million good reasons to show up."

Fitzgerald frowned and shook her head. "Let's say the seller *does* show. How do we know he'll give up everything he has? His copies. Not try to stiff us?"

"You mean like we did to *him* outside Grand Central? To his late representative, I should say."

"Hey, he's the bad guy, remember, O'Hara?"

"I think I've got that part down. *He's the bad guy, he's the bad guy.*"

Just then, O'Hara got word in his earpiece. "He's coming. We know who it is. He came himself this time."

Fitzgerald didn't get it yet. "So why did he come here? Didn't he know this could be a trap?"

O'Hara leaned in close to her. "Ask him yourself. I'll bet he has a good answer."

A guy in his early thirties, blue business suit, aviator sunglasses, briefcase, sat down at the table. He got right to it. "So, you have my money this time?"

O'Hara shook his head. "Nope. No money. *Don't* get up, though. We're all over the food court. Taking your picture for *USA Today* and *Time* magazine. The *Sing Sing News.*"

"You're making a big mistake, my friend. You're fucked," said the guy in the suit. He started to get up.

But O'Hara pulled him down again.

"Obviously, we don't think so. Now, listen to me, because here's the deal. You *don't* get any money for the file you stole and then tried to sell back to us. But you *do* get to walk away from all this. Of course, you leave the briefcase and the copies you made. We know who you are, Agent Viseltear. If you come at us again, or if any of this ever gets out, we take you down. And I mean *down.* That's the deal. Not too bad, huh?"

O'Hara stared long and hard at the guy in the suit, Viseltear, who was an analyst at Quantico and a thief. "You follow all of this? You get it?"

Viseltear shook his head slowly. "You don't want me in a court of law," he said. "You can't have this go to court. I get it."

O'Hara shrugged. "If you come at us again, we take you down. *That's* what I need you to get."

And then he punched Viseltear squarely in the jaw. Almost put him out. "Just like you tried to take me down with your pizza delivery guy in Pleasantville. Now get the hell out of here. *Leave* the briefcase."

Still rubbing his jaw, Viseltear stood up from the table.

He was a little wobbly but he walked away, and it was over.

Well, not exactly over, O'Hara couldn't help thinking—because *he* knew too much about what had really happened, didn't he?

He'd looked inside the suitcase, looked at the flash drive, read that little piece in the Style section of the *Times.* Put one and one together. Came up with 1.2 billion.

But maybe, just maybe, that could turn out to be a good thing for him.

And maybe not.

Things aren't always as they appear.

Chapter 104

"O'HARA."

"Susan. Nice to see you."

"Even under the circumstances?"

"Always. Under any circumstances."

We were on our way to Frank Walsh's office on twelve in the FBI building in downtown Manhattan. Susan and I worked under Walsh's supervision, though usually in separate divisions. Frank Walsh controlled several departments in the New York office.

"Susan. John," he said, and showed his teeth when we arrived at his office. Walsh is an accomplished smiler, raconteur, and glad-hander, but that doesn't mean he isn't smart. He's Susan's and my boss after all.

We moved the conversation into his conference room. "I'd like to shoot the breeze with you two bullshit artists for a while, but I'm very tight on time today. Maybe dinner at Neary's some night soon. Susan, you can't come in here for this. Sorry."

"Of course," said Susan. She doesn't think Frank is as smart as I do, but she tolerates him.

"So, let's get down to business," Walsh said as he and I walked into the next room. "This hearing is now called to order."

The room had that uncomfortable, tight-collared, shame-on-you air to it. It was the kind that immediately announced loud and clear without a single word being spoken: *You fucked up good, O'Hara.*

I sat down in the lone chair facing the disciplinary panel. Since the night Nora disappeared, I'd gone from the hospital to the hot seat, with a week of recuperating time in between for my shoulder. Not to mention a little undercover work I'd finished out at La Guardia Airport. I was guessing the panel wanted me good and healthy before officially kicking my ass.

Frank Walsh got things started with a brief run-through of my background. The panel listened intently while a tape recorder in front of Frank recorded every word.

Agent John Michael O'Hara . . . former U.S. Army captain . . . former NYPD officer, decorated twice . . . Currently special agent with the FBI's Counterterrorism Division, specifically the Terrorist Financing Operations Section . . . Several important undercover assignments . . .

"Frank?" came a voice. It was an older man sitting at the far right end of the table. In addition to his involvement with the disciplinary committee, his day-to-day was the serial murder unit. His name was Edward Vointman.

"Could you please elaborate on how it is that Agent O'Hara was involved with the Sinclair investigation in the first place?"

I held back a smirk. Vointman's question was the politically correct way of asking what he really wanted to know. *Why the hell wasn't I aware of this?*

Walsh frowned. In most any company, let alone a government agency, the left hand rarely knows what the right hand is doing. In this situation, however, the breakdown in communication was a little more suspect. The right hand didn't know what one of its own *fingers* was doing.

Walsh reached out and turned off the recorder. When the tape stopped, so did his stiffness.

"Here's the story, Ed," he began. "The Joint Terrorist Task Force here in New York has been working with the financing group from the Counterterrorism Division *and* Homeland Security on monitoring money trafficking in and out of the country."

Vointman opened his mouth as if to say something—most likely, "What do you mean by monitoring?"—when Walsh stopped him.

"I can't tell you anything more on that, Ed, so don't bother." He cleared his throat. "Anyway, what happened was we got a red flag on a large transfer from a Connor Brown in Westchester a while back.

"Upon further investigation we turned up an odd coincidence. The guy's fiancée, Nora Sinclair, was previously married to a doctor in New York who died the same way. Get this, he was a cardiologist. The good news is she probably wasn't a terrorist. The bad news is she was probably involved with both deaths."

Again, Vointman opened his mouth, his original question even more valid. As a section leader of the serial murder unit, the case definitely should've been thrown his way.

As before, Walsh cut him off. "Here's the thing," he said. "We couldn't turn it over to your group, Ed, without being a hundred percent sure this Nora woman wasn't a shill for someone or, unlikely as it may seem now, some sort of operative herself. Long story short, we went with O'Hara because he was experienced with both those scenarios. He worked undercover for four years with the NYPD, and his profile matched well with the mark. He was even working on another related assignment at the time.

"In other words, he had the right look and—at least, we thought—was good at using his head." He turned to me with a steely glare. "Of course, we were thinking about the one *above* the waist."

Walsh reached out again and hit the RECORD button. "But I disagree," he said.

It was all downhill from there.

For the next hour I fielded questions on every aspect of my investigation into Nora Sinclair. Every decision I made, and those that I didn't. *Especially* those that I didn't.

The panel was relentless. I became their human piñata, and everybody was sure to take their whacks.

When it was done, Walsh gave his thanks to everyone, then excused the room. I assumed I was free to go as well. That's when he told me to stay put.

Chapter 105

THE REST OF THE disciplinary panel had filed out, and it was just the three of us. Walsh. Me. The tape machine. Everything was very still. For twenty, maybe thirty seconds, all he did was stare at me.

"Am I supposed to be saying something?" I asked.

He shook his head. "Nope."

"Are *you* supposed to be saying something?"

"Probably not. But I'm going to ask the question anyway." He leaned back in his chair and folded his arms tight against his chest. His eyes bore right into mine. "I'm going to get a phone call from upstairs, aren't I?"

The man was uncanny. "What makes you say that?"

"Let's say it's a hunch," he said with a slow nod. "You're too smart to be this dumb."

"I guess I've had worse compliments."

He ignored the sarcasm. "You got caught with your pants down, literally, but something tells me you've still got your ass covered."

I didn't answer right away. I wanted to see if he'd keep talking, maybe reveal the source of his "hunch." He didn't.

"I'm impressed, Frank."

"Don't be," he said. "It was written all over your face."

"Remind me not to play poker with you."

"I can still make this exceedingly tough for you."

"I'm very aware of that, too."

"Nothing changes what you did, how badly you screwed up."

"I'm very aware of that."

He closed his file. "You can go."

I stood.

"Oh, one other thing, O'Hara."

"What's that?" I asked.

"I know all about your *other* assignment. I knew from the start. I'm in the loop. I know you're the Tourist."

Chapter 106

WHEN I WALKED into Susan's office a few minutes later, she was standing at the window, staring out on what was a drizzly afternoon. It was hard not to notice the symbolism of her having her back to me.

"How bad was it?" she asked without turning around.

"It was really bad."

"Scale of one to ten."

"Eighteen, nineteen."

"No, seriously."

"A nine, maybe," I said. "I won't know anything for a week."

"Until then?"

"They chain my ankles to my desk."

"They really ought to chain something else."

"For the record, that's now the second dick joke I've gotten today."

"What'd you expect?"

"I don't know, but I'd appreciate it if I didn't have this entire conversation with your back."

Susan turned around. She was a tough cookie and almost always unflappable, though you'd never know it to see her face at that moment. The concern and disappointment were unmistakable.

"You made me look bad, John."

"I know," I said quickly. A little too quickly.

"No, I mean, *really* bad."

I gave a good, long stare down at my feet. "I'm sorry," I said softly.

"Hell, you knew that working this through my department was bending the rules to begin with."

I said nothing. To know Susan as I did was to know she was trying to get it out of her system. The anger, the frustration, the letdown. I figured she probably had one more good primal scream left in her before she could move on.

"Damn it, John, how could you be so fucking stupid!"

And there it was.

When the foundation of the building stopped shaking, she resumed her calm, stoic demeanor. There was still the matter of a serial killer on the loose and the need to catch her. Unfortunately, the reports from the field continued to offer little cause for optimism. Even the media coverage yielded nothing. Nora seemed to have completely disappeared.

"What about our people in the Caymans?" I asked.

"Nothing," said Susan. "The Caribbean, the entire town of Briarcliff Manor, her apartment here in the city, and all points in between; she hasn't been spotted anywhere."

"Christ, where is she?"

"That's the sixty-four-thousand-dollar question." Susan glanced down at a piece of paper on her desk—scribbled on it was the amount of money frozen in Nora's account. "Or should I say, the eighteen-million, four-hundred-and-twenty-six-thousand-dollar question?"

It was a staggering number.

"That reminds me," I said. "What about the tax attorney, Keppler?"

"The one you strong-armed?"

"I prefer the term *cajoled*."

"Either way, Nora hasn't contacted his office."

"Maybe I could pay another visit to the guy and—"

She stopped me. "You're chained to your desk, remember? And who knows what's going to happen after." She managed a slight smile. "On the bright side, if you are suspended, perhaps you'll have more time to spend with your boys."

"I don't know," I said. "That all depends if their mother will let me."

Susan turned around again and gazed out the window. "You know, if you were as good a husband as you are a father, we never would've split up."

Chapter 107

I WAS ALWAYS lousy at sitting still. Now I was supposed to be doing it for an indefinite period. After two days of being chained to my desk, I was already stir-crazy. There was paperwork to be done, but I wasn't doing it. All I could do was stare out the office window at the gray gloom of downtown New York. And wonder.

Where the hell is she?

The reports coming back from the field were short but hardly sweet. No sign of Nora anywhere. No trace of her. How the hell could she disappear?

The routine was maddening. The phone

would ring in my office, I'd listen to the update, and then I'd slam the phone back down. I was being consumed by frustration. The sign on my back was clear for everyone: WARNING! CONTENTS UNDER EXTREME PRESSURE.

The phone rang again. I picked up and braced for more of the same. "O'Hara," I said.

I heard nothing back.

"Hello?"

Still nothing.

"Is anyone there?"

"I've missed you," she said softly.

I shot up in my chair.

"Well, aren't you going to say something?" Nora asked. "Did you miss me? Not even the sex? Not even that?"

I was about to answer—I'd opened my mouth, prepared to unleash a venomous rant, but then I stopped myself. I needed to keep Nora on the line.

I hit the RECORD button on my phone, followed by the button next to it, which triggered a trace. *Deep breath.* "How are you, Nora?"

She laughed. "Oh, c'mon, at least yell at me. The man I knew wasn't the type to hold back."

"You mean Craig Reynolds?"

"You're not going to hide behind the Insurance Man, are you?"

"He wasn't real. None of it was real, Nora."

"You wish that were true. Right now the only truth is, you can't make up your mind. You don't know if you want to fuck me or kill me."

"I'm pretty clear on that," I said.

"That's your wounded ego talking," she said. "Speaking of wounded, how are you feeling? You didn't look too good that night."

"No thanks to you."

"I'll tell you something, O'Hara. It hurts knowing we won't see each other again."

"I wouldn't be so sure about that," I said through clenched teeth. "Trust me, I'll find you."

"That's such a funny word, isn't it? *Trust.* I'd imagine your wife doesn't have much of it for you these days. Gee, I hate to think I broke up your marriage."

"You can rest easy, your timing was a little off. She's been my ex-wife for two years."

"Really? So you are available, O'Hara?"

I looked at my watch. She'd been on for over a minute. *Keep talking, O'Hara.*

I shifted gears. "How are you managing without money?" I asked.

She snickered. "Plenty more where that came from. It's everywhere."

"Is that all this is about? Money?"

"You say it like it's a *bad* thing. A girl needs to look out for her future, doesn't she?"

"What you did goes a little beyond retirement planning."

"Okay, so maybe there's a little bit of sport, too. We're angry, O'Hara. Most women are seething at men. Wake up and smell your bacon burning, sweetie."

She was beginning to get worked up. Maybe I'd touched a nerve. Good for me.

"What do you have against men, Nora?"

"Do you have an hour? Several, actually."

"I do. I have all the time you need."

"But I'm afraid I don't," she said. "It's time to go."

"Wait!"

"Can't wait, O'Hara. I'll see you in your dreams."

Click.

I flipped my wrist and locked in on the second hand of my watch. "Please," I whispered. I called down to the tech guys. "Tell me you got a location!"

The initial silence ripped through my ears. "Sorry," I was told. "We missed her."

I picked up the phone, base and all, and whipped it against the wall. It shattered into pieces.

I'll see you in your dreams.

Chapter 108

THE GRAY-HAIRED GEEK installing my new phone the next morning gazed down at the scattered pieces of my old one. Then he looked at me with a knowing, seen-it-all smile. "It just fell off your desk, huh?"

"Stranger things have happened," I said. "Trust me on that one."

Minutes later the new phone was up and running. At least something was. I remained deskbound, tormented by boredom, not to mention self-doubt and a whole lot of guilt, truckloads of the stuff.

The new phone rang.

My first thought was that an encore was

on its way—Nora wanted another conversation, another chance to turn the screws. On second thought, I knew better. Everything about her call the day before said it was a one-time-only event.

I picked up. Sure enough, it wasn't Nora.

It was the *other* woman in my life who currently had it in for me. Needless to say, Susan and I weren't exactly on the best of terms. Still, we remained professional.

"Any word yet from the audio lab?" I asked right away. The recording of my conversation with Nora was being analyzed for possible background noises that suggested her general, if not specific, location. An ocean wave; a foreign language being spoken by a passerby. Just because I couldn't hear it didn't mean it wasn't there.

"Yeah, I got the report back," said Susan. "Nothing they could pick up."

Technically, it was more bad news, but the way she delivered it—as if it were irrelevant—told me something.

Susan knew something.

"What's going on?" I asked.

"What's going on? You're still *incredibly fucking stupid,* John. If you *could* hurt me, you would have broken my heart again."

She was holding out on me.

"I know that, Susan. There's something else."

She chuckled at my intuitive grab. "How fast can you get to my office?"

Chapter 109

TWENTY MINUTES LATER Susan and I were speeding north out of New York City, and after an hour-fifty on the road we pulled onto the grounds of the Pine Woods Psychiatric Facility in Lafayetteville, New York.

"This should be interesting for you," Susan said as we got out of my car and headed toward the main building, a brick tower of eight floors. "Meet the parent. Nora's *mom* lives here, O'Hara."

I gave a half smile. I could tell that Susan was enjoying this.

Soon we were sitting in a small conference room on the psych facility's top floor. Seated across from us was the head nurse on the disturbed ward.

I couldn't tell if the heavyset woman was scared or simply nervous. Either way, she looked extremely uncomfortable. Meeting a couple of FBI agents does that to some people.

"Agent John O'Hara, I want you to meet Emily Barrows," said Susan, who had made the original contact with the folks from Pine Woods.

I turned to the woman, extending my hand. "Pleasure," I said.

"I think Emily has valuable information for us about Nora," said Susan.

I sat there with all the anticipation of a kid on Christmas Eve. Not once did I take my eyes off this woman, who was wearing white slacks and a simple white blouse, her hair pulled back and held with bobby pins. She was no-frills all the way down to her rubber-soled cordovans.

"Well," she began, her voice shaky, "one of our patients at Pine Woods is a woman by the name of Olivia Sinclair."

This much I knew.

"Nora is Olivia's daughter," said Emily. "At

least, I'm pretty sure she is. It just dawned on me that I never saw any proof of that."

"I have," said Susan. "After I spoke with you on the phone, Emily, I pulled the prison file."

I raised an eyebrow at Susan. "*Prison* file?"

"Olivia Sinclair began a life sentence when Nora was six," she said.

"For what?"

"Murder," said Susan.

"You're kidding me."

Susan shook her head. "It gets better, O'Hara. She murdered her husband. And the couple's little girl, Nora, was there when it happened."

Susan went on. "A few years after Olivia Sinclair was sent away, she seemed to lose touch with reality. That's when she was transferred to Pine Woods. In the meantime, Nora bounced from one foster home to the next. She moved so much, there was never a cohesive file on her."

Susan glanced at Emily, who now looked completely lost.

"I'm sorry," Susan said to her. "We have good reason to believe that Nora killed her first husband a couple of years ago. Based on that, and everything else that's happened, we have even better reason to believe she killed her *second* husband."

"She and Connor Brown were only engaged to be married," I said, reminding Susan.

"I'm talking about Jeffrey Walker," she said.

I was now more lost than Emily. "Jeffrey Walker?"

"You know—he writes all those sappy historical novels. Or at least he did."

"Yeah, I know who he is. You're saying that Nora and he were—"

"Married."

"Christ," I said, putting the pieces together. "The news reported that he died of a heart attack. And let me guess," I said. "He lived in Boston."

Susan touched her finger to her nose.

"Which brings us back to Emily," she said. She turned to the nurse. "Go ahead, tell him what you have. This is good, O'Hara."

Emily nodded and asked that we follow her. "I'll show you," she said. "Let's go see Olivia."

Chapter 110

WE WALKED DOWN the hospital corridor to meet Nora's mother, Olivia.

"One day I'm talking to Nora about the writer Jeffrey Walker, and the next I'm reading in the papers that he's dead," said Emily as we walked.

Susan and I just listened. "Of course, I didn't think there was any connection. I didn't even know Nora was in trouble until I saw it on TV."

Emily stopped walking in the hall. There was obviously something she needed to tell us before we got to Olivia's room. "A couple of weeks ago, I happened to read a note that

Olivia had passed to Nora. In the note was a secret that blew all of our minds. But it also told us a lot about Olivia, and maybe Nora as well. You'll see in a minute."

Emily started to walk again. She continued past another few doorways, then she reached out for one of the handles. "This is Olivia's room."

The nurse opened the door and I could see a very old woman propped up in bed. She was reading a novel and she didn't look up from it as the three of us entered her room.

"Hello, Olivia. These are the visitors I told you about," said Emily in a clear, loud voice.

Finally, Olivia looked up. "Oh, hello," she said. "I like to read."

"Yes, Olivia likes to read." Emily nodded, and then a smile pulled at the corner of her mouth. The nurse turned to face Susan and me.

"For a long time, Olivia fooled us about her actual condition. She used to play all kinds of tricks to make us believe she was a lot worse off than she actually is. One time, when Nora was here, she pretended to have a seizure because her daughter was going to reveal something she shouldn't, and

Olivia knew we tape all patient visits. Olivia is a very good actress. Isn't that right, dear?"

Olivia was watching Susan and me, but she had listened to what the nurse had to say. "I suppose so."

"Well, we've pretty much agreed to let Olivia stay here at Pine Woods anyway. But only if she agrees to help you."

Olivia nodded, still staring at Susan and me.

"I'll help," she said in a whisper. "What choice do I have?" At which point, Olivia set down her novel and climbed out of bed.

As Olivia walked over to the closet, Emily spoke. "Every time Nora would visit, she'd bring a new novel for her mother to read, even though she didn't believe Olivia actually read the books."

Olivia was reaching into her closet and then pulled out a cardboard box. I could already see that it was filled with books and also some wrapping, some envelopes.

"Then Nora stopped visiting. But then a package arrived, addressed to Olivia. It was from Nora. There was even a note," said Emily.

I started to get excited. A *package.* Surely, this was about tracing where it came from.

Had Nora been foolish enough to include a return address? That would've been too good to be true.

And it was.

Emily explained that there was nothing on the package to reveal anything about Nora's whereabouts.

"No return address. No foreign postage stamps or markings. Only a smudged, unreadable postmark."

She turned to Olivia. "Please give Agent O'Hara the note you received."

I took it, unfolded the paper, and read it aloud.

"'Dear Mother, sorry I can't be there to visit with you. Hope you enjoy the book. Always with much love. Your daughter, Nora.'"

I re-read the note, then shook my head. "What's so special about this?"

Susan fielded this one. "Everything. As careful as Nora was, she wasn't careful enough."

She stared at Emily.

I stared at Emily.

Finally, Emily explained what she'd obviously already told Susan. "Look very closely at the piece of paper, Agent O'Hara. Hold it up to the light," she said. "Do you see it? Lower right corner."

I held the note to the window and then placed it close to my eyes.

Holy shit.

The stationery had a custom watermark.

I looked back at the others—and saw that Olivia had begun to cry. "She's such a good daughter. Such a love."

Chapter 111

NORA STROLLED OUT to her private terrace in the afternoon sun, wearing nothing but a pale blue bikini bottom and a brilliant smile. She sipped from a bottle of Evian, then pressed it against her cheek. She'd yet to tire of the view of the Baie Longue beach and its glowing white sand, the way it seemed to melt into the turquoise waters of the Caribbean. She couldn't have designed it any better herself.

La Samanna on the island of St. Martin had a well-deserved reputation as an exclusive hideaway resort. Nora was employing the *hideaway* part. During the day, behind her Chanel sunglasses, she was a rich socialite lounging by the pool. And at night—well, the way she and Jordan had been heating up the bedroom, dinner was always courtesy of room service.

In fact, on some days, like honeymooners, they never left their villa. Thankfully, La Samanna also had a great room-service menu for breakfast and lunch.

"Darling, do you want the Duval-Leroy or the Dom Pérignon today?" Jordan called from the bedroom.

Decisions, decisions . . .

"You pick for us, honey," said Nora.

Jordan Mauch, Dallas real-estate tycoon, was a born decision maker. The one that had made him the most money was recognizing Scottsdale, Arizona, as the next West Palm Beach before anyone else did. His latest decision involved his personal life. *What a good move to hire Nora Sinclair to decorate my new house just outside Austin and then reward her with a little trip to the Caribbean.*

He called to her again from inside the bedroom, the lunch order placed. "Darling, do you realize that you're not exactly dressed out there?"

Nora replied, tongue in cheek, "I'm just trying to even out my tan lines." She listened to him laugh. "Besides, this is the French side of the island, honey," she said.

Earlier in the week, she and Jordan had driven up past Grand Case, over to the nude beach at Orient Bay. Were it up to Nora, she would've stripped and made herself at home. Not Jordan. Nothing doing. That was one local custom he had no intention of partaking in. Nora didn't even try to talk him into it. She'd already come to learn that very rich men with overseas accounts never want to take their clothes off in public. No doubt it has something to do with shielding their assets.

Nora went back inside the villa and slipped into one of the resort's fluffy white robes. It felt cozy against her skin. She climbed into bed with Jordan and snuggled up against his broad chest.

There was just one problem.

She couldn't get John O'Hara out of her head. His smell, his taste, the way he seemed to get inside her head better than any man she'd ever been with.

And it made her angry. She didn't want these thoughts, she didn't want to be in the arms of someone else, Jordan Mauch or anyone, and be thinking about O'Hara. It hurt too much. *What the hell is wrong with me? I don't fall in love.*

"Earth to Nora . . . ," Jordan said.

She snapped out of her faraway gaze. "I'm sorry, honey," she said. "I was just thinking how perfect everything is."

He smiled. "Just another day in paradise."

They shared a kiss, only to be interrupted by a knock at the door. Lunch had arrived.

Jordan climbed out of bed and pulled open the door. "Thank you," he said as the room-service attendants wheeled in their large serving table. They were wearing the usual Docksides and shorts, with linen shirts and large straw hats.

Suddenly, off came the hats.

"Hello, Nora. I told you we'd meet again," said O'Hara.

"Don't you dare talk to her!" snapped Susan. She drew her gun and took perfect aim at Nora on the bed. "You're busted, you bitch!"

Then she turned to Jordan Mauch. "And you . . . you're the luckiest man alive."

Chapter 112

THAT AFTERNOON A VERY strange and unexpectedly nice thing happened—I got some time off, and I got to spend it with Susan. We wisely decided to check out the beach at La Samanna, which was long, wide, and dazzlingly white. There was even an old shipwreck down the shoreline.

"Are we sure we can trust these local guys?" I asked Susan as we caught a few rays.

"You're acting like they're the Keystone Kops, or something," she said.

I was referring to the *gendarmerie,* the police on St. Martin.

They'd taken Nora into custody until the extradition papers could be finalized for her return to New York.

"Maybe it's just me," I said, "but it's hard to put a lot of faith in policemen who wear shorts. We're not even talking about normal ones, either. Did you see those things? They were so tight, I could tell their religion."

Susan turned to me with an incredulous stare I'd seen many times before. "Shut up and drink your drink, John."

She had a point. As she always does.

Our police work there was done. Nora was safely in custody, and the case was closed. We'd even checked in with John Jr. and Max back home to see that they were okay with their grandparents, Susan's mom and dad, who still sort of liked me, in spite of everything.

If just for a little while, Susan and I deserved to be sitting right where we were. Side by side on comfy beach chairs at this unbelievably ritzy resort, watching the sun go down against the backdrop of a beautifully illuminated orange sky. Hell, we'd even gone for a swim together.

I reached over with my mai tai. "Here's to Nurse Emily Barrows."

Susan clinked my glass with her piña colada.

I leaned back in my chair and sighed deeply. I felt a sense of satisfaction and an equal amount of relief. I also felt a twinge of something I couldn't quite put my finger on, but it wasn't very comforting. Let's call it guilt.

I glanced over at Susan, who looked incredibly pretty and serene. I'd caused her so much pain and I felt horrible about it. She deserved better.

I took her hand and gave it a gentle squeeze. "I am so, so sorry."

She squeezed back. "I know you are," she said softly.

And there it was. A happy ending if there ever was one. Me with a mai tai in one hand, the first woman I ever truly loved in the other. And Nora Sinclair soon to be serving a life sentence for the murders she'd committed.

Of course, I should've known better.

Chapter 113

THE FOLLOWING FRIDAY I was in Susan's office in New York. I had been *summoned.* She'd just gotten off the phone with Frank Walsh.

"O'Hara, I don't even know how to tell you this."

"Straight up, I guess. I made my own bed, didn't I?"

"It's not that, John. It's . . . they're dropping the charges against Nora Sinclair."

The news hit me like a sucker punch. Hard, painful, and completely unexpected. It took me a few seconds before I could even string together a sentence.

"What do you mean, they're dropping the charges?"

Susan stared at me from across her desk, unblinking. I could see in her eyes how upset she was, but it was a very controlled anger.

Unlike mine.

I started to pace and curse and threaten everything I could think of, beginning with going to the *New York Times.*

"Sit down, John," she said.

I couldn't sit. "I don't understand. How could they? She's a cold-blooded murderer."

"I know she is. She's an incredible snake. She's psycho."

"Then, why would we let her walk?!"

"It's complicated."

"Complicated? It's bullshit. It's unacceptable."

"I don't disagree," Susan said in a measured tone. "And if yelling and screaming now is going to make you feel better, be my guest. But when you're finished, it's not going to change a damn thing. It's a done deal upstairs."

I hated it when she was right. Like the time Susan told me I was too self-involved to salvage our marriage. Bull's-eye.

I finally took a seat and drew a deep breath. "Okay, why?"

"Actually, if you think about it, you already know."

She was right again. Call it denial, or wishful thinking, but I was always aware that Nora's indictment could present a serious problem for the Good Guys. My behavior would come out during the trial, and the powers that be at the Bureau were none too pleased at the prospect of suffering through the embarrassment. Still, suffer they would, if that were the only problem.

But I knew there was more—much more.

Hell, I'd been involved in it when I went undercover as the Tourist.

The suitcase was part of it. The list of names and accounts inside was part of it.

My dalliance with the suspect paled in comparison to a larger concern. Something far more sensitive and, potentially, more embarrassing. That is, if ever it became public.

Frank Walsh had alluded to it during my disciplinary hearing—*the monitoring of money being trafficked in and out of the country.* Needless to say, it wasn't being done through voluntary surveys at the local bank. It was being accomplished with private agreements among Homeland Security, the Bureau, and several multinational banks. The rationale? The only thing more dangerous than a terrorist group is a terrorist group with solid financial backing. The logic was supposed to be simple. Stop their money and you stop them. Or, even better, *find* their money.

And find them.

The only rules were that there weren't any. Which is to say that a lot of this was, well, illegal. No one was considered safe or above reproach. Casinos to charities, big corporations to day traders. Anywhere and everywhere in the world. We hacked them all. If money was moving, we were watching. And if money was moving in apparent secrecy, we were *really* watching. Suddenly, private numbered accounts were anything but.

Hello, Connor Brown.

And hello, Nora.

"So, that's it, huh?" I said to Susan.

"What else can I tell you? Nora represents the lesser of two evils to them." She smirked. "I mean, what's a few dead rich guys compared to keeping the world safe for democracy, or whatever. They're going to set her free, O'Hara. For all I know, she might be out already."

Chapter 114

NORA DROVE the red Benz around lower Manhattan—fast—until she was sure no one was following her. Not the press, not the police. *Nobody.* Then she gunned the Benz up onto the decrepit roller coaster known as the West Side Highway and headed north to Westchester. She needed some time by herself.

Soon she was breezing along in the convertible at close to ninety. God, she was free—and it felt good. This was the best thing that had happened to her. She'd hang out at Connor's house for a few days, finally sell off all the furniture there, then plan her next move.

Funny, she was thinking, *maybe it's even time for me to settle down. Marry somebody for real, have a kid or two.* The idea made her laugh, but she didn't dismiss it. Stranger things happened—like her getting out of jail.

Before she knew it, the Benz was pulling up in front of Connor's—the scene of the crime, as it were. How strange, and delicious, this was. She was totally free; she'd gotten away with murder. And her few days in jail, at the famous Riker's Island near La Guardia Airport, actually made this all the more special. Extraordinary, really.

Nora got out of the car, thought she heard a sound—and it reminded her of Craig, of O'Hara. What had all *that* been about? She still didn't know, except that the attraction had been huge and real and very emotional for her.

But she was over Craig now, right?

You're over him.

Nora let herself inside, and the house was a little musty, and definitely dusty, but not too bad. She'd be there for only a short while anyway. She could deal with a little hardship, right?

She went into the kitchen and swung open the door to the fridge, the Traulsen. Oh God, what a disaster! Rotting vegetables—and *cheeses!*

She grabbed a bottle of Evian that was sitting in front, then quickly shut the refrigerator door before she gagged.

"Gross me out, would you, please."

She wiped off the bottle with a clean towel, twisted it open, and drank nearly half.

Now what? Maybe a hot bath? A swim in the pool? A sauna?

Her mouth remained open, but there were no more words.

Just a moan.

Then a scream.

And incredible pain!

Suddenly Nora was holding her stomach. She could barely stand.

My stomach is burning up, she thought as she looked around the kitchen—but no one else was there.

The pain exploded into her throat, and Nora felt as if she couldn't breathe. She wanted to throw up, but she couldn't do that, either. Everything was spinning until down she went, helpless to break her own fall.

She might have hit the tile floor face-first,

but she didn't even care. Nothing mattered except this incredible fire eating her from the inside out. Her vision was fuzzy. The worst pain in her entire life was taking over her body, inhabiting her.

Then Nora heard something—footsteps approaching the kitchen.

Someone else was in the house.

Chapter 115

NORA DESPERATELY NEEDED to find out who was there. *Who is it?* She couldn't see very well. Everything so blurry. A feeling that her body was disintegrating.

"O'Hara?" she called out. "Is that you? O'Hara?"

Then she could see someone walking into the kitchen. It wasn't O'Hara. *Who, though?*

A blond woman. Tall. Something familiar about her. *What?* Finally she was standing over Nora.

"Who are you?" Nora whispered as terrible heat seared her throat and chest.

The woman reached up—and she took off

her head. No—it was her *hair,* a wig that she'd removed.

"That help, Nora?" she asked. "Recognize me now?"

She had short, sandy blond hair underneath—and then Nora knew who it was. *"You!"* she gasped.

"Yes, me."

Elizabeth Brown—Connor's sister. Lizzie.

"I followed you for a long time, Nora. Just to make sure about what you did. Murderer! I wasn't even sure if you'd remember me," she said. "Sometimes I don't make much of an impression."

"Help me," Nora whispered. The terrible burning was in her head now, on her face—everywhere—and it was horrible, the worst pain she could imagine.

"Please help me," she begged. "Please, Lizzie?"

Nora couldn't make out Connor's sister's face anymore, but she heard her words.

"Not a chance in hell, which is where you're going, Nora."

Chapter 116

SOMEONE HAD CALLED in a mysterious message to the Briarcliff Manor police: "I caught Connor Brown's murderer for you. She's at his house now. Come and get her."

The police contacted me in New York City, and I got up to Westchester in record time, about forty minutes of daredevil driving through the city, then the Saw Mill Parkway, and finally treacherous Route 9A.

There were half a dozen local police and state trooper cars parked in the circular driveway at the Brown house. Also an EMS van from the Westchester Medical Center. I took a deep breath, let it out slowly, then hurried inside. Man, I was shaking like a leaf.

I had to show my badge to a patrolman in the foyer. "They're in the kitchen. It's straight—"

"I know where it is," I said.

I realized that I wasn't ready for this as I walked past the living room and formal dining area on the way to the kitchen. Everything in the room was familiar to me, and maybe that made it harder, I don't really know. I was there but I kind of wasn't, like watching yourself in a bad, bad dream.

The forensic technicians were already at work, which meant that the investigators were finished. I recognized Stringer and Shaw from the White Plains field office. I'd worked with them briefly when we set up the insurance scam to get Nora.

Her body was still there, lying beside the kitchen counter. A broken water bottle was near it, shards of glass all over the floor. A police photographer was starting to take pictures, and the flashes seemed like explosions to me.

"Well, somebody got to her." Shaw came up and stood next to me. "She was poisoned. Have any bright ideas?"

I shook my head. I didn't have anything close to a bright idea. "I don't. But somehow I don't think we'll look too hard to try and solve this one."

"Got what she deserved, eh?"

"Something like that. Bad way to go, though."

I walked away from Shaw because I was feeling a need to shove him, or maybe punch out his lights, which he didn't really deserve.

Then I went to see Nora.

I waved off the photographer. "Give me a minute here."

I crouched down, readied myself as best I could, and looked at her face. She had suffered at the end, that much was clear, but she was still beautiful, still Nora. I even recognized the white linen blouse she was wearing, and a favorite diamond bracelet on her wrist.

I don't know what I was supposed to feel, but I was incredibly sad for her and I was starting to choke up. I was also a little sad for myself, and for Susan, and our kids. How the hell had all of this happened? I don't know how long I stared down at Nora's body, but when I finally stood up again I saw that the kitchen had gone quiet, and everybody was watching me.

Inappropriate, I knew. Ought to be my middle name.

Chapter 117

I DROVE BACK to Manhattan that afternoon. The radio was on pretty loud, but it
didn't much matter. My mind was someplace
else. I knew exactly what I wanted to do now,
what I needed to do. Nora's death had
brought things into clear focus for me. I was
even certain that I had never loved her. We'd
used each other, and the result had been
just terrible.

I returned to my office and stayed there
just long enough to grab a file. There was
another office I had to visit right away.
Upstairs, where the big boys roam.

"He'll see you now," said Frank Walsh's secretary.

I walked in and took a seat in front of Walsh's imposing oak desk.

"John, to what do I owe the pleasure?" he asked.

"I need to talk to you about some things. Nora Sinclair is dead, by the way."

Walsh looked surprised and I wondered if it was genuine. Not much got past him, which was probably how he'd survived all these years with the Manhattan Bureau.

"Simplifies things, I guess," he said. "Are you okay?"

"I'm fine, Frank."

He tented his thin, gnarled fingers. "But not too fine, am I right? What's up?"

"I want a leave of absence. With pay, Frank. I've been working too hard. Double shifts and all that."

Well, at least something could still surprise Frank Walsh.

"Wow," he finally said. "Before I deny your request, John, is there anything else you'd like to tell me?"

I nodded. "I made a copy," I said.

Then I pushed the file forward.

"You want to tell me what's inside?"

"Contents of a well-traveled suitcase, Frank. There was also some clothing, which I guess was just there for padding, or maybe in case the wrong person opened up the suitcase."

Walsh nodded. "Looks like the wrong person opened it."

"Or maybe the right person. Susan said that this was all about making the world safe. Monitoring terrorist funds in and out of the country, checking out illegal offshore accounts. That was how we accidentally found out about Nora. She transferred a lot of money, all at one time, and we caught her."

Walsh nodded, then smiled. It was the greasy smile that gave him away. Kind of insincere, definitely nervous. "That's what happened, John."

"Sort of," I said, "but not exactly. Susan believed your story, Frank, but I had some trouble with it. So what if the FBI and Homeland Security were tracking terrorist funds and bending the law here and there? John Q. Public would probably understand."

Frank Walsh wasn't smiling anymore, but he was listening intently.

"So, yeah, I looked inside the suitcase.

When I did it, I thought I might need some leverage someday, and maybe what was inside might help me. Purely self-serving. I had no fucking idea. Open the manila envelope, Frank. Take a look. Get ready to have your mind blown. Or maybe not."

He sighed heavily, but then opened it.

What he found was about the size of a forefinger. It was a small flash drive. *My* copy of the original.

"There's a printout in the file, too. Funny thing, though. It's *not* terrorist funds, Frank."

"No?" said Walsh, and calmly shook his head. "What is it, John?"

Finally I had to smile. "You know, I'm not entirely sure, and I have to preface this by saying that I'm not a huge fan of either political party. I've sort of liked presidents along the way, on *both* sides. Don't know what that makes me. Agnostic?"

"What's on the printout, John?"

"What I think it is, somebody in the Bureau tracked money coming and going to several offshore accounts. People trying to hide cash, lots of it, close to a billion and a half dollars. And as best I can tell, Frank, *everyone* on the printout is a contributor or 'friend' of the political party not currently in power. How about them apples?

"Now that *would* be embarrassing to the Bureau, and the administration, if it had come out during Nora Sinclair's murder trial. That would be considered very unlawful, highly unethical too. Even worse than screwing Nora Sinclair, which I'm incredibly ashamed of, by the way."

I stood up and noticed that my legs were a little shaky now. For some odd reason, I reached out and shook Frank Walsh's hand, maybe because we both knew I was saying good-bye.

"Leave of absence, with pay," he said. "You've got it, John. You deserve it."

Then I walked out the door and headed home—to Riverside.

To Max, John Jr., and Susan—if she'd have me. And I'll tell you what, the whole ride to Connecticut, I prayed that she would.

And that Susan, that incredible, wonderful Susan—eventually she did.

About the Authors

JAMES PATTERSON is the author of the two best selling new detective series of the past decade: the Alex Cross novels, including the #1 *New York Times* bestsellers *The Big Bad Wolf, Four Blind Mice,* and *Violets Are Blue,* and the Women's Murder Club series, including the #1 bestsellers *1st to Die, 2nd Chance,* and *3rd Degree.* He is also the author of the bestselling love stories *Suzanne's Diary for Nicholas* and *Sam's Letters to Jennifer.* He lives in Florida.

HOWARD ROUGHAN is the author of *The Up and Comer* and *The Promise of a Lie.* He lives in Connecticut with his family.